REMEMBER LOVE

SAINTS PROTECTION & INVESTIGATIONS SERIES

By

Maryann Jordan

Cover Design by: Becky McGraw
Editor: Shannon Brandee Eversoll
Format: Paul Salvette, BB Ebooks

ISBN: 978-0-9975538-2-6

DEDICATION

To those who keep our airports, borders, schools, and communities safe, this book is dedicated to you. Your tireless efforts to assure our safety is noticed...and appreciated.

ACKNOWLEDGEMENTS

First and foremost, I have to thank my husband, Michael. Always believing in me and wanting me to pursue my dreams, this book would not be possible without his support.

My best friend, Tammie, who for twenty years has been with me through thick and thin. You've filled the role of confidant, supporter, and sister.

My dear friend, Myckel Anne, who keeps me on track, keeps me grounded, and most of all – keeps my secrets. Thank you for not only being my proofreader, my marketing assistant, but my friend.

Going from blogger to author has allowed me to have the friendship and advice of several wonderful authors who always answered my questions, helped me over rough spots, and cheered me on. To Kristine Raymond, you gave me the green light when I wondered if I was crazy and you never let me give up. MJ Nightingale and Andrea Michelle – you two have made a huge impact on my life. EJ Shorthall, Victoria Brock, Jen Andrews, Andrea Long, A.d. Ellis, ML Steinbrunn, Sandee Love, thank you from the bottom of my heart.

My beta readers kept me sane, cheered me on, found all my silly errors, and often helped me understand my characters through their eyes.

Shannon Brandee Eversoll as my editor and Myckel Anne Phillips as my proofreader gave their time and talents to making Love's Taming as well written as it can be.

My street team, Jordan's Jewells, you all are amazing! You volunteer your time to promote my books and I cannot thank you enough! I hope you will stay with me, because I have lots more stories inside, just waiting to be written!

My Personal Assistant, Barbara Martoncik and Marketing Assistant, Myckel Anne Philliips, are the two women keep me going when I feel overwhelmed and I am so grateful for not only their assistance, but their friendship.

Andrea Michelle of Artistry in Design has now created all of my covers and she is amazing at taking my vision and creating a reality. Eric McKinney, my photographer and his wonder models, grace my covers.

Most importantly, thank you readers. You allow me into your home for a few hours as you disappear into my characters and you support me as I follow my indie author dreams.

CHAPTER 1

B LAISE HANSSEN REACHED his large hand over to
the seat next to him and gently petted the small
kitten. The thin, scraggly body fell to the side, its little
claws coming out as it tried to defend itself. "Ow! It's
okay, lil' bit," he said, scratching the soft ears. "I'll get
you home and fed in just a minute."

He drove down the long, rural road, his workweek
ended, and looked forward to the weekend. The woods
on either side grew thick with the summer foliage.
Smiling, he felt the stress of his job fade away as his old
jeep bounced along the ruts.

He had stopped by the grocery on his way home
and found the stray hiding under his vehicle when he
got back. He guesstimated the little ball of fur was
about two months old, but had probably been living on
its own for a while. The slight rumble of a tiny purr
sounded underneath his fingertips and he grinned once
more. *Always another stray...how the hell do they find
me?*

Lifting his gaze back to the gravel driveway, he
turned and appreciated the view. He bought the

property over a year ago from the daughter of an old man who had passed away. She wanted to divest herself of the eyesore as quickly as possible and Blaise scooped up the acreage for very little money. The old man's house was not in terrible shape, but it took a few months and quite a few do-it-yourself projects to make it a comfortable home for himself and his constant furry houseguests.

Coming around a curve in the driveway and into a clearing, he grinned again when he viewed one of his favorite houseguests lounging on the front porch waiting for him.

Parking, he scooped up the kitten and stepped out of the jeep, walking toward the beauty, while calling out, "Ransom!"

Standing as fast as his old, arthritic bones would allow, Ransom greeted him with a joyous lick, nuzzling his hand to see if there was a treat. Sniffing the spitting kitten instead, Ransom turned his reproachful eyes up toward him. Putting his hand in his pocket, Blaise pulled out a milk-bone, ruffling the furry head of the beautiful collie. He was one of his oldest pets and the most loyal.

"Come on, boy. I've got to get everyone fed and then it's back out on the town for me tonight."

The old dog ambled through the house with Blaise as he greeted his menagerie of cats, and into rooms he built onto the back, behind the kitchen and laundry room. One door led to a large space, resembling a veterinarian's office and another led to a room full of feed. Setting the small kitten into a crate, he quickly filled the water and food dishes before closing the door. "Sorry, lil' bit. I've got to keep you quarantined until I can check you out and make sure you're up to date on your vaccines." The small kitten, eyes large, sniffed the proferred food suspiciously before greedily digging in.

Blaise then filled a multitude of containers with feed and headed out the back to a special area. Barking filled the air, as he moved toward his kennels of rescue dogs. They jumped, yelped, barked, and tail-wagged their excitement over both getting fed and seeing their caretaker.

"Yeah, yeah, I know," he laughed, as he made his way down the row. "Some for you King, and you Sasha, and we mustn't forget you, Bossco."

As he finished their runs and feedings, he headed back inside the house, storing the containers and then following Ransom into the kitchen. Preparing the special dinner for the few elderly dogs and cats, he fed them inside.

By the time all of the animals were cared for, he realized he needed to rush. Tonight, the Saints were all meeting at Chuck's Bar and Grille. He chuckled as he made his way upstairs to the bathroom, thinking about their ever-expanding group. Stepping into the shower after stripping and tossing his clothes onto the bed, he let the hot water ease his muscles as he reflected on how lucky he felt to have such a rewarding job with the best of the best.

When Jack Bryant, a former Special Forces sergeant, retired he re-created one of his last assignments, where he worked with a diverse group of men on a mission in Afghanistan. Jack discovered that the group worked coherently and without egos, making the experience a life-changing one, as well as a successful mission. It took Jack over a year to build his compound underneath his massive, luxury house on over twenty acres at the base of the Blue Ridge Mountains. Jack recruited men from the FBI, CIA, SEALs, Special Forces, ATF, police, and DEA to create his new business—Saints Protection & Investigations.

Upon graduating from a school for Veterinary Medicine, Blaise decided that instead of joining a practice, he would pay off his student loans by becoming a government veterinarian, first for the Department of Agriculture and then recruited by the DEA. His work with the canine program quickly moved him into a Veterinary Medical Officer position. He had hoped for a more exciting career, but red-tape had sapped the energy out of him even though he loved the idea of investigating. Finding Jack's Saints had been a dream come true.

Originally all single men, they were slowly finding women that fit their lifestyle and so the bar nights took on a completely different role. Instead of a chance to pick up the flavor of the evening for many of them, it was time spent with their co-workers, friends, and their women.

Ransom bumped Blaise's hand with his nose, having followed him upstairs, as he stepped out of the shower. "Hey, boy. Did you finish eating? I hate leaving, but it's a Saints night at Chuck's."

Dressing in faded jeans that fit his muscular thighs and a polo that stretched over his massive chest, he stood in front of the mirror staring at his reflection. His Nordic heritage showed in his blond hair, square jaw, and blue eyes.

"Don't worry, old boy. I won't be bringing anyone home tonight." He chuckled to himself, realizing that he almost never brought a woman home. At least, not after a few attempts, during which he found that the seduction of a woman was difficult with barking, wet noses, and the occasional cat sitting in front of his date with their leg up, licking their bottoms. *Yeah, that's a mood killer!*

"But I'll be back early," he promised Ransom, then turned to see two cats now curled up on his bed, sleeping on the clothes he tossed there earlier. He started to shoo them away but knew the clothes were destined for the washing machine anyway. *What's a little more cat fur?*

The thought of fur had him remembering several dates where, even if they went back to her place, the women complained of getting fur on their clothes when their bodies were flush in a deep kiss. With one last look at the cats on the bed, he headed back downstairs.

The realization that bar pickups were just not his thing anymore hit him. *I can't even remember the last one!* Now that so many of his friends had settled down, he yearned for more. Closing and locking the door behind him, he got back into his jeep. As he turned the vehicle around in his yard, he knew it would take a special woman to be able to accept his life. A very special woman. *And I don't have a clue where I'll find her.*

~

BLAISE ARRIVED AT Chuck's at the same time several of his co-workers drove into the parking lot. He grinned as Cam assisted his very pregnant wife, Miriam, from their vehicle, followed closely by Jack and his pregnant wife, Bethany.

Hustling to open the door for them, the women greeted him with hugs and kisses. Walking in behind the others, he allowed a moment for his eyes to adjust to the dim lights of the bar. Chuck, behind the bar with his usually surly expression, offered a head jerk to Blaise in greeting.

"Yo, big fella!" called out Trudi, the longtime waitress at Chuck's. "I ain't seen the whole crew here in a while."

Blaise grinned at the bar's iconic waitress, complete with tits, ass, big hair, and big attitude. The kind-hearted, but sharp-tongued, waitress tended to mother-hen the Saints when they were around. Walking over, he hugged her, careful not to unbalance the tray of drinks she was carrying. She might have been in her mid-forties, but she still managed to out-serve the younger waitresses that she kept in line.

"I swear, every time you guys come in, another one of you has fallen," she pronounced, nodding toward Chad, escorting his new wife, also pregnant. "And honest to God, you all must be as fertile as can be. You all hardly get with a good woman before she ends up in your house, with a ring on her finger, and pregnant!"

"Well, the only thing at my house that's pregnant is one of my rescue dogs," Blaise countered, a twinkle in his eye.

Trudi looked him up and down carefully. "Hmmm, I could easily see you being next. But, then, you only seem to pick up strays…not women!"

Laughing, he replied, "Ain't it the truth!" He followed the group toward the back where several tables were pushed together, making a large seating area for the seventeen of them. It did not take long for the beer and Chuck's wings to be served. Trudi kept them well supplied, including water for all of the expecting women.

Soon the assembly was circled around, sharing food, drinks, and tall tales of missions gone awry. The laughter rang out and camaraderie encompassed the newest Saint, Patrick, and his girlfriend, Evie. Blaise noted they fit right into the group, as though they had been there since the beginning.

Leaning over to Marc, he said, "You usually bring a

date. What's wrong? You off your game tonight?"

Chuckling at the good-natured teasing, Marc replied, "Look around, man. This group used to be a bunch of men, all on the take. Now, we look more like a domesticated bunch of—"

"Careful," Monty said, throwing his arm around his grinning fiancé, Angel. "You'll soon have seven women trying to fix you up!"

"Heaven help us all, then," Marc called out, to the laughter of them all. "No need to worry, ladies, I am perfectly capable of getting my own dates."

The others looked at the tall, rugged man and knew his words were true. He preferred the outdoors and the woman that captured his heart would have to love the same.

"Yes, but what about Blaise?" asked Dani. Married to Chad, she was also one of the newer additions to the group.

"Oh, Blaise is more suited to picking up strays than women," Bart quipped. The former SEAL won the glare of Blaise but did not back down. "If it doesn't have four legs and fur, I'm not sure it'll be able to fit in with his menagerie."

At that, Blaise hung his head, chuckling with the group. *It's true. God, that's sad!* Several minutes later, as the food continued to be consumed, the conversations became quieter and Blaise settled back in his seat, allowing his gaze to roam fondly over his friends, and then around the bar. The usual Friday night crowd was present with a few groups at the pool tables and a few couples dancing to the jukebox in the corner. *Wonder how old that jukebox is?* Chuck had refused to add anything newer, saying if people wanted a nightclub they could go to Charlestown.

Several people sat at the bar, casually talking to Chuck or with their eyes glued to the baseball game on the TV mounted in the corner. A slight movement in the shadows at the far end of the bar caught his eye. The bowl of peanuts disappeared from sight. Leaning over slightly, he saw a small hand scooping the peanuts out and shoving them into an oversized coat pocket. Curious, he shifted his seat closer to the wall in order to have an unobstructed view of the miscreant.

Shocked, he stared at a woman, her thin arm poking out of a jacket sleeve, as she slyly grabbed more peanuts. Her long, brown, somewhat ratty hair was pulled back into a ponytail. Her face bore no makeup but was striking nonetheless. Her dark eyes, huge in her face, darted around as though making sure she was not seen. He noticed a glass of water sitting on the bar next to her.

A piercing stabbed him in the heart, as his protective nature roared to life. *She looks like she hasn't eaten a decent meal in a while. She's lucky to be in Chuck's. He'll not mind the missing bowls of peanuts and is probably sending more down her way, knowing she's hungry.*

Excusing himself, he casually walked to the other end of the bar and nodded toward Chuck. When the owner reached him, he leaned in and said, "The woman at the end of the bar—"

"I've been feeding her peanuts," Chuck said quickly. "Trudi's keeping an eye on her. She's been in here before but is real skittish. When Trudi asked her if she'd like something to eat, she skedaddled out. She didn't give Trudi a chance to tell her it'd be free."

Blaise nonchalantly looked over Chuck's shoulder at the woman. Her face down, she kept her eyes moving around, seemingly observing her surroundings. He slid his gaze around, glad that she had not attracted the attention of any of the men at the bar. *It's no wonder, with her clothes. It appeared she wore a man's t-shirt with an old faded jacket over it. While her face was beautiful, to the casual observer she was no more than a down-on-her-luck woman looking for a handout.*

A swelling of protectiveness overcame him again and he said, "Get her some food. Just sit it down in front of her and don't tell her it's from me. Just put it down and walk away. She might eat it then if she feels like no one is watching." Realizing he just sounded like he was approaching one of his skittish strays, he shook his head. *People aren't so different. If she doesn't trust…she won't eat.*

Chuck nodded and moved to the kitchen as Blaise headed back to the table, having grabbed another pitcher of beer. Sitting down next to Bart's new wife, Faith, she looked up at him. Feeling her small hand on his arm, he gazed down at her, a questioning expression on his face.

"I can tell you noticed the woman sitting over there. I feel…" shaking her head in confusion for a few seconds, she continued, "danger with her. But mostly a great deal of fear."

Checking to see that no one else from their group was listening, he said, "Anything else?"

"No. But approach…cautiously."

Nodding, he smiled at the petite, dark-haired beauty. Faith, while never claiming to be a seer, did get visions at times and had assisted them in a case last fall. In fact, that was how she met Bart. He mouthed, *Thanks,* and went back to his conversation with Marc. Out of the corner of his eye, he observed as Chuck set a plate down in front of the woman at the bar. The woman's eyes jerked open wide and it appeared she was about to slide down off her chair. Chuck leaned over and whispered to her before walking away. *Good man. Just let her be, and she'll soon eat.*

As her eyes darted around the room he quickly looked away, not wanting her to see him staring back at her. Engaging Chad and Marc again in conversation, he was determined to let her eat in peace. Forcing himself to wait at least five minutes before looking at her again, he watched the seconds crawl by. Finally, shifting his chair slightly, he looked toward end of the bar.

She was gone. The plate was still there, but the food was gone as well.

CHAPTER 2

WHAT THE FUCK? Where the hell did she go? Irritated that he had allowed her to be out of his line of vision, with the crowded bar, she had slipped away unnoticed. *Some investigator, I am,* he thought angrily.

Standing, he headed back to the bar. Chuck, seeing him scowling as he came over, threw his hands up. "Hey man, I didn't see where she was going. But the plate was left empty, so she must have eaten."

"Yeah, all right," Blaise grumbled, then shook his head. "It's okay. Her getting some food in her is the most important thing anyway."

No longer in the mood to join his friends, he moved down the hall past the bar to the men's room. Finishing there, he decided he needed a breath of fresh air. A door to the back of the bar was located near the restrooms and was the quickest way outside. Pushing open the door, he stepped out and almost tripped over the crouching woman, holding a bite of chicken out to a huge German Shepherd.

The woman, startled, jumped up as the dog placed its body in front of her, its bared teeth and snarl declaring the warning to Blaise. Stunned, he jerked his hands up and took a step back, making sure he let the dog know he was no threat.

The dog continued its low growl but made no threatening approach. The woman reached down, fingers outstretched, and gently touched the animal with her fingertips. The barely-there touch was all that was needed. The dog immediately softened its growl, relaxing its stance slightly.

"I mean you no harm," Blaise said. "I just came out for some air." His eyes lingered on her face, entranced now that he obtained a clearer view of her. Dark hair, not dirty, but looking as though it had not been brushed recently, was pulled back into a ponytail with escaping tendrils blowing in the breeze. Her face, cheeks slightly hollow, were clean and her complexion clear. A scar ran across the side of her forehead. Red and angry. It appeared to be fairly recent and had not been treated.

But it was her eyes that captured his attention, rendering him almost speechless. Large, dark, brown—so dark that it was difficult to tell where the iris stopped and the pupil began.

His gaze dropped to the napkin full of food clutched in her hand before moving to the dumpster behind Chuck's, where he noted a paper plate with rummaged food on it. *Jesus, has she been eating out of the garbage?*

Her gaze followed his and he watched as her chin

lifted in defiance. She did not speak, but her eyes were wary and her body tense, as though ready to take flight.

"I'll be glad to get you some more food…for your dog," he hastened to say, catching the flash of fear in her eyes. A furtive shake of her head was her only answer.

His eyes dropped to the beast in front of her. Beautiful dog…well maintained, until recently, he guessed. Very similar to its owner. Perhaps they haven't been on the street too long. His assessing gaze then noticed the dog favoring one of its back legs.

"Is your dog injured?"

Her eyes barely left his as she quickly glanced down to the animal, but she said nothing.

"I'm a veterinarian," Blaise explained. "I'll be glad to take a look for you."

Once more, a quick shake of her head was all he received.

Frustrated, he continued, "Well, at least let me get you and your beautiful dog some more food that's…uh…healthier." At this, he noticed her tongue dart out as she licked her lips. The small nod was the first positive encounter he had, and he breathed a sigh of relief.

Grinning, he backed slowly toward the door and said, "If you're comfortable here, just stay and I'll be back in a few minutes. I'll bring some food and water for you and your dog."

Quickly turning, he rushed back into Chuck's, bypassing the bar and heading straight into the kitchen. "Trudi, I've got the woman outside and she's feeding her dog. I told her I'd bring more food."

"Just like you to pick up a stray!" Trudi said, hustling around, filling another plate with chicken, baked beans, coleslaw, and potato salad. "Here's a bag of chips as well." Grabbing a quart of milk from the refrigerator, she shoved it all into his hands.

Hustling back out the door, he said, "I've got a feast for you and your dog!"

Only the silence of the night, mixed with the distant noise from inside the bar, greeted him. She...and her dog...were gone.

~

AFTER SEVERAL MINUTES running behind Chuck's looking for her, Blaise gave up, furious that he had not made sure to have her enter with him. Walking back to the table, he saw the silent, curious stares of his entire group of friends. Sitting down heavily, he pursed his lips in anger and, for a moment, considered not saying anything. Quickly realizing that was a stupid reaction, especially if they could help, he looked up and said, "You're not going to believe it."

Having everyone's attention, he related the events of the past hour, captivating them with his story. "So, I guess, I'd just ask that you all be aware and if you see her, call it in to me. She may be hurt...I think her dog may need attention. I...I...just want to make sure she's okay."

True to their nature, the group immediately began to brainstorm. "She touch anything?" Jack asked.

Fingerprints! Fuck! "Yeah, the water glass on the bar, but I can see it's already been put in the tray with all the other glasses to be washed. We won't be able to tell which one was hers."

"You said Chuck reported that she had been here before?" Bethany asked hopefully. "Maybe she'll come back. Maybe we can find her another night."

"Maybe," Blaise agreed doubtfully, "but I've probably scared her to death."

"What about the dog?" Cam pondered. "You said it looked well cared for...healthy. A homeless person might not have a pet that nice. Do you think she just found it?"

"The way that dog was guarding her? It had to be hers."

"Maybe she's running," Miriam offered softly. "Maybe from an abusive relationship."

Luke, the former CIA, computer guru of the Saints, said, "If Chuck'll give us the security tapes from tonight, I can see if I can get a visual hit on her."

At that, Blaise's eyes jumped back to life. "Good idea. I'll get 'em."

The party began to break up, with promises from everyone to keep their eyes open for the woman and her dog. Blaise told Chuck he would swing by the next day and pick up the evening's security tape. With hugs and kisses in the parking lot, each moved to their vehicles.

Blaise got in his jeep, but sat for a long time, unable to keep his eyes from roaming over the parking lot, especially into the dark corners. His blood fired with concern...and interest...he knew he would not rest until he could find her again. *And next time, you won't get away until I'm sure you're okay.*

THE WOMAN HUNKERED down in the shadows, completely hidden, with the large dog lying on her feet, watching the man from Chuck's sitting in the jeep. Sucking in her lips, she lovingly moved her hand over the dog, scratching behind its ears and down its long back.

"I wonder who he is, Gypsy."

He was handsome—almost breathtakingly so. She had noticed his group, sitting around tables pushed together. Laughing, talking. Enjoying each other's company. *Did I use to do that? Did I have friends like that?*

There had been an air about the gathering. The men were all good looking and appeared as though they could handle themselves in a fight and, yet, were so gentle with their wives and girlfriends. She sighed. They seemed to be having a fun time.

When the man started his jeep she instinctively moved further back into the shadows, watching as he drove away. "It doesn't matter who he is, does it, girl? We won't see him again." Sucking in a deep breath, she stood and, with the dog faithfully at her side, slid off into the darkness. A few blocks away, she came to the house she had been calling home for over a week. Deserted, it was old, set back off from the road. With no neighbors around, it had been easy to go in through a window the first time. Now she let the two of them in through the back door, quiet as always with no lights to guide their way.

She heard scuttling in another room and hoped the mice…or rats…would keep away. Reaching into a deep pocket of her large jacket, she pulled out the napkin full of food, setting it down on the floor of the kitchen before plopping down cross-legged next to the dog. Gypsy, as always, looked at her with golden brown eyes, not moving…waiting.

Smiling, she said, "Eat," and the dog immediately began lapping up the food. The woman pulled out some more of the food from her other coat pocket and began nibbling. It was not much, but it was the first real food she had all day.

Sighing, she scrunched up the papers, walking outside with them in her hand and placing them in a trash bag she had found. "We don't want anymore bugs or rats in our house, do we, Gypsy?" Looking around to make sure they were still alone and hidden, she said, "Go on, do your business."

Needing to take care of business herself, she nervously walked into the edge of the trees behind the house and relieved herself before quickly heading back inside with her dog. Once back inside the kitchen, she took the old broom and swept the floor clean, making sure to leave no crumbs. Replacing the bare broom in the corner, she wandered through what had been the living room toward one of the tiny bedrooms in the back. This room still had glass in the window, although dust and dirt had mostly obliterated the view. *That's fine with me…keeps peeping eyes from being able to see me!*

❧

BLAISE LAY IN bed that night, the full moon peeking through the window of his second story bedroom. He left his blinds up, preferring the illumination provided by the moon. Ransom used to sleep on his bed, but these days he preferred a pallet next to him; two cats curled up at the foot of his bed instead. He had checked on the new kitten in the vet room and was pleased to see the food had been eaten and the tiny animal was curled up, safe and sound.

Who are you, Mystery Lady? He was anxious to get the security tapes tomorrow to see if Luke would be able to divine anything. Worry kept sleep at bay. *Are you all right? On the streets? In danger? Running? And if so, from what? Abuse?* He pondered if she were mentally ill, as many of the homeless are. *What's your story?*

The questions continued to plague him as the

moon moved across the sky. Something about the woman called to him…her large, guileless eyes, while frightened, were as protective of the dog as it was of her. *I'm used to trusting animals…and that dog trusted its mistress.*

Finally deciding to spend the weekend staking out Chuck's and the surrounding areas, he fell into a fitful sleep.

A PILE OF old, but clean, blankets were on the floor and the woman curled up on them, patting the area beside her. She kept her shoes on in case she needed to make a quick getaway but took off her jacket to use as a pillow. Gypsy trotted over, turned around a few times and then settled in, close to her mistress. The moonlight streamed through the grime in the curtain-less window and she knew sleep would not come easily.

Her mind filled with images of the blond man in the alley with her, his hands up in a gesture of conciliation. He was tall, at least a head taller than she. His square jaw, thick muscles barely contained in the tight polo shirt. The baby blue shirt only served to make his blue eyes even brighter. *Oh, yeah. He could be right at home standing on the bow of a pirate ship.* Chuckling, she wondered where that thought came from.

That must have come from a previous life. The one before…everything went black. Heaving a deep sigh, she curled up tighter with Gypsy. "Thank goodness you have a collar with a nametag girl, or I wouldn't even know your name," she whispered. As the dog slept beside her, she watched the moon move across the sky and wished she wore a nametag around her neck as well. *Because, maybe, just maybe...I'd remember who I was.*

CHAPTER 3

AFTER A FITFUL night of non-sleep, Blaise rose from his bed and walked to his window overlooking the kennels. The dogs were waking, beginning to move around and he knew he needed to get out to feed them. A wet nose nuzzled his hand and his fingers absent-mindedly rubbed Ransom's head. Images of the large, protective German Shepherd and its beautiful mistress filled his mind. *Huh, not like I didn't think of them all night.*

Sucking in a deep breath, he glanced down at Ransom, saying, "All right, boy. Let's get the morning going." Pulling on sweatpants and an old t-shirt, along with boots, he tromped down the stairs, the cats darting ahead of him and Ransom following behind at a slower pace.

Entering the kitchen, he slid a coffee pod into his machine and turned it on. An image of Luke's complicated coffee maker flitted through his mind. "Luke likes his coffee strong even if it scares the rest of us," he said. Realizing he talked to his animals as though they were people in the room, he chuckled. *Well, I guess I under-*

stand animals better.

Making his way into the clinic, he checked on the little kitten, now wide eyed and playing with a toy mouse in its cage. The kitten gave off a tiny hiss and swatted at his hand when he tried to pet it. "Hey, I'm trying to help," Blaise protested. Filling the dishes with food and clean water, he wiggled his fingers at the tiny tiger.

Twenty minutes later, he had finished feeding the dogs in the kennels outside and walked back into the house. His house was in a constant state of evolvement. He had the clinic and feeding rooms built first, wanting to make sure his animals were taken care of more than his own comfort. Marc and Chad had helped with the kitchen and bathroom upgrades. Other than that, the rest of the house remained very much the same as when he bought the property.

Moving into the kitchen, he grabbed his coffee. Looking down at Ransom, he said, "You wanna share my breakfast?" Indulging the older dog was a morning ritual for them and he quickly plated bacon and eggs for himself and another plate for Ransom. He smiled indulgently as he ate slowly, Ransom lifting his eyes to his master when he had finished before ambling over to his soft bed in the living room as Blaise finished eating.

Glancing at his watch, he hoped Chuck would be up at this hour, unable to wait any longer to get his hands on the security tapes. Locking up, he headed out, arriving at the bar about fifteen minutes later. Walking around to the back, he knew if Chuck were there, it would be to accept deliveries. Sure enough, the owner was there and, surprisingly, so was Trudi.

Chuck's arms were full of boxes of beer as he unloaded them from a delivery truck, helping the driver. The bulky owner, his shirt slightly pulling at the button at his stomach, looked up as Blaise approached. With a head jerk toward the door, he indicated for Blaise to follow.

Trudi, right on their heels, was already asking questions. "What happened last night to that girl? Did you see her again? Do you know where she went?"

"Hold on, Trudi," Blaise said. "Give me a minute and I'll tell you what I know."

Trudi patted her big hair in place, while a pout settled on her expression. "Fine, but don't take too long!"

Once inside the kitchen storeroom, Chuck set down the box he was carrying and called out to the driver, "I've got somethin' to do. You can bring the rest of it in and put it here."

Gaining a nod, the driver headed back to his truck. Chuck went into his small office and came out with a disk. "Don't know what you'll find, but I reckon you Saints'll be able to gain some kind of clues."

Nodding gratefully, Blaise laid the disk down on the counter next to him, his hands resting on either side of it. Shaking his head, he confessed, "Can't tell you much. I found her out back and she had a big dog with her. She was feeding the dog, as well as herself.

And…not just what you had given her. It looked like she had been digging through the garbage to find some food."

"Fuck!" Chuck growled, at the same time Trudi cried out, "Oh, hell no!" Blaise looked at their faces, seeing anger written on both.

"No fuckin' way is someone gonna eat my garbage," Chuck continued. "You think she'll come back? I could start leaving some food out for her."

"That girl needs help!" Trudi announced as if no one else had thought of that. "What are you and that group of big men gonna do about it?" she demanded.

"We're working on it, Trudi. That's why I had Chuck give me this security disk."

Trudi huffed as though the men were inefficient. "Well, I'd think a bunch of you trying to find one little woman with a big dog would be able to track her easily. And when you do," she added, poking a long, red fingernail in his chest, "I want to know. I'll make sure that girl's got some clothes and food!"

Blaise glanced down at the finger jabbing his chest and grinned. Chuck and Trudi might run the bar with a bit of surly, down home, no frills manner…but they had two of the biggest hearts he knew. *Well, besides the Saints and their women!*

"We're gonna work on it right now," Blaise replied, snagging the disk off the counter and, with a kiss to the top of Trudi's hair, he headed back out the door. Stepping around the delivery truck, he glanced about, his mind replaying the events of last night. *Wherever you are, Mystery Lady, I'm going to find you. And whatever it is you need...I want to help you get it.*

PULLING INTO JACK'S driveway after passing through the security gate, Blaise drove to the front of the house. There was a rear entrance to the underground compound, but the Saints always parked in the front and entered through the front door. Jack wasn't just a boss—he was a friend. All of the Saints were.

Entering the large, luxury log cabin, he immediately moved to the kitchen bar where Jack's wife, Bethany, was just pulling out a large cobbler. Her baked treats were one of the reasons no one was ever late to meetings. Taking a plate from her with a wink and sincere thanks, he turned and appreciated the view out of the floor to ceiling windows on the other side of the open space of the living room. The two story stone fireplace stood as a sentinel between the windows. The backdrop of the Blue Ridge Mountains completed the majestic view.

"It never gets old, does it?" Bethany asked.

Jerking his head around, he smiled. "No, this place is really great."

"But not for you?" she added, with a knowing grin.

Chuckling, he dropped his head. "No, you're right about that. I'm afraid I can't live without my little house full of animals."

She walked by, touching his arm as she moved passed. "You have a good soul, Blaise." As she disappeared down the hall, she called out over her shoulder, "Don't worry. You'll find her."

Jolted out of his musings, he jogged down the stairs to the conference room—the hub of the Saint's compound. The compound consisted of a spacious conference room, complete with computer equipment, security monitoring screens for the security aspect of the business, secure video conferencing equipment used for the many virtual meetings with government officials, and Luke's station where he managed to hack into most systems needed. Other rooms were filled with ammunition, weapons, safety equipment, and just about anything else they might need. A locker room, complete with bunk beds, was in another area for times when they worked around the clock at the compound.

Luke, already on his second cup of coffee, held his hand out, obviously sure that Blaise would be bringing the security tapes from Chuck's. Accepting it, he immediately popped it into one of his computers.

Marc plopped down in a chair, staring at the empty plate in his hand. Running his fingers through his hair, he complained, "Boss, I hate to sound ungrateful, but do you think Bethany could make bigger cobblers? I gobbled this up in no time."

Jack laughed, saying, "Maybe you should eat more breakfast before you come!"

"I do, but it's not nearly as good as what she bakes!"

Turning to see Monty coming into the room, Marc added, "Hey, you're engaged to the famous cupcake baker. How come you don't come in with some of her goodies when we meet?"

The quiet-natured, former FBI agent looked at him as one would a petulant child. "Marc, as big as you are, you'd eat up all her profits."

Blaise slapped his friend on the back as he sat down next to him. "Looks like you're on your own, buddy."

Cam and Bart came in next, the two best friends good-naturedly bantering amongst themselves.

"Bartholomew is a perfectly good name. I can't understand why you wouldn't name your kid after me!"

Cam rolled his eyes, answering, "You know my parents. And Miriam's. Both sets are about as traditional as they come. If it's a boy, he'll be named after our fathers."

Jude, just polishing off his treat, grinned. "But which father's name will be first?" Chad, still eating, just grinned. He and his wife had already named their unborn daughter and he was glad it was not a boy.

Cam's face fell as he sat down. Appearing disconcerted, he admitted, "We don't have a decision yet and it'll be a fuckin' battle no matter which one we choose."

"All the more reason to name him after me!" Bart insisted.

"Got her!" Luke called out, instantly sobering the group as Blaise jumped up and peered over Luke's shoulder.

"I'll send it to the screen," Luke said, projecting the image on the large white board on the wall.

Blaise continued to stand as he watched the bar video from the previous night. Luke had started with the inside views. *There she is!* The group watched as she walked in, unassumingly, looking around before quickly taking the bar stool at the very end. It was obvious her eyes continued to dart around at first. "She's checking out the place. She appears uncomfortable," Blaise said.

Her eyes then landed on the bowl of peanuts in front of her. She slid her hand out hesitantly, snatching a few and bringing them in front of her. Shelling them, she ate a few and stuck others into her jacket pocket.

Blaise could not take his eyes off her large ones, her flawless face a mask of uncertainty. Her fingers daintily worked at the peanuts.

They watched as Chuck brought her a glass of water, saying nothing. Her large eyes jumped up to his in appreciation and it appeared she thanked him.

"Chuck said she had been in there twice before. Both times trying to not be seen, but obviously hungry. She eats peanuts and he gives her water," Blaise reported. "The first night, Trudi wasn't there, but the next time she was. Chuck said that when Trudi approached to offer food, Mystery Lady ran."

"Mystery Lady?" Marc asked, lifting his eyebrow in question.

Blushing, Blaise admitted, "Yeah, I guess that's how

I've been thinking of her."

The other Saints grinned silently but continued to watch hawk-like at the screen in hopes of helping to identify Blaise's Mystery Lady.

They observed as Chuck set the plate of food in front of her. She appeared frightened, but Chuck just nodded and walked away. Her head twisted around to see if anyone was watching and then she picked up one of the chicken wings, biting into the meat.

Blaise's heart squeezed when he saw the look of ecstasy on her face as she tasted the savory goodness. *Fuck, when was the last time she had a decent meal? I have got to find her.*

"You got that right, brother," Marc said, the other Saints following in agreement.

Jerking his head toward them, Blaise realized he had spoken his thoughts aloud. Not embarrassed, he gazed back to the screen. The Saints watched as she carefully wrapped up the extra meat into a napkin and slid off the stool, slipping unnoticed out the front door.

"Go to the back of the bar camera angle," Blaise said, but Luke was already on it. He projected the images from the camera attached to the back of the bar that included the delivery area as well as the garbage dumpster.

"There she is," Jude announced to no one in particular.

Blaise's gaze moved across the men in the room, finding each one entranced with the video...or perhaps with the woman in the video.

They saw her step around the corner, an intent expression on her face. Suddenly, from behind the dumpster, came the large German Shepherd trotting over to her. Nuzzling her hand, it sat at her feet. She bent, offering it the rest of her food. As the dog ate, she moved to the dumpster and leaned over, plucking out what appeared to be some bread and other unidentifiable food.

The quiet room resounded with sounds of *fucks, holy hells, damns,* and other curses as the men watched the woman gathering food from a dumpster.

Jack, showing more emotion than normal, growled, "I know you described this last night, but it's a fuck-of-a-lot more potent seeing it."

The video continued as they watched Blaise on the camera with her and their interaction. As he re-entered the building, she grabbed the food and, with the dog at her side, ran off into the night.

Luke stopped the camera and the group continued sitting in silence for a moment, none quite sure what to say.

"Right," Jack said, slapping his hand down on the table. His eyes lifted and met Blaise's. "We've got several jobs the others are working on now, but no large-scale mission that requires everyone's participation." Pinning Marc with his gaze, he said, "We've got some security flights I'll be sending you on later in the summer. Chad...you, Bart, and Monty will continue assisting the FBI on the ISIS cells from our last major mission."

Receiving nods from those men, he turned his gaze back to Blaise. "If you want to utilize us to assist this woman, I'll back you."

"Boss, I gotta be clear about something," Blaise said tentatively. "I don't mind doing this alone. I have no idea who this woman is or what she's running from. But there's no way she'd be able to afford the Saints for our assistance."

Shaking his head, Jack declared, "Look around. We're sitting in a state of the art security and investigation compound. Got lucrative contracts from government agencies and corporations. If we can't utilize some of our time and resources to aid someone in trouble, then we're not the kind of men I think we are."

Grinning as he breathed a sigh of relief, Blaise observed the nods from every man in the room. "Okay, then. I'll start working with Luke to see if we can get an ID from her image."

CHAPTER 4

THREE HOURS LATER, Luke and Blaise looked at each other in frustration. "The problem is that in trying not to draw too much attention to herself, she keeps her head down and barely looks up. The closest image is when she looks up in surprise at Chuck when he sets the food down, but that is only a partial image with her body facing almost away from the camera."

Blaise leaned back in his chair, rolling his shoulders to ease the tension. They had compared the data to missing persons, domestic violence complaints from police files, runaways going back almost five years, and even the FBI database.

Blaise had even reached out to veterinarians in the state, sending a mass email inquiring about a woman bringing in a German Shepherd who may have been injured. Several had emailed back with possibilities, but in checking them out, none of them were the Mystery Lady.

"Well, we've collected data on a number of possible hits, so we can start going through them one at a time," Luke said. "Why don't we get started again after lunch?"

Blaise nodded in agreement and headed out of the compound. He bypassed the fast food chains and headed home instead, taking the opportunity to check on his animals. Taking his sandwich with him in his jeep after making his rounds petting his menagerie, he turned toward Chuck's instead of heading straight back to Jack's.

Walking in, he caught Chuck's head jerk and plopped down at the bar.

"I see from your expression, you ain't found her yet."

"Not yet, but we're working on it. Thanks for the video disk. Luke's processing it to see if we can figure anything out."

Chuck lifted his eyebrow, staring at his long-time customer. "This woman's got a hold on you, don't she?"

Shaking his head, Blaise replied, "I just know she needs help, Chuck. Can't explain it, but now that I've seen her, I want to help…in any way I can. I'd like to—"

"Thank God you're here!" Trudi screamed as she came running into the bar, her face flush with excitement. "I saw her!"

"Where?" Blaise shouted, jumping from his seat and turning to face Trudi, who was still trying to catch her breath.

"I saw her crossing between some buildings and it

looked like she might be heading to the park on the campus side of town," she panted. "I was stuck in traffic and couldn't get turned around. Then I didn't have your cell phone number but thought maybe Chuck would know how to get hold of you guys."

She barely finished before Blaise bolted from the establishment, buckling only as his jeep peeled out of the parking lot. Placing a call to Luke he promised he would be careful, but would try to get fingerprints, even if by subterfuge. *Jesus, that sounds creepy, even to my ears. But if she's in trouble, it'd be nice to at least know who I'm trying to help. I could find her house...or job...or something.*

Heart pounding, he drove to the large park in Charlestown, near the campus. The sunshine had brought out the families and college students, and quite a few dog walkers. *A perfect place for her to blend in for a while.*

Driving by the perimeter of the park for a few minutes he finally realized he did not have a clear enough view of the acreage. Parking, he began to walk swiftly along the sidewalks meandering throughout the park. Forcing himself to slow down so as to not draw attention, he continued to search.

Every single, dark-haired woman caught his gaze, quickly dismissed as soon as he could ascertain they were not who he sought. So caught up in his surveillance, he missed the disappointed expressions on several women he walked by, his gaze looking right through them.

His eyes darted to every dog chasing balls, catching Frisbees, or just walking along with their masters. He made his way past the picnics and the college students lounging in the sun. Basketball courts were on one side with tennis courts on another. A large, flat area, big enough for a soccer game, had children running around kicking balls.

Turning around and around, he grew frustrated when there was no sign of her. *How big is this place?* He had driven by it many times but had never taken the opportunity to walk around. The enormity of the park when trying to find one woman was overwhelming, especially if that woman did not want to be found.

Privacy…she'd be looking for somewhere private. Seeing a small pond in the distance, he headed toward it, noting benches along the path and into the trees bordering two sides of the water.

He was almost two-thirds around the pond when a deep bark sounded from the edge of the woods. His gaze jerked quickly to the sound and he saw a German Shepherd bounding toward a bench, partially hidden in the shadows of the trees. A few more steps and he could see…her. His Mystery Lady.

He let out a breath he did not realize he had been holding. She did not see him, but he could not take his eyes off her. Her hair, pulled back into a braid hanging over her shoulder, looked like it had been combed then braided. Still wearing the oversized jacket, on a warm day, he wondered now if it was to give her a place to put food if she came across it. His suspicions were confirmed when she reached into her pocket and pulled out a treat for the dog as it bounded back to her.

Blaise, rooted to the sidewalk, stared at her large eyes, sparkling in the daylight as her head was thrown back in laughter before she bent forward, grabbing the dog's furry face in her hands and kissing its nose. Squatting, she wrapped her arms around the animal, both creatures sharing a moment of unadulterated love. *Beautiful.* And his heart squeezed once more.

Suddenly, the dog turned toward him and growled, planting its body protectively in front of the Mystery Lady once more. He watched as her gaze jerked to his and her body readied for flight.

"No, no," Blaise begged, lifting his hands upwards. "Please don't go, Miss. I only want to help. You and your dog. Please."

She stood, her body tense, staring at the man she recognized from the previous night at the bar. Warily, she watched as he once again kept his distance, his hands up. "What do you want? Have you been following me?" she asked, fear evident in her voice.

"I just want to help."

Licking her dry lips, she kept her fingers lightly on Gypsy's fur, both calming the growling dog and calming herself.

"I don't want to frighten you," he said. "If you want, I can sit on the ground, not too close to you."

She stared a moment, uncertain of his intentions. Watching as he sat down cross-legged about ten feet away, she noted he kept his hands on his knees where she could see them. Her head lifted in pride, although her eyes shifted nervously. "Why do you think I need help?"

Shaking his head, he said, "Miss, I'm sure you were hungry last night." His eyes dropped to the dog, no longer growling, but watching him with the same wariness as his mistress. "And no one, not even a dog, should have to eat from a trash can."

A flash of embarrassment crossed her face, quickly replaced by irritation. "I...I do what I have to do."

"I'd like to check out your dog," Blaise continued. "I'm a veterinarian. What's its name?"

The woman was quiet for a long moment and he thought she was not going to answer him. He waited patiently, his gaze moving between the beautiful woman and the dog, who had now relaxed its stance.

Finally, she spoke, softly saying, "Gypsy. Her name is Gypsy."

"Gypsy," he repeated with a smile, thinking of the similarity between the dog and the woman. "That's a beautiful name for a beautiful dog." He held out his hand, palm up, and waited.

The woman nudged Gypsy and the dog trotted over to Blaise, immediately sniffing him, allowing him to run his expert hands over the dog's body.

No broken bones, hips good, teeth good. Probably

about three years old. Coat in decent condition. Glancing back up to the woman, he wished that she would accept his offer of assistance.

Continuing to ruffle the dog's fur, he said, "She's a beauty, Miss, that's for sure. Have you had her since she was a puppy?"

The change in the woman's breathing was instant and Blaise was aware his question sent her into anxiety, but had no idea why.

"Gypsy," she called sharply, "we have to go."

The dog immediately trotted over to her and Blaise stood slowly. "Hey, I'm not trying to cause a problem. Please let me help. If nothing else, let me provide some food for both of you."

That appeared to cause the woman hesitation and he continued to pursue that line of persuasion. "The dog's bones and musculature are good, but the coat could use a good brushing and is definitely showing signs that the diet is lacking in some vitamins." He pierced her with his gaze, a smile playing on his lips, and said, "Look, you're completely right to be scared of me. I'm a stranger and you've got no reason to trust me. But, I swear, we can walk to one of the food trucks nearby for lunch. We'll be out in the open and you won't have to be afraid. Okay?"

Please, come on Mystery Lady…say yes.

SHE HAD BEEN stunned when the man from the bar

stepped off the path near her and her instinct was to run. *Why didn't I?* She felt safe with Gypsy guarding her, but it was more than that. It was the way he did not try to approach. The way he held his hands up again. Then it was the way he looked over her dog, carefully examining it. *And the way he calls me Miss.*

His offer of help was so wanted…needed. But, not knowing what might be out there…if anyone…held her back. He looked so kind. So trustworthy. *How would I know?* she chastised herself. Just then her stomach growled loudly and the idea of eating something from one of the food trucks around the edge of the park had her mouth watering. Sparing a glance down to Gypsy, she looked into the dog's trusting eyes. *How can I refuse?*

Lifting her gaze once more to the man, patiently waiting for her reply, she allowed herself a moment of wishing he really could help her. *I need someone. I can't keep living this way.*

Nodding slowly, she said, "Okay. Yes. Uh…I'd like some lunch."

Stepping back onto the path, Blaise grinned, making sure to give the woman and Gypsy a wide berth to walk beside him without crowding them. She offered a small smile in return for the gesture.

The dog trotted between them as they walked at an easy pace. "I know Gypsy's name, but we haven't been introduced. I'm Blaise. Blaise Hanssen." A few steps passed and he looked over at his companion. "And you are?"

Stumbling, she blurted out, "I'd rather not say." Breathing rapidly, she cringed. *That sounded rude! Why couldn't I have come up with a name…any name?*

Noting her hesitancy, he simply nodded. "I can understand you wanting to be cautious. I'm a strange man to you."

They stood awkwardly for a moment before he said, "I hate not calling you anything. How about you tell me what you'd like me to call you." As she seemed to hesitate, he added, "I hate to call you the Mystery Lady."

At that, she smiled and appeared to relax. "It was nice when you called me Miss."

Keeping the pleasant smile on his face, he now knew she might be running from something or some-one. *Her hesitancy is more than just being wary of a strange man.* Wanting to alleviate the panic from her face, he simply nodded and pointed to a few of the trucks on the park's edge. "What are you in the mood for, Miss? Looks like we have tacos, barbecue, hot dogs, Korean, and," he stretched over to look further down the road, "probably meatball subs."

Her stomach growled loudly again, the intoxicating smells holding her hostage. She wavered on her feet, suddenly overwhelmed with the choices. Blaise reached out and grabbed her arms to steady her.

"Hey, let's get you some water first," he said. Quickly paying for two water bottles, he ushered her to a seat nearby. Most of the lunch crowd had passed and they sat in silence for a few minutes, drinking the water after she offered some to Gypsy.

Blushing, she gazed up at Blaise. "I'm sorry," she said. "I felt a little…" her voice trailed off, not knowing what else to say. Swooning at the handsome man's feet was hardly what she expected to do.

Pleased to be sitting close to her, he smiled. "Look, Miss. Let's be honest. I know you're hungry. I know your dog must be hungry. I don't know what your situation is, but honest to God, I only want to help."

She peered deeply into his eyes, searching for…and finding…sincerity. Nodding slightly, she agreed. Looking over at the trucks again, she said, "It all sounds so good, but I think what I'd really like is a hotdog."

Grinning at the progress, Blaise confirmed, "Then hotdogs it is! Come on, you can fix them the way you and Gypsy like them." Standing, he reached for her hand without even thinking about it.

Startled, she held on tight as his long legs headed toward the hot dog truck with her dog trotting right along with them. And for the first time in weeks, she smiled. Her heart felt ever so slightly lighter. And it looked like her stomach was going to soon be full. Allowing him to link fingers with her, she eagerly walked toward food.

❧

AN HOUR LATER, both woman and dog were sated, full

of hotdogs, fries, and even a milkshake from an ice cream vendor.

The conversation was slow, as Blaise realized it would take more than a full stomach to earn her trust. He was cognizant that she kept the conversation light and definitely off of anything to do with her.

Looking over, he grinned, seeing the satisfied expression on her face. He had pretended not to notice when she snuck a few pieces of her second hot dog into the pocket of her jacket, sure that it was for Gypsy later on in the evening. He had no doubt she took care of the dog before her own needs. *A woman after my own heart…wait, what?* His smile slipped as the thought ran through his mind.

"Are you alright?" she asked, her face full of concern.

"Yes, yes," he hurriedly answered.

"Okay, well, I should be going," she replied. "I want to thank —"

Just then Blaise's phone rang. Seeing it was Luke, he said, "Please stay…I just need to take this call."

Receiving her nod, he only walked away a few feet, unwilling to let her out of his sight again. "Luke, sorry. I'm talking with *someone.*"

Luke, catching on, asked, "You found her? Where?"

"I'm having lunch at the park."

"Can you get any info from her? Does she need our help?"

"I'm working on the file you're interested in. I

think it needs more work," Blaise responded cryptically. He caught her smile and he smiled in return.

"Got it," Luke answered.

"Right," Blaise replied before disconnecting, walking back over to the picnic table.

"Sounds like I'm keeping you from work," she said, standing, wiping her hands delicately on the napkin.

"No, no, it's fine. I'm okay. In fact, I'm having a nice time," he said honestly.

She peered up into his face once more as though searching for something. He had no idea what she was looking for, but hoped she found it in him.

Sticking out her hand, she said, "I really need to go, but I want to thank you. I appreciate you buying us lunch." Her other hand was fingering Gypsy's fur.

Blaise took her hand in his much larger one. Giving it a small shake, he discovered he did not want to let it go. Staring into her dark chocolate eyes, he was stuck with the thought that she was not just a charity case. A mystery. A mission to assist someone down on their luck. *I want to know this woman. I want her to trust me enough to tell me what is going on in her life. I want—*

Her hand pulled back from his, jerking him out of his musings.

"It was nice meeting you, Blaise."

"And you too…uh…Miss." He caught the slight wince as he hesitated over what to call her. "I'd like to see you again. Is there any chance that perhaps we can meet tomorrow?"

Seeing the wariness come across her face once more, he rushed to say, "We could...I don't know...uh...maybe meet right here again?"

She looked around in indecision, biting her lip. Finally, she nodded slowly and said, "Sure. I'll be around. There's no pressure. If you come, you come. If not...well, thanks for today."

With that, she turned and hurried down the sidewalk, Gypsy by her side as always.

Blaise stood rooted to the path, not moving until she was no longer in sight. Letting out a deep breath, he moved to the picnic table they had sat at. His mind churning, he tried to make sense of his emotions. He always collected strays...*isn't that what everyone says? I just wanted to help her. No one should go hungry. And she gave half her food to her dog.* He smiled, thinking of the dog's absolute trusting loyalty to her.

Always one to trust an animal's instinct over a human's, he knew the woman was a good person. *One I want to help...yeah, right,* he thought as his gaze traveled down the street where she had disappeared. *She's one I want to know.*

CHAPTER 5

BACK AT THE place where she and Gypsy stayed, she wondered, *Why the hell did I agree to let him buy me lunch? I've been avoiding people for weeks. Now he wants to meet me again.* Looking down at Gypsy's body, napping on the blanket now that she had a full stomach, she knew she had the answer. *We both needed that, didn't we girl?*

She rubbed her head in frustration. Her fingertips ran over the scar on her forehead. When she had woken up, that morning weeks ago, she felt blood running down her face but had not sought help. It was frightening not knowing whom to trust. *How can I trust anyone…when I don't remember who I am?*

It was amazing how much more complacent she felt now that hunger pains were not stabbing at her. *I don't feel the pervasive fear that's plagued me.* Glancing back to Gypsy, she thought of how Blaise had quickly earned her dog's trust. *I don't understand why, but if you trust him, it seems like I can too.*

Deciding to follow Gypsy's example and take a nap, she lay beside the large, warm dog. For the first time in weeks, slumber came easily, with dreams of a tall, muscular, blond, blue-eyed man staying with her.

THE NEXT DAY, by noontime, Blaise paced the sidewalk in front of the park where the food trucks were stationed, his eyes scanning the area. Fifteen minutes passed and his frustration grew with each minute.

Finally, a deep bark sounded behind him and he turned quickly, already recognizing the German Shepherd's bark. Gypsy bounded over to him and as he bent to ruffle the dog's fur, he lifted his eyes, seeing Miss walking toward him. Her hair, brushed again, was pulled back in another braid. She wore the same old jacket, but he could see a different t-shirt underneath. Her shy smile made her large eyes shine even brighter. *She really is quite beautiful.*

As she approached, he noticed her face glowed from a scrubbing but, while her hair was neat, it appeared that she had not washed it in a few days. A slight frown crossed his expression as he realized wherever she was staying, running water might not be readily available. *Fuck! I never thought of that.*

Miss watched his face change from one of excitement to one of disgust and her steps faltered. His eyes were latched on her hair and she unconsciously lifted her hand upward, wondering if she had something on her. *No, he's just disgusted.* Halting several feet away, uncertainty filling her soul, she felt the sting of tears hit the back of her eyes. Breathing deeply, she willed them away.

Blaise noted her hand shaking as it reached up, patting her hair, then dropped down to her eyes, filling with tears as an embarrassed blush crept up her face. "Hey, what's wrong?"

She stared at him. His voice sounded so concerned, but mixed with the expression that had been on his face, she was confused. "I…um…haven't had a chance to…um…shower…um today."

Understanding hit Blaise as he realized she had noticed him staring at her, and misinterpreted his concern over her lack of water. "No, you look great!" he said, taking her hand. Pinning her with his gaze, he smiled. "Really great."

She peered once again, looking deeply into his eyes, searching for deceit but finding none. Sighing, she nodded but said nothing.

He gave a slight tug on her hand, saying, "So what's lunch going to be today?"

The corners of her mouth turned up in a smile again, and her gaze moved past him to the trucks. "I don't care. Why don't you surprise me?"

Grinning widely, he agreed. "Okay, you and Gypsy go sit on that bench and face the park. I'll get some lunch for all of us."

Cocking her head to the side, she asked, "Why do I need to face the park?"

" 'Cause if you're watching me, then it won't be a

surprise!"

Laughing, she agreed and moved over to the bench with Gypsy close at her heels. In a few minutes, he returned, carrying a bag filled with tacos. The tantalizing scent of the spicy beef assaulted her nostrils and had Gypsy's nose quivering and tail wagging.

The three of them dug into their lunch, the sounds of the others in the park fading into the distance as the world seemed to narrow to just the trio.

An airplane flew overhead and Miss looked up at the same time Gypsy stopped eating. The dog stood rigid, as though at attention, and Miss casually commented, "Must be landing. Their flaps are down."

The taco halted on its way to Blaise's mouth as he turned in surprise toward her. "How can you tell?"

"The sound," she replied, still focusing on her lunch. "Landing planes make a different sound." As the aircraft continued on its downward path out of sight, Gypsy relaxed, returning to her food as well.

Blaise wondered, *How would she know that?* Looking back down at the dog, he wondered about its behavior as well. Wanting to understand more, he asked, "Have you spent much time at an airport?"

He watched as her forehead crinkled in thought, then her hand jerked to the scar. A look of panic formed on her face and she immediately set her food down, her body tensed for flight again.

"I'm sorry," Blaise quickly said, putting his hand on her arm. "I was just curious." He kept his eyes on hers, realizing what he saw beyond the panic…was confusion. *Something's happened to her…something traumatic.* Understanding she was not just a homeless person, but could be in trouble, ratcheted up his concern even more. "Please, let's just enjoy our food."

She would not make eye contact with him, but simply nodded. The silence stretched as they both finished their meals and she bent down to pick up the well-licked wrapper off the ground, petting Gypsy's head. Leaning back, Miss patted her stomach, unused to being full for two days in a row.

"This was amazing. Thank you," she said. "I can't remember food tasting so good."

"When was the last really good meal you ate?" Blaise asked gently, his gaze roaming her satisfied expression, hoping she would be honest with him.

A long minute of silence passed as she appeared to be working something out in her head. At long last, she said, "I don't remember."

Unsure what to say to that, he continued to sit silently. His mind whirling at the myriad of possibilities concerning her past, he pondered how to get her to confide in him. *Animals are so much easier than people to figure out!* Deciding to plunge ahead, he asked, "How did you get here?"

A slight giggle erupted and she said, "I walked, of course!"

Chuckling, he noted the deep chocolate eyes, normally full of doubt, now full of mirth. Once more struck with her beauty, he hesitated, not wanting to scare her away. "No, I meant how did you get to Charlestown? Are you from here?"

Her brow crinkled again, as she looked down. "No...I came from somewhere else."

No further response was given, so they sat in silence for a few more minutes. Finally, Blaise placed his hand on her arm, saying, "I don't want to make you uncomfortable. I...well, I just wanted to know more about you."

"Why?" she asked, this time, no suspicion in her expression.

Shrugging, he admitted, "I'm not really sure. I guess because at first I noticed you seemed to need some help. And now...I'd like to know you better."

She turned toward the park, her face now wistful, and said softly, "There's not much to tell."

Deciding he had pushed his luck for the day, he asked, "Can we meet tomorrow?"

Smiling shyly, she turned back to face him. "Are you going to keep buying me lunch?"

"If you'll let me."

Standing, she took Gypsy's leash and nodded. "Okay, then. Tomorrow." With that, she walked away, leaving Blaise once more watching her disappear.

"WHAT'S THE LATEST on the new assignment, Boss?" Marc asked, the Saints sitting around the conference table discussing upcoming cases.

Jack handed him a file. There's a conference in Alaska and we've been tasked to provide security and flight arrangements for one of the participants.

Marc nodded and began perusing the file. Blaise walked in, apologizing. "Sorry, I'm late."

Luke looked up, saying, "You still meeting the mystery woman?" This comment drew the attention of the other men.

Sliding into his seat, Blaise nodded. "Yeah. Today made the fourth day she has met me at the park and I buy lunch for her and her dog."

"What has she told you about herself?" Cam asked.

"Not much," Blaise admitted, "but each day she seems more comfortable." Looking at Luke, he added, "I don't get the feeling that she's scared of men, which makes me think she's not running from an abusive relationship. She's not giving her name, and seems very reticent to give me any information."

"I've gone through the missing person reports from Charlestown and Richland. I've also now been looking at the ones from around the state. I'll branch out if you want."

Cam cleared his throat and spoke hesitantly, "You don't think she might be running from the law?"

Blaise shook his head slowly, responding, "I know I need to look at all possibilities, but I don't get that vibe. She's not hiding. She's out in the open." Looking back up, he affirmed, "No, no way."

"Good enough, man," Cam replied, a smile replacing his concern. "I gotta tell you that Miriam was asking about her last night. Wondering if you had found out more. She was worried that you said the woman had a scar on her forehead that might not have been taken care of."

"Do you think Miriam would take a look at her if I could get her to agree?" Blaise asked.

"Hell, yeah."

"Okay, tomorrow, I'll see if I can step things up more."

Jack brought the meeting back to the other missions at hand, but Blaise found his thoughts wandering back to the beautiful, lost, and very alone woman…and her protective dog. Seeing her each day had quickly become the highlight of his week—a thought he refused to spend any time analyzing. He looked up and caught Marc smiling at him, a knowing expression on his friend's face.

~

FOR THE NEXT three days, Blaise met with Gypsy and her beautiful owner. Each day they had something different to eat and he realized that he looked forward to meeting them. She relaxed bit by bit, her skittishness easing each time they met. He was pleased to see her eat and at least knew she and Gypsy had one full meal a day.

Days later Blaise paced back and forth wearing the

grass down near the picnic table they always ate at. Constantly looking at his watch, he wondered where she was. *Is she hurt? Sick? Did she take off again? Did I scare her off?*

Thirty minutes passed and he grew more worried by the moment. Running his hand through his thick hair, he began to curse under his breath, drawing the censure of a few moms passing by.

Where can she be? Why, oh why didn't I get her—

"Blaise!" her voice cried, the sound almost drowned out by the pounding of her feet on the pavement as she ran toward him.

Relief flooded him until he caught sight of her face as she came closer and his eyes dropped to her side. *Where's Gypsy? Fuck!*

She did not stop running until she collapsed almost at his feet. His arms reached out, gathering her, as he dropped to the ground with her.

Panting to the point of not being able to speak, she tried nonetheless. "Gyp…sy…some…thing…wrong."

He brushed her hair, now loose from its braid, away from her flushed face. "Breathe, sweetheart. Slow it down, and breathe."

Her breath hitched as she continued to speak, "You…got…ta…come…Gyp…sy."

He stood, assisting her from the ground, and said, "Let's go. I'll drive and you can show me where she is."

A nod was her only answer as he kept his arm around her waist offering her support. Thankful, because he parked his jeep close by, they were inside and pulling away from the park within a few minutes.

"Where are we going?"

Her head jerked around, looking out the windows. "I don't know the street names. But turn around and I'll take you the way I come."

Following her directions, it took fifteen minutes to drive and Blaise realized how far she had been walking every day, just to meet him at the park. *Why didn't I ever ask? I could have saved her all this walking!* His face, a mask of irritation, matched his tight grip on the steering wheel.

She looked over, seeing his anger. Hanging her head, she realized he was going out of his way to help her—again—and this time, it appeared that he was mad about it. She felt guilty, but pushed that emotion to the background, willing to face his ire to help Gypsy.

"Here, turn here," she said, pointing down a long drive at the end of a cul-de-sac.

He followed her pointing finger, noting the weeds were tall, the grass not trimmed in what appeared to be years. His curiosity piqued, he wondered what dwelling he would find at the end of the drive. His answer appeared before him, but it was all he could do to not gawk.

A ramshackle shack stood amongst the weeds. The windows were broken out and it appeared uninhabitable...possibly for years. *She lives here? No fuckin' way!*

She jumped out of the vehicle, almost before it

came to a stop, rushing toward the back of the house. Blaise followed closely as they rounded to the back door and watched in horror as she simply gave it a strong push to open it. *The lack of basic security almost drove him to his knees.*

Inside, she rushed through what was originally the kitchen and into the front room. On a pallet of old blankets, laid Gypsy. She dropped down next to the dog, who whimpered its greeting.

"What happened?" Blaise asked, immediately squatting next to the dog as well.

"She was fine this morning and I let her run in the yard for just a bit. Then she came limping back, barely putting any weight on her front right leg. By the time this happened, it was almost time to leave to meet you. I kept trying to see what was wrong, but she snapped at me. Then it was so late to meet you, but I knew you could help her, so I ran all the way."

Blaise glanced at the woman, seeing the tears form, stunned that she had run the several miles to get to the park. "It's fine. She wasn't upset with you. She was just protecting her injury," he said, gently.

She sniffed, wiping her nose and nodded forlornly. "I don't know what's wrong. If something happens to her, I don't know what I'll do…she's my only friend." This time, the battle to keep the tears at bay ended and a choked sob broke through.

"She's not going to die, sweetheart," he assured, capturing her chin with his fingers, lifting her face to his. "Promise."

She held his gaze for a moment and then sucked in a ragged breath, nodding her affirmation.

"It appears she stepped on something in the yard and she's injured her paw." He noticed Gypsy's understanding gaze, as he gently probed the injured area and ran his hand lovingly down her fur.

"We need to take her to my house. I have a clinic there. I do not have a private practice here, but I am licensed to treat animals, including the many strays that are given to me." He expected her to hesitate, but her love for Gypsy was evident as she jumped up and immediately agreed.

As they stood, his eyes now roamed around the room. Completely bare except for the pile of blankets, which he realized was her bed as well. *Fuckin' hell!* An old broom stood in the corner, obviously used recently because, while the house itself was a barely-standing dump, it was swept clean. The windows, while dirty, would do nothing to keep someone from seeing her. He was sure there was no running water—no shower, no toilet, no drinking water.

His eyes pierced hers and he ordered, "Grab whatever you want to take with us. She'll need to stay overnight and I'm not letting you come back here."

She had no idea where she would stay but, if he allowed, she would bed down with Gypsy at his clinic. *And his voice did not seem as though he was giving her a choice.* Strangely, that was okay. Nodding, she said,

"Let's go. I want her taken care of. And anyway…" her voice grew soft. "I've got nothing to take, other than a change of clothes." She bent and grabbed a small backpack, hoisted it over her shoulder and then bent toward Gypsy.

Blaise gently pushed her out of the way, handing her his keys. "Go open the door and I'll carry her."

Within a few minutes, they were back on the road. Blaise glanced in the rear-view mirror at Miss sitting with Gypsy's head in her lap and smiled. As crazy as it seemed…this felt right.

CHAPTER 6

S HE LOOKED THROUGH the window as they pulled
onto a gravel driveway through the woods, suddenly realizing her situation. *I'm in a vehicle, with a
stranger, who's taking me to his home. Oh, Jesus, don't let
this be a mistake!*

As if reading her thoughts, he said, "I know you're
scared. Please, Miss. I swear I only want to help you
and Gypsy."

Holding his gaze in the mirror, the tight band
around her throat eased and she breathed deeply.
"Okay," she whispered. "I trust you."

She jerked her head around as they parked, seeing a
neat, older house at the end of the drive. The sound of
dogs barking their greeting filled the air, causing Gypsy
to lift her head, ears perked in alarm.

Blaise hopped out of the driver's seat and opened
the back door. Leaning in, he handed his keys to her
before lifting the dog into his strong arms.

Following the pair, she noted how effortlessly he
carried the large burden, as though it was nothing.
Stepping around him, she unlocked the door, opening

it for them. Blaise moved through the house with a purpose, straight past the living room, kitchen, stairs, and into a back room. At a quick glance, she could see it did resemble a veterinarian's office.

He placed the dog on the examining table and murmured comforting words. Gypsy laid quietly, her eyes full of trust. Taking the dog's cue, she stayed by her side, petting her and feeling at ease in his home.

She watched in fascination as Blaise immediately began to examine Gypsy. After he worked his way from her nose to her tail, soothing the animal constantly, he moved to her injured paw. Gypsy stayed still, comfortable with his examination. "You're good at that," she said. "It's like she completely trusts you."

"I like animals," he admitted. "Sometimes more than people."

Grinning, she nodded her understanding, running her hand over the thick fur.

"Be careful," he warned. "She might snap as I probe her paw."

"She won't."

"You have a lot of trust in your dog. How long have the two of you been together?"

No answer was forthcoming, causing Blaise to look up at the woman's face. Her expression was indiscernible—part sadness, part fear, part longing. Before he could question her further, she whispered.

"As long as I can remember."

He wanted to ask her what that meant. The dog

was only a couple of years old...*certainly not old enough for her to not be able to remember when she got her.* Turning his confused mind back to the task at hand, he probed the paw with a pair of forceps.

"Looks like she's got a small piece of glass embedded." He continued to gently extract the offensive material, speaking softly to Gypsy throughout the procedure. Turning, he grabbed swabs and chlorhexidine. Treating the entire paw, he wrapped it up in gauze.

"Will she be all right? Will she need stitches?" she asked, concern in her voice.

As he answered, Blaise lifted his gaze and was struck dumb by the large, warm eyes staring right at him. Trusting. Mesmerized, he stumbled over his words, saying, "Uh...uh...no...um, no stitches." Giving himself a mental headshake, he brought his mind back to the task. "But she needs to stay off of the outside ground for a few days. She needs to stay indoors, where she won't get a chance to re-injure herself or step in something that can bring on infection."

She nodded, biting her lip. "Okay..." she agreed hesitantly. "But, I don't know where we'll—"

"You'll stay here," Blaise stated as though the matter was decided, then saw the error of his ways when he observed the narrowed eyes of his guest. "I mean," he hastened to say, "that Gypsy needs to stay here and there's no way I can allow you to go back to that tumble-down shack. It's a miracle you haven't been attacked."

"I think having a guard dog probably kept me safe," she mumbled.

"Well, since your source of protection needs to be taken care of, I'm the next best solution."

Her eyes shifted around the room as she asked, "Where would I sleep? Can I get some blankets to sleep in here?" Her gaze suddenly jumped to his as she stammered, "Or I can sleep outside. I didn't mean to imply that I'd—"

"Shhh," Blaise admonished. "I don't know what all's gone on in your life, but I promise, you're safe now. I've got a spare bedroom that has its own bathroom."

Looking askance, she shook her head. "Oh, no. I couldn't impose. You've got a small barn out back. Gypsy and I'll be fine in there."

"I know you're scared and that makes you smart, and I'm racking my brain trying to figure out a way to let you know you're safe with me." Placing his hand on his hip, he blurted in frustration, "But there's no way I'm letting a woman sleep in a shed when I've got a place for her here. Please. I just want to help."

She continued to hesitate and Blaise knew it was a risk to offer a defenseless woman his spare bedroom. The silence stretched between them as he let her ponder her choices. Her eyes glanced back down to a resting Gypsy and her expression softened as she slowly nodded. "Okay. Gypsy trusts you, so…I'll stay." Lifting her gaze back to his, she said, "And thank you…for everything."

Letting out his breath, he grinned. "Let's get you situated. I'll fix something to eat since we didn't have lunch and you can take a shower if you'd like."

Her warm eyes sparkled as she tried to hide her pleasure, but she nodded enthusiastically. "Yes, please! I haven't had a full shower since…well, in a long time." Ducking her head as she stumbled over her comment, she was grateful when he left it alone.

She followed him dutifully as he led her back through the house, noting that even with an older dog following them and several cats around, the space was neat and clean. The kitchen was not large, but sufficient. The living room was much bigger since it appeared to be combined with what would have been a dining room as well. He led her up the stairs and she accepted the towels he handed her.

"My room and bathroom are here on the left," he said, "and the second bedroom is on the right, with the bathroom here." He opened the door at the end of the short hall, exposing a small, but clean, bathroom.

Her breath caught in her throat as she looked at the facilities. *I've sponged bathed in public bathrooms for…how long now? Weeks?* The white tiled room, gleaming in cleanliness, overwhelmed her. She looked up, realizing he had been speaking and she completely missed what he had said.

"I'm sorry," she gushed, tucking a strand of dirty

hair behind her ear. "What did you say?"

"I just wanted to know if you needed anything."

"No, no, this is more than enough."

He stood for a moment, her words striking deep inside of him. *A small bathroom is more than enough. Where have you been? What happened to you?* Sucking in a deep breath, he said, "Well, I'll be downstairs if you need anything." He glanced down to the small backpack she carried. "Hang on," he said, as he turned and headed into his bedroom. Returning, he handed her one of his old DEA t-shirts. "I know it'll be big, but it's clean. We'll wash clothes tonight."

As the worn-soft material slid through her fingers, she clutched it tightly, bringing it to her chest, catching the clean scent of detergent. "Thank you, again," she whispered, not trusting her voice.

"Um, there's some shower gel, shampoo, and some…um…products under the sink in there. My sister comes for a visit occasionally and she leaves things here so she doesn't have to bring them with her. She'd be happy for you to use anything."

Sucking in her lips, knowing if she spoke now she would burst into tears, she simply nodded.

With a grin, he turned and headed back down the stairs. She watched him until he disappeared, his large body moving gracefully. Swallowing the lump in her throat, she hoped she was not making a mistake staying at his house. *I'm not afraid of him…I'm afraid of feeling something for him.*

Taking a deep breath, she hurried into the bathroom, locking the door behind her. A few minutes later, stepping into the shower, letting the water sluice over her body, she luxuriated in the simple act of washing every part of her body. She found a razor and sweet smelling shaving cream, coconut body wash, shampoo, and conditioner. After scrubbing her hair, she stepped out of the tub, into the steaming room, not minding that the mirror was foggy. She allowed the steam to slowly dissipate as she took her time using coconut lotion over her entire body. By the time she finished and towel dried her hair, she could see her reflection in the mirror.

Her skin was pink from the heat and scrubbing. Fresh. Clean. Her long hair hung down her back in wet tendrils. Her eyes drifted downward, taking in her body. *I've definitely lost some weight since…being on my own.* Moving her gaze back to her face as she applied lotion, she noted the reddish scar marring her forehead. Her fingertips moved over it gently, a grimace replacing her complacent expression. *How the hell did this all happen?*

BLAISE MOVED ABOUT the kitchen fixing the late lunch, three cats swirling between his legs. "Come on, guys. Let me get this going and then I'll feed you." His mind had stayed on the woman upstairs in the bathroom. Grabbing his phone from the counter, he called Jack.

"Hey, boss. I wanted to let you know that I've got the Mystery Lady here with me. Her dog was injured and she came to our meeting place to find me."

"They okay?" Jack asked.

"Yeah, but I'm going to have to keep him and I'm letting her stay here while the dog's recuperating here as well."

Silence greeted him and he rushed to explain. "I saw the hovel she was living in. Jack, it's amazing she hasn't been attacked."

"Don't take this the wrong way, Blaise, because there's not one of us that wouldn't have stepped in to help this woman, but are you sure about having her there? You do have a propensity for—"

"Picking up strays," Blaise finished, irritated that his boss would make the comparison. "But this is different. There's something about her that draws me in. I want to unravel the mystery of who she is."

Jack chuckled, saying, "You got it, man. Do you need us?"

"Maybe. I'm going to find out what's going on with her, hopefully, tonight. Then, if she's in trouble, I'll contact you."

"Whatever you need," Jack agreed.

"Thanks, boss," Blaise replied, disconnecting. By now the three cats had jumped on the counter in a more desperate effort to gain his attention. "Get down," he admonished, moving into the back room, putting food down in their dishes. "You'd better appreciate the fact that you're getting fed early."

Walking back into the kitchen, he ran into Miss. She yelped as she stumbled backward, his arms rushing out to grab her shoulders.

"Sorry!" they both exclaimed at once.

Blaise's hands did not leave her as his mind rushed to catch up to his vision. Soft, dark waves of shiny brunette hair flowed down her back. Her face scrubbed clean exposed light freckles across her nose. Her cheeks blushed a rosy pink. Her lips, curved in a smile, captured his attention as he longed to pull her in the rest of the way. Moving his gaze around, it finally landed on her wide, dark eyes, startling him back to his senses.

Letting go of her shoulders as though burned, he exclaimed, "I'm sorry, Miss. How was your shower? You look amazing, just amazing. Not that you weren't…um…nice before…but now…well—"

She giggled, watching the normally self-assured man stumble and bumble over his words. "The shower was fabulous. And thank you for letting me use your sister's toiletries. I haven't been this clean in…well, a bit."

Her words brought him back to reality. "We've got to talk. But first, let's eat." He noticed her immediate concern and said, "Remember, I just want to help."

Opening up slightly, she said, "That's sweet, but I don't think anyone can help me."

Hating the despondency in her voice, he placed his

hands on her shoulders, turned her around and gave her a little push toward the kitchen bar stools. "Well, we'll fill our bellies and then see what we can do."

The sight of a large salad, huge triple-decker club sandwich cut in quarters, and chips was enough to stop her worry for the moment.

"It's not much, but—"

"No, no, it's perfect," she gushed.

The two sat down at the stools and ate in companionable silence for several minutes. She finally turned to him, saying, "When I came down, I heard you talking to someone in the back room. Is Gypsy all right?"

Nodding while chewing, Blaise swallowed and replied, "I was talking to the three house cats. They were annoying me while I was trying to fix the sandwiches so I put them in the back room with some food."

"Do you talk to your animals a lot?" she queried. "I find myself talking to Gypsy all the time like she's a person."

Grinning, he allowed his gaze to move over her face once again, his cock instinctively jumping at the sound of her voice, and those beguiling eyes staring at him. Irritated with his lack of self-control, he willed it to behave. "I think that happens when you live alone," he replied. "My animals are my world."

Nodding her agreement, she continued to eat. Stopping only halfway through, she pushed the plate back gently. "I'm stuffed," she confessed.

"Are you sure? You look like you need to eat more."

Giggling, she patted his muscular bicep, saying, "Not all of us are so big!"

He reached over, snagging the rest of her sandwich, finishing it off as well. Standing, he took the plates to the sink and left them, wanting to learn more about her. Holding his hand out to her, he said, "Come on, sweetheart. We need to take care of the animals and then we need to talk."

Licking her lips nervously, she agreed. *I've got no idea if you can help me, but Gypsy and I are running out of options.*

She trailed behind him, observing as he filled a wheelbarrow with buckets of feed before they walked outside to the kennels. It only took a moment for her to quickly follow his lead and begin filling the dishes of food as he hosed out the kennels.

"Are you keeping them?" she wondered aloud.

"No, they're boarding here while recovering from one thing or another. They'll be adopted out as soon as they're able."

He looked over his shoulder as she playfully talked to and petted each one. With the setting sun casting a glow over the yard, her eyes were alight, the genuine smile on her face taking his breath away. *She's got a way with animals.* The strange realization sent pleasure throughout him as he smiled at her obvious joy.

Finishing with their work, they pushed the now empty wheelbarrow back to the door and went inside the house. Washing at the large industrial sink in the clinic, she followed him into the living quarters.

Placing her small hand in his much larger one, she relished the feel of his fingers closing around hers. Protectively. *Possessively? No, get that idea out of your head, girl. He's just helping.* But as he led her to the sofa in the living room, she knew she was in danger of falling for her rescuer.

CHAPTER 7

H E SETTLED HER down on his worn, but comfortable sofa, making sure to sit close, but not too close. Treating her like a skittish animal, he needed to provide comfort without appearing threatening.

She watched him closely, not sure what he wanted to talk about. Heart pounding, she sat straight, hands clasped in her lap. Then he smiled and her breath rushed out of her lungs. *I think I'd follow that smile to the ends of the earth.* Her lips curved softly in response.

"I want to tell you about me," Blaise started, "so you'll know how I can help. I'm a veterinarian, but I don't own my own practice. I worked for the DEA as a vet with their drug dogs. It allowed me to pay off my student loans. When I got out, I started a new career." He chuckled, adding, "Well, a couple of new careers, actually. I run this shelter and have a state license to treat the animals here. And, I'm a private investigator with a firm that specializes in big contracts."

At his last statement, her eyes widened as her mouth hung open. "I…I…don't understand," she confessed.

"I work for a company of investigators. We don't take the small time PI jobs. My boss gains government contracts, such as working with the FBI or other agencies or large private companies. We provide security and investigations." He held her gaze for a moment, seeing her mind turning over his words. "Miss, whatever's going on with you...I can...we can help."

Oh...I'm a case to him, she realized with disappointment. Looking into his eager face, she "Blaise, unless you're a mindreader, there's no help for me."

Not understanding her words, his eyes found her scar again. She noted his observation and lifted her fingers unconsciously to the injury.

"What happened?" he asked softly. "Let's start there."

Shaking her head sadly, she said, "I don't know."

The silence stretched uncomfortably. "Okay," he began again. "Let's start with who you are. What's your name? Where did you come from?"

Swallowing hard, she bit her bottom lip, wanting to look anywhere but into his eyes. He lifted her chin with his fingers, forcing her gaze to fall upon his. Taking a deep breath, she answered truthfully, "I don't know."

Cocking his head to the side, his lips turn down. "You don't know who you are?"

Shaking her head, again, she replied, "I can't remember anything."

The unexpected answer had Blaise dropping his hand, leaning back heavily as his breath left his body in an audible whoosh. *Can't remember? Amnesia?*

"I can see your mind working," she said. "Believe me, I've tried to understand what happened to me, but I don't."

"What's the first thing you remember?" he asked, his mind now working in a completely different direction. *Hell, I thought she was running from an ex or the law. Amnesia? What the hell?*

Shifting slightly on the sofa so that she was no longer facing him, but rather toward a view of the window overlooking his yard with the woods behind, she said, "I woke up. Out there somewhere."

Deciding to stay quiet so she could tell her story in her own time, he settled back as well, keeping his eyes on her.

"I was in the woods. In a car. It was at the bottom of a big ravine, with brambles all around. The car was crushed, but I was able to crawl out. My head was bloody. I looked inside the car to find something to wipe the blood away, but there was nothing in the car, so I took off my sweater. I got the dried blood off." She touched her scar again, her expression pained. "I didn't remember anything. My name. What I was doing. I don't even know if that was my car."

Blaise stood, moving to the kitchen to pour a glass of water, bringing it back and handing it to her. She took it gratefully, swallowing deeply, draining the glass.

"I heard a whimper…kind of a soft bark. There was a large dog next to the car. I was scared at first, but it came right to me, as though it knew me. There was a collar with a nametag. The only word on it was Gypsy."

"Was it your dog? Did the name mean anything to you?"

"No. I assumed it was my dog since we were deep into the woods and no one else was around."

"What did you do?"

"I climbed out of the ravine, which I discovered was very deep. When I got to the road above, you couldn't even see my car, nor were there any tell-tale signs." Giving a shrug, she said, "I had no idea what happened, but I thought my memory would come back. A trucker passed by and gave me a lift."

"You hitchhiked?" Blaise asked, unable to hide his protective irritation.

"Sure," she said. "How else was I going to get anywhere? The trucker was nice. He didn't ask any questions and dropped me off at the park in Charlestown. I stayed a few nights on park benches and then tried to find a homeless shelter when my memory did not return. But none of them would take me with a dog and I wasn't about to part with Gypsy. After all, she was the only friend I had."

Rubbing his hand over his face in frustration, Blaise tried to still his wildly tossing thoughts, for the first time unable to think methodically. He noticed her growing still and the doubtful expression on her face. Forcing an encouraging smile, he said, "So how long ago was this?"

"About three weeks," she replied. "I found the abandoned house and made a home for us there. It's horrible not remembering. I wanted to try to find someone to help me but didn't know whom to trust. What if someone was trying to harm me?"

"I've got to ask, why didn't you go to the police?" He knew his question sounded accusatory, but he was desperate to understand her motives.

Her face twisted in a mask of frustration. "You can't imagine what it's like…I didn't even know who I was. I couldn't think well and the fear…the overpowering fear. Even fear of the police."

"Were you not afraid of the trucker?"

Reaching up to touch her forehead, she said, "I remember that he offered to take me to a hospital. He seemed kind and Gypsy wasn't afraid of him. I think that's why I trusted him."

"And nothing has returned to you?"

"Sometimes, I have dreams…nightmares…but when I awake, I can't recall. Just images, darkness, fear." Her eyes implored him to understand. "I just can't remember anything about who I was before I crawled out of the wreck, with Gypsy at my side."

"A chip!" Blaise said suddenly, leaping from the sofa. "God, what an idiot I am!"

"Huh?"

He turned back to the wide-eyed woman on the sofa looking at him as though he was crazy. "If Gypsy was your beloved pet, you probably had her implanted with an identifier chip! I can't believe I didn't think to scan for that."

Leaning down to snag her hand, he escorted her to the back room, where Gyspy laid on a blanket, eyeing the three cats invading her space. He walked to a cabinet and grabbed a microchip scanner, before kneeling over the dog.

Running the scanner over the dog, his heart leaped when an identifier had been found. His eyes showed his enthusiasm as they sought hers. "We've got a number!"

"Will that tell me who I am?" she asked excitedly.

"Well, it will tell us who had the dog registered. Since you are the probable owner, then at least we'll know more than we did."

Taking the scanned number to the computer on the counter, he began to search. It did not take long for a hit to come up, but he stared at it in confusion. Turning slowly to her, he said, "I've got an identifier chip. It says TSA-GMK and then a number. I don't know what the rest of this means, but this identifies a Transportation Security dog."

~

TWO HOURS LATER, Blaise pulled into the driveway of Jack's property, Miss sitting stiffly in the passenger seat of his jeep. Glancing sideways, he noticed her posture and instinctively reached over to gather her hand in his, giving it a gentle squeeze.

Her gaze cut over to his before staring out of the window again. As Jack's large house came into view, she gasped. "Oh my goodness, this is beautiful." Then her eyes landed on the number of vehicles in the front. "Who all is here?" she asked, her voice tremulous.

"My boss called everyone in. Don't worry, sweetheart. I'll be right with you."

Nodding, she tamped down her desire to flee. *You wanted help and now you have it. Suck it up, girl and accept what's coming.*

Fifteen minutes later, she was ensconced on a large, overstuffed sofa, Blaise protectively at her side. She looked around in awe at the nine other large, handsome men in the room. They had been introduced but she would never remember all of their names. Bethany, a pretty blonde and Jack's wife, welcomed her before sitting down with her husband.

Blaise smiled at Bethany, glad that Jack asked her to join them, knowing her presence would have a calming effect on the inquisition.

Reining in her nervousness, she retold her story and then answered their questions to the best of her ability.

No, she did not remember her childhood or parents.

No, she did not remember her job.

No, she did not remember how she came to have a TSA dog.

The man identified as Luke, said, "We can try fingerprinting. We didn't get any hits on reported missing women, but if she had anything to do with the TSA, they'd have her fingerprints on record."

She jerked her gaze to Blaise, gaining his approval. Looking back to the dark-haired man, she nodded. "Let's do it."

He left the room for a few minutes, coming back with a fingerprint kit. Taking careful prints, he handed her the wipes as he stood.

"Bethany is going to keep you company for a while, Miss, and we'll be back as soon as we know anything," Jack said smoothly.

The men stood, all filing out of the room, Blaise leaving last. Kissing the top of her head, he said, "You'll be fine." Gaining her nod of acceptance, he followed the others out.

"Come on," Bethany smiled. "I've got a few friends coming over in a little bit. They want to meet you and I was just ready to pull some desserts out of the oven!"

Going willingly, she was tempted by the smell of the berry cobbler, but her mind stayed on the men delving into her identity.

~

BLAISE LOOKED AROUND the table once everyone was in the compound's conference room. "I really want to thank everyone for coming back in today."

The sounds of *no problem, anytime, and hell yeahs*

resounded around the group. Luke began the process of running her fingerprints through the various databases he had, slurping down more of his juiced-up coffee.

"Gotta tell you, your habit of picking up strays has landed you with a full blown mystery this time," Marc joked.

"What have you divined from talking to her over the past week?" Monty asked. The former FBI agent's analytical mind was already calculating the possibilities.

"She's intelligent. She's very literate. I'd say, definitely educated," Blaise began.

"Why didn't she seek help sooner?" Bart asked. "Why didn't she immediately go to the police?" A bit of a skeptic, he wanted to know her motives for staying hidden.

"She's been having nightmares. Says things appear as black…or dark, was her exact words. And she says she wakes up frightened. Doesn't know who to trust."

Jude smiled, saying, "Just seeing her in the bar that night, I have to say she cleans up nicely. You've done a good thing, man."

Smiling, Blaise replied, "Giving her access to my shower and all the girlie shit my sister leaves there, you woulda thought I'd given her the best present ever."

Getting back to business, Jack asked, "If that dog worked for the TSA and she's the owner or handler…or both, then why did something not come up in the missing report searches earlier?"

Luke, glancing over his shoulder, replied, "If no one

reported her as missing, then there'd be nothing to find."

The Saints pondered that for a moment, before the questions began flying.

"Why would no one report her missing?"

"What about family?"

"What about employers?"

"What the hell?"

Jack lifted his hand, calling for silence. "Let's work the problem instead of making it more complicated than it already is."

Cam added, "If she has no immediate family or is estranged from them, there wouldn't be a report."

Nodding, Chad added, "The TSA chip could have been implanted before she obtained the dog. Maybe it's not her dog. Or it is her dog and the TSA was just an added identifier."

"How's it going, Luke?" Blaise asked, anxious to find out any information.

"It normally takes about two hours, but I'm narrowing the search down to TSA right now to see if we get a hit."

The Saints continued to toss around possibilities with no perceivable results until Luke's voice called out over the group. "Got it," he stated proudly, followed by a more subdued, "Holy shit."

Blaise, jumping from his chair, rushed to peer over Luke's shoulder before he had a chance to project the information onto the screen.

A picture of a smiling, uniformed, dark-haired woman kneeling beside her dog filled the screen. The woman's smile lit the photograph, piercing Blaise's heart. His eyes moved quickly over the screen before dropping to the caption underneath.

Grace Kennedy, TSA trainee, and her dog, Gypsy.

CHAPTER 8

I N THE KITCHEN, Bethany pulled out two large cobblers from the oven, placing them on cooling racks. "Can you grab some plates? They're in the cabinet next to you."

"Sure," Miss replied, getting two down.

"Oh, we'll need more than that," Bethany said, laughing. "You'd better get down about fifteen."

Eyes wide, she did not have time to say anything before the front door opened and a group of women came in, all chattering away. Their eyes landed on the newcomer and she immediately felt self-conscious. That emotion only lasted a minute as the women instantly welcomed her.

Just like with the men, she knew it would take a while to remember names, but smiled through the introductions anyway. *I won't be around long enough for it to matter.*

A beautiful, curvy blonde with pink, purple, and teal stripes in her hair set down a couple of large white boxes tied with the same colored ribbons. ACH in scrolled letters adorned the boxes. Lifting a questioning gaze to her, the woman grinned. "I'm Angel of Angel's Cupcake Heaven. Monty's my fiancé and its been requested that I bring enough to keep all the Saints happy. One mountain man in particular."

Angel winked and opened the box, allowing Miss to peer inside at the delectable confections. The frosting colors matched the colors in Angel's hair.

"Have you been to my bakery?" Angel asked. Before Miss had a chance to respond, Sabrina sent a glower Angel's way.

"Um, I don't think so," Miss replied tentatively.

Shrugging, Angel looked apologetically toward Sabrina, mouthing *I thought she might recognize them.*

Catching the exchange, Miss shrugged, saying, "I'm sorry, but so far nothing I've seen has triggered my memory."

Though slightly surprised that the women knew about her, she did not let on. She just assumed the men had called the women in to keep her company and shared her story.

A petite, dark-haired, heavily pregnant woman approached. "I'm Miriam, Cam's wife. I'm also a nurse. Would you allow me to take a look at your injury?"

Her hand flying to her forehead, she grimaced. *It must look horrible.* "Sure," she agreed, suddenly very self-conscious.

Miriam took her hand and led her to a bathroom down the hall. She sat on the toilet seat, while Miriam began to examine the jagged scar. "Can you tell me about this?"

"I ran off the road…um…in my car…so, um…had an accident about three weeks ago."

"No medical treatment?"

Sucking in her lips, she replied, "No. I was…confused…scared."

Miriam smiled gently, soothing, "Of course you were. I think you're very brave to face what you have faced alone."

"But you're not alone anymore," came the declaration from the hall.

Glancing out, she saw the women all nearby. Bethany stepped forward with some bandages and blushed while saying, "Sorry, but you'll find in this group, there are few secrets."

"It's okay," she replied, wishing she would be spending more time with the women. *But Gypsy will soon be better and I'll be back on my way. To where, I have no idea.*

Before she had a chance to respond further, Blaise appeared at the door. "Come on, sweetheart. We need to talk."

The women immediately backed away and a glance passed between him and Miriam. Offering a smile, Miriam said, "I'll finish this later."

Blaise closed the bathroom door, wishing for a different location to talk, but wanting to speak to her immediately. He lifted her up onto the counter to raise her closer to his eye level, wanting to keep a check on how she reacted.

"Do…do you know?" she whispered, fear gripping her heart.

Nodding, he said, "Yes. But the answer will only produce more questions. I promise we will find all the answers. But to start with…your name is Grace. Grace Marie Kennedy."

HEART POUNDING, a roar in her ears, she sat perfectly still, her eyes fixed on Blaise's. She did not realize she had not taken a breath until he whispered, "Babe, breathe."

The air left her lungs in a rush and she raggedly pulled more back in. "Grace? My name is Grace? How can you be sure?"

"I'll show you our proof when you're ready, but I wanted a chance to talk to you first." Lifting his hand to her cold cheek, he caressed her soft skin. "Does the name sound familiar?"

Not answering, she closed her eyes, swaying against the warmth of his hand. *Grace. Grace Marie Kennedy.* She said the name out loud, letting it roll off her tongue, trying it out. Seeing what memories it might invoke. *It doesn't feel strange…but it doesn't remind me of anything.*

"Are you sure?"

She jerked her eyes open, realizing she had spoken out loud. Nodding, she sat up straighter and asked,

"What else do you know about me?"

"That's all right now, babe. Luke is doing more looking and he's bringing some equipment upstairs so that we can go over it with you. I wanted to tell you alone. If you don't want anyone else around, I'll tell Luke to set us up in Jack's private library." He was about to insist on that when she slid off the counter and peered up into his concerned face.

"No," she said. "It's okay, Blaise. I've been alone for three weeks, not knowing who I was or how I got hurt, but feeling as though someone was the cause of it. So I was afraid to trust anyone. You've become a good friend and those people out there," she motioned toward the closed door, "are your friends. So if anyone can help me, then it's here."

For the first time since he met her, he stepped closer wrapping his arms around her, pulling her into his warmth. Cradling her head against his chest with one hand, he secured her body with his other arm. Kissing the top of her head, he whispered, "We're going to find out what happened, Grace. And I'll be with you every step of the way."

She felt his strong heartbeat against her cheek, drawing comfort from it. Leaning her head back, she held his eyes, feeling the power of the intensity of his gaze. He bent slightly, moving forward until his lips were a breath away, then hesitated. She took the step herself and lifted up on her toes, meeting his lips with hers in a barely-there kiss. But one that left them both breathless.

Giving him a nod, she allowed Blaise to link fingers with her and together they walked back into the living room, where the large gathering awaited anxiously.

LUKE HAD SET up his laptop on the dining room table and, once Grace assured everyone she was ready to find out who she was and did not mind doing it publicly, she settled in a chair next to him with Blaise taking the seat on her other side. The other Saints had their tablets, so they would be able to see the information without hovering. But even so, their women were doing enough hovering for all of them.

Jack gave Bethany a silent signal to move the women back, but as she was about to do so, Grace spoke up quickly. "No, no, it's okay. If they want to stay, they can."

Luke turned to Grace and said, "I want to let you know how I went about this, okay?" Gaining her nervous nod, he began. "Because the chip in your dog identified her as a TSA dog, I narrowed my search to fingerprints within their employee database. That's where we got a hit."

He pulled up the TSA badge photo of her kneeling next to Gypsy. Grace stared at the picture for a silent moment. *That's me. That's Gypsy.* Grace Marie Kennedy, TSA trainee. *So I worked for the TSA? Or wanted to?* Knowing no more answers would come from that photograph, she nodded and Luke added more information.

"Here is your birth certificate and driver's license," he said, flashing those on the screen as well.

I'm twenty-seven years old, she noted.

"Now," Luke stumbled, clearing his throat, "this is where it will get more personal. Are you ready?"

Her eyes moved from Luke's to Blaise's, the distress evident on her face. Blaise wrapped his arm around her shoulders giving her a little squeeze. "We're here for you, Grace."

Sucking in a deep breath, she nodded toward Luke again. This time, he said, "I think I found the reason you weren't reported missing…at least not by family. Your parents are deceased. They were older when they had you and you had no siblings. They've both been dead for a couple of years…um…I'm checking on the details." With a few more clicks of his keyboard, he brought up a picture of an older couple, smiling, with a young woman standing between them.

Grace stared at the couple, trying to memorize their faces since recognition did not come. *Mom. Dad.* At her feet was another dog, possibly a Golden Retriever. *It seems as though I liked animals.*

Luke continued, "You also aren't married and from a quick look at your social media, it seems you are not dating anyone."

The Saints were viewing the same information that she was looking at, but their eyes continually moved back to the woman sitting in front of them, carefully peering at the screen. She showed no recognition but stared intently at each picture Luke pulled up. The women began to nervously eye each other.

"So…" she spoke for the first time since seeing the pictures, "no one was around to report me missing? I…I… had no friends?"

"Grace, we're just beginning our investigation," Blaise said. "There's going to be a lot of information we need to pull together to find out what happened."

She nodded jerkily, a choking sensation climbing into her throat. Blaise and Luke shared a look behind her back.

Jack, sitting across from Grace, spoke, calling her attention to his kind face. "Ms. Kennedy, we're going to find out what happened to you. We don't need to do any more today."

"Mr. Bryant—"

"Jack, please."

Breathing deeply, she offered a small smile and said, "I suppose you should call me Grace." Turning to Blaise, she tried to joke, "It's better than Miss or Mystery Lady."

He felt the shaking of her body next to him and tightened his embrace. "You're not alone anymore, babe."

Luke's soft gaze fell on her and he said, "I've got your address."

Jack looked up sharply at Bart and Cam. No words

were needed and they grinned at the silent order. Blaise knew the two men would break into her apartment this evening to see what they could find.

Grace caught the meaningful glances and sat up straighter. Determined to face whatever was happening, she asked, "What are you planning?"

"A couple of us will go to your apartment tonight to see if there are any clues to your disappearance."

"Can't I go too?" She turned toward Blaise, "I'm dying for some of my clothes. And maybe it would spark my memory."

Shaking his head, he disagreed, "Not until it's been checked out and then secured by the Saints. For all we know there may be evidence there and we want to keep you safe until we know it's clear."

Seeing the reasoning, she agreed. The pervasive fear continued to rear its ugly head, even now in this room full of kind-hearted people...*who are fast becoming friends.* "What about my employer? What about the TSA?" she asked tentatively.

"I think we've done enough digging for now," Blaise cautioned. Seeing her about to protest, he added, "We need to get back and check on Gypsy." Looking at his boss, he added, "Jack will keep us apprised of what is found in your apartment and I promise, as soon as it can be cleared, I'll take you there myself."

Realizing she had gotten all the information she could handle she nodded, strangely relieved someone else was taking charge. *It's been exhausting these past several weeks.*

"Grace, why don't you come upstairs with me and the girls and we'll find a few things to tide you over until you can get your own clothes," Bethany encouraged.

Jack, smiling at his wife's ability to know what was needed—both for Grace and for the Saints—winked as she passed him by, her fingers trailing over her husband's shoulders.

As the women left the room, Blaise turned to Luke and asked, "Okay, what about the TSA?"

"It looks like she had completed the training classes with her dog but had only been recently hired with TSA. She was still in their trainee initiation but had not become a full-fledged employee yet."

"Why the hell would no one report a missing woman and the dog?" Blaise groused. "She deserves so much more than this!"

The other Saints grinned at each other, recognizing Blaise's concern morphing into deeper feelings.

"We're gonna find out," Jack assured. "Monty, get with Mitch and let him know what we're onto. This may just be a case of a woman having an accident, who was not close to anyone to alarm them…or this could be something more. I don't want our speculations to get to her until we have more intel."

"Agreed," Blaise said. "She said she has fear and nightmares anyway. I'm going to take her home and have her sleep in a real bed for the first time in almost a month."

Just then, the women reappeared, Grace following Bethany, clutching a small overnight bag. Smiling as her dark eyes landed on Blaise, she said, "I've got what I need until I can get into my place."

Not embarrassed to pull her into a public embrace, he held her tightly, eyeing the other women over the top of Grace's head. *Thank you*, he mouthed, realizing once more that not only were his co-workers good friends, but their women were just as amazing. Looking down at the beauty he escorted out of the house, the thought slammed into him...*she'll fit right in.*

As soon as that crossed his mind, he stumbled. *What will we find? Someone who wished her harm?* Catching himself, as he settled her inside his jeep and headed back down the Saint's drive, he vowed to keep her safe...and with him for as long as she would have him.

CHAPTER 9

ARRIVING BACK AT his house after picking up drive-thru hamburgers, Blaise once more glanced to his right, Grace's quiet demeanor giving him concern. *Grace.* He liked the way the name rolled around in his mind. *Grace and Gypsy.* The names sounded right.

Parking, he said, "Let's go on in. We can check on Gypsy, eat, and then I'll take care of the animals while you can get ready for bed."

At the mention of the word *bed*, Grace perked up, a smile lighting her face. "I'm embarrassed to admit that I can't wait to sleep tonight on a real bed."

"Why would you be embarrassed?"

Twisting to face him, she replied, "Because you've done so much for me. I'm a complete stranger and yet you've offered me the safety and protection of your home. And…I've got nothing to offer in return."

"Just your company," he answered. "I've never really thought about how lonely it can be sometimes out here with just the animals. So you, here with me, gives me someone to talk to."

Laughing, they entered his house, the cacophony of

animal sounds greeting them. "I'll go check on Gypsy. Why don't you take care of your animals before we eat. I hate to eat first when they're hungry."

Blaise nodded, knowing she was right. *A woman after my own heart.* Heading out to feed the dogs in the kennels, he tried to guard his heart. *Watch your step...she may be gone out of your life very soon.* But now that she had been in his house, it was hard to image her not staying.

Grace's thoughts were a tangle as she knelt by Gypsy's bed in the back room. The faithful dog's tail wagged and she stood licking her owner. "So we now know that I'm Grace," she said, earning a bark from Gypsy. "Oh my God. You recognize my name! Grace!"

The dog barked again and Grace felt lighter than she could recall since the accident. She still did not remember anything, but realizing Gypsy was confirming her name, brought tears to her eyes.

A few minutes later, Blaise came back into the room and found Grace petting Gypsy, tears running down her face even as a smile played on her lips.

"Grace? Are you okay?" he asked, hustling over to her.

Gypsy barked again.

"See?" Grace laughed. "When she hears my name, she barks. She affirming it's really my name."

Thrilled to see her excited, he joined in the playful exchange, Ransom joining in as well. A tiny mewing sounded and Grace looked up, surprised to discover the little kitten. "I didn't see it earlier." Jumping up, she poked her fingers through the bars of the crate and wiggled them. The kitten pounced and played for a few minutes, until Blaise poured food into the dish and it immediately began purring as it gobbled the kitten chow.

"Why is it crated?"

"I just found her and wanted to separate her from the other animals until I had a chance to make sure she wasn't sick."

"Does she have a name?"

Grinning, Blaise shook his head. "How about you do the honors?"

"Oh, I'll need to think about a good name." Ruffling Gypsy's fur once more, she left the back room and went into the kitchen. After washing her hands, she took the bag of takeout and set it on the kitchen bar.

After the hamburgers had been consumed, and they were lingering over their fries, Blaise said, "I know today's been crazy for you. You must be exhausted."

"I woke up this morning in a shack, and the only thing in my life that I could think about was having lunch with you," she confessed, staring down at her plate. "I couldn't understand why you were so persistent in helping me, but now that I've met your friends, I understand why. It just seems to be in your nature to want to help. And now? I've had my dog cared for, food, a shower, and a bed to sleep in tonight."

"Is that okay?" he asked. "I know some people are

very…reticent to accept help."

Her gaze jumped to his. "Blaise, I had nothing to lose. I have no memory, no knowledge of who I am. I have fear when I go to sleep and dream…as though when my mind is relaxed it allows me to remember the fear of someone wanting to hurt me." Rubbing her face, she sighed. "I thought about going to the police, but…"

"What, babe?"

"But what if I had done something wrong? What if I were the one that someone was chasing because of something I had done?" Sighing, she said, "I know it doesn't make rational sense, but when you can't remember anything, everything is scary. Even the police."

He nodded, understanding for the first time why she stayed hidden. "You kept thinking your memory would come back to you? Your past?"

"Yes, yes," she enthused. "But it didn't." She lifted her gaze to his and added, "Will you please let me know about my parents as soon as you learn? I might not remember them, but I want something to hold on to."

"Absolutely," he promised, his voice warm and soothing. Stooping to grab the overnight bag Bethany loaned her, the two of them walked up the stairs. At the entrance to the small guest room, he handed her the bag. "We'll know more tomorrow and see where to go from there." Kissing the top of her head again, he said,

"I hope you sleep well, Grace."

SEVERAL MINUTES LATER, Grace slid beneath the covers, the sheets feeling like silk although they were just department store cotton. The scent was from a dryer sheet, enveloping her in a floral cloud. The mattress underneath, supporting her weight in comfort, felt…familiar. Closing her eyes, she could almost imagine herself in a bedroom like this one. A flash of an image flew through her mind—*a room smelling much like the floral scent she now experienced, painted pale yellow on three walls with one wall a forest green.* Her eyes jerked open and the image was gone.

I'm not crazy, she told herself. *I'll remember…I've just got to remember.*

Rolling over in the soft bed, she allowed the events of the day to melt away, leaving only the thoughts of the man in the room across the hall. *He's so beautiful,* she thought. His muscles, barely contained in the navy polo shirt he wore or the jeans that fit his form so well. Closing her eyes, she remembered the idea that he could be on the cover of a romance novel. *I must have read some of those for me to make the comparison! I've had no memories until being with him and something about him is making me feel again.*

But what do I feel? Oh, girl. Watch your heart. He might be a knight in shining armor but that doesn't mean he's for you. You're just one of his strays he helps. Don't confuse kindness with love.

Sighing, Grace turned over one more time, her exhausted body almost tumbling into slumber. *Yeah, but if I were to have someone fall in love with me…the gorgeous, giving man across the hall would be the one I would want.*

With that last thought, sleep finally claimed her.

~

ACROSS THE HALL, Blaise laid in a similar state of unrest. His normally ordered mind was swirling with the unexpected events of the day. Starting out, only looking forward to his lunch with Grace, hoping he might have a chance to get her to divulge a little more about herself. And now, she slept in the room across the hall.

We know her name. We know a little about her family. We know where she lived. We know where she worked. But why the fuck was she missing for three weeks and no one reported it?

He heard a whimper and sat up, seeing Ransom lying on the floor near his bed, sound asleep. Throwing back the covers, he stood, slipping into the hall. Hearing the sound again, he headed downstairs. Gypsy was at the door leading into the kitchen, whimpering for her mistress.

"Come on, girl," he called softly, leading the dog upstairs. Not wanting to disturb Grace, he knocked gently and, hearing no answer, turned the knob slowly.

Opening the door, Gypsy trotted into the bedroom, hopping up onto the bed as though she belonged. Curling up at her mistress' feet, she took her place of protection.

Smiling, he gazed at the pair as the moonlight poured through the window. Drawn into her room, like a moth to the light, he peered down at Grace's face, peaceful in slumber. He lifted his hand to his chest, rubbing over his heart as a slow ache began.

Her beauty stunned him, from her thick, luxurious hair to her pure complexion. Her pert nose, slightly turned up and, when awake, her huge, dark eyes. In sleep, thick lashes laid against her cheeks. Her kissable mouth slightly opened as she breathed deeply made him fight the urge to lean down and taste her.

I'm such a stalker, he admonished inwardly, but could not bring himself to leave quite yet. As he watched the pair, he understood that while it was her beauty that captured his attention, and her vulnerability that first caused him to seek her out...it was her strength that brought him to his knees. *Thank you, Lord, for watching over her.*

As he made his way back to his bed, his thoughts turned over to what Bart and Cam would find tonight in her apartment. He had wanted to go himself but knew there was no way he could leave her...not even with another Saint. *No, she's mine to protect.*

BART AND CAM, completely in sync after numerous missions together, slipped effortlessly into Grace's apartment under the cover of darkness. Bart's former SEAL missions enabled him to take on any job Jack had given him yet. A planner, he knew the best way to get the job done. His best friend, Cam, came from a different background. Cam may have come to the Saints by way of the Richland Police Department, where he had been an undercover cop, but it was his days as a juvenile delinquent that aided him now. Cam joked that breaking and entering were second nature to him.

Her apartment was located in a nice suburb of Richland, on the western side of town toward Charlestown. The neighborhood was neat and filled with middle-income family homes, condos, and apartment buildings.

Once inside, the pair moved through the modestly furnished rooms. The kitchen was directly to the left, U-shaped, with a bar that separated it from the living room. Cam examined the kitchen while Bart moved on into the larger room. A single door from the living room led to the single bedroom and bathroom.

A few packing boxes still stood in the corner, and only a couple of pictures were hung on the wall. Walking over, Bart examined the collage. Pictures of Grace, from childhood to recent, each with her animals, ending with a snapshot of she and Gypsy. Checking the boxes, he found out of season clothes in one and books in another.

The minuscule bathroom held the expected toiletries, but nothing else. Cam stuck his head into the bedroom, saying, "I'm done out here."

Slipping back through the small, dark apartment, it was evident to their experienced eyes that someone had searched the place. The sofa cushions were in place but slightly skewed. Cans in the cabinets had been moved about, left turned over. Her clothes were partially hanging out of drawers, although the drawers were almost pushed back in.

"What does your gut tell you?" Cam asked, taking pictures of the rooms.

Bart stood for a moment, coming out of the bedroom. "It's been searched, but not tossed. Why? Why go to this much trouble to search someone's place, not trashing it, but not taking the time to thoroughly put everything back?"

"Someone didn't expect her to come back. Someone thought she was dead," Cam stated, his voice hard.

CHAPTER 10

LUKE SAT AT his computer early the next morning, grouchy without his super-charged coffee. As Jack came downstairs, he halted in his steps, staring at the glass of milk sitting in front of Luke. Lifting his eyebrow in a sardonic expression, he stood with his hands on his hips waiting for an explanation.

"Shut-up, boss," Luke groused.

Laughing, Jack said, "Figured that high-octane coffee you've been downing for years would finally eat it's way through your stomach."

Saying nothing, Luke absentmindedly rubbed the center of his chest.

Jude and Monty walked into the room, hearing the last comment. "No shit, Luke? You've got an ulcer?" Jude asked.

"Jesus, can't a guy drink milk if he wants to without everyone jumping down his throat?" Luke complained.

Marc, Patrick, and Chad entered next, eyeing the glass and seeing everyone standing around staring at Luke. Before they could comment, Bart and Cam hustled into the meeting room as well.

Blaise was the last to enter, not surprised to observe he was last, considering he had insisted on making a full cooked breakfast for Grace.

As they all settled around the table, Luke downed the milk, slamming the glass onto the table. Lifting his eyes to the silent stares, he said, "Yes, I am drinking milk. No, I am not happy about it. Yes, I may be suffering from an ulcer and before you think of giving me a problem, Jack, I have seen a doctor. So I am perfectly able to do my job. Just not as well since I can't seem to get my eyes open! Any questions?"

The others grinned at Luke's crabbiness replacing the normally easy-going, but hyper, mood of the former CIA computer expert. Shaking their heads, they quickly got down to business.

Monty patched in Mitch Evans, their FBI contact. "I've filled Mitch in on what we've discovered so far."

"Saints," Mitch greeted. "We don't have an open case on anything to do with Grace Kennedy, but with her involvement with the TSA and a missing drug-trained dog, I told Monty that I wanted to be kept apprised of anything you find."

"No problem," Jack agreed.

"How's Grace this morning?" Marc asked Blaise.

Smiling, Blaise said, "Really well, considering how intense yesterday was for her. I think sleeping in a real bed and getting food inside was the best thing that could have happened. She's thrilled to know what her name is, but so far did not say she had any memories." Suddenly looking over at Bart and Cam, he said, "Except she said, last night, before she went to sleep, she remembered sleeping in a bed before. She said the room colors were pale yellow on three walls and green on the other one."

"Damn," Bart said, nodding. "Those were the colors in her bedroom."

Breathing a sigh of relief, Blaise said, "Maybe, just maybe, it'll all start coming back to her."

Cam spoke up, "Miriam suggested a counselor for Grace. Both she and Bethany have seen a really good trauma counselor in Charlestown."

"Dani's started going to the groups with Miriam and Bethany now and she likes this lady," Chad added.

"You're right. No matter what happened to cause the accident and her memory loss, I feel like Grace is going to need some help to work through the memories," Blaise conceded. "She has a great deal of fear, but can't figure out why. I checked on her in the middle of the night and she was curled up tightly with her dog."

Jack nodded toward Luke and said, "Okay, tell us what you've got and then we'll hear about Bart and Cam's visit last night."

"Can you start with her family?" Blaise interjected. "She's really wanting to have some facts to help her with her memories."

"Sure," Luke said. "Her parents, Elizabeth and George Kennedy, were in their early forties when they had her and she was an only child. They owned a small family farm northwest of Richland and moved to a house in the suburbs about eight years ago, shortly after Grace went to college. Two and a half years ago, they were on an icy road and slid down into a ravine. Both were killed upon impact, according to the police report."

Blaise, silent for a moment as he digested another piece of sad information about Grace, looked up at Luke for him to continue.

Accepting a nod from Blaise, Luke said, "Grace Marie Kennedy, twenty-seven years old. Graduated from VCU with a degree in Criminal Justice. She worked for a county Sheriff's department for about two years before becoming involved in their canine program and did that for another two years. Last year, she left her job and went back to a K-9 school for training with the TSA canine program. She had just completed that and was in the process of becoming a full-time employee with TSA in Richland." As Luke recited his findings, he continued to glance up at Blaise.

"So how the hell does she go missing for three weeks and no one notices? Searches for her? Contacts the police?" Blaise growled. Catching the expressions of the others feeling the same way, Blaise looked back at Luke and said, "Keep going, man. I'm all right."

"Here's where the info gets tricky," Luke continued, as everyone's attention ratcheted up, instantly more on alert. "From her social media accounts, it looks like she's not very active. There were only a couple of friends from VCU that she kept up with and that was sporadical. There were pictures of her going away party from the Sheriff's office and that split appears amicable, but there also hasn't been much contact between her and her former co-workers. The training classes just graduated a month ago, and most of them are in the process of getting new jobs with their dogs as well. She also just moved. The apartment that Bart and Cam went into last night had only been rented for about two months."

"So her life was right in the middle of change when she had the accident," Marc stated. "Almost like the worst time for someone to go missing—right when there was no one steady that she saw on a daily basis to notice her gone."

"Let's talk about the accident," Blaise demanded. "What do we know?"

Luke continued, "She drives an older model Nissan Altima, black with grey interior. She bought the car from a reputable used car dealership and has had it for almost two years."

"Blaise, is there any chance she would remember where the accident occurred? I know she said it was at the bottom of a ravine, not noticeable from the road since it was covered in thick brambles and trees, but we could search," Patrick added.

"I don't know, but it's worth shot to find out."

Jack nodded, jotting down notes on his tablet.

Looking up, he asked Luke, "What else?"

Shaking his head, Luke replied, "Not much. She has a checking and savings account. Nothing remarkable in either. Regular deposits from her jobs. Normal deductions. She got a sizeable insurance benefit from her parents' deaths, but that was put in her savings and she hasn't touched the money."

"Bart. Cam. What'd you find last night in her apartment?" Jack asked.

Bart began, "We entered with no problems. The apartment was furnished, nice but not new. But…" he paused, sparing a glance toward Blaise, "it had been searched."

At that, the Saints' attention narrowed to a focal point of what Bart was saying. "They did a half-assed job of covering up. Done, but sloppily."

"As though someone didn't worry about her coming back and knowing her place had been searched. But also that it wouldn't look searched to the common eye if someone else came in."

"Came in," Blaise repeated, his voice hard. "Like the apartment super who would come in after her rent went unpaid, to ensure that he wouldn't call the police."

"Exactly," Bart agreed. "There was no laptop or computer of any kind in the apartment. Since she said there was nothing in the car, maybe someone wanted to make sure there was no link to her that someone could find."

The group was silent for a moment until Mitch spoke up from the video-conference. "Jack, right now, I'd say you've got enough to start an investigation. What do you want from the FBI?"

Jack shot Blaise a look, then said, "The Saints are taking on the mystery of Grace Kennedy. I don't think we'll need your office until we obtain more evidence, but we'll keep you informed."

Obtaining Mitch's affirmation, he disconnected, leaving the Saints to begin processing the new case.

"I've got a bad feeling about this," Blaise admitted, piercing his co-workers and friends with his gaze. "The truth could be as simple as she was out with her dog, had a car accident and, suffering from amnesia, became disoriented and afraid. But...it's too clean. Too neat. With someone searching her apartment... that indicates she had something that someone wanted. Wanted enough to stage an accident, assumed she was dead, and banked on her being at an in-between phase of her life so there was no one to report her missing."

"We need to look at anyone in her life before the accident, as well as try to find her car," Jack said.

"Do we want to keep her status secret?" Monty asked. "After all, if someone wanted her dead, don't you think that they would be upset to know they had not finished the job?"

"Fuck!" Blaise cursed at the thought of her still being in danger.

"Monty's right," Jude agreed and the others nodded.

"So, for now, in our investigation, as far as anyone knows, Grace Kennedy died in that car accident. We'll conduct our interviews as though she is missing."

Jack continued to divvy out the assignments. "Jude, Patrick—I want you two to take whatever information Grace can give you about where she remembers the ravine and begin combing the area. Marc, you're our outdoorsman—you take charge of that part of the investigation."

"What about her friends and workplaces?" Blaise asked. "I want to be in on some of the interviews."

Jack nodded, acknowledging Blaise's professional ability to hold on to his temper if he did not receive answers he liked. "You, Monty, and Chad split up the interviewing. Check out the K-9 training facility, any friends she had there, and the TSA coordinator for hiring trainees. Blaise, you can take Grace to her apartment, but have Bart and Cam go with you since they were there last night. Get her to tell you if she remembers what's missing, what's out of place, and dust for fingerprints. If the intruder wasn't expecting her back they may have been careless."

Cam spoke again, saying, "Blaise, Miriam looked at Grace's scar and said she really needs to have her forehead seen by a doctor. The injury is healing, but a doctor…or maybe a plastic surgeon, can make it less noticeable. But one way or the other, it should be looked at."

"I'll take her to Doc Sanderson, if that's okay with you, Jack?" The doctor treated the Saints' injuries, not asking questions, knowing they were investigators. He was efficient and understood the nature of their business, having been a former Army doctor.

"He'll be good. Hell, he'll be surprised to see a pretty face," Bart laughed.

The meeting dismissed, the Saints broke up into groups to plan their parts of the mission. Marc pulled Blaise to the side. "We're going to need to interview Grace to find out what she says about the car. Can we do that before you take her to her apartment?"

"Yeah. Follow me and we'll do it first." Realizing she did not have a cell phone, he turned to Jack and asked, "Can I get a burner cell phone for her to use in case of emergencies?"

Luke went to the storage room, returning with one, handing it to Blaise. "This'll be good for her." He hesitated a moment, drawing Blaise's attention.

"What is it?"

"I was just wondering if you wanted…well, if you felt about Grace…"

"Just say what's on your mind!"

"I wondered if you wanted me to put a tracer on your Saint medallion?" Luke finally got out.

Blaise did not hesitate as he reached under his shirt and grabbed his St. Blaise pendant and pulled the chain off his neck. "Abso-fuckin'-lutely," he said, handing it to Luke, who grinned as he walked into the back room with the medallion in his grasp.

Standing, legs apart, hands on hips, Blaise noted the others grinning at him. "What?" he asked testily. "I'm gonna keep her safe at all costs."

"Watch your heart, man," Bart laughed. "You put that medallion around her neck and she's claimed."

Grinning back, Blaise nodded. "Damn straight!"

SITTING IN BLAISE'S living room an hour later, Grace clutched his hand as Marc questioned her. Jude used his tablet to map out what she remembered and Patrick, still learning some of the finer points of investigating, watched and listened carefully.

"I remember, when I crawled out of the car, I heard water. When I looked down the hill, I could see a fairly large creek. The car had come down the ravine and stopped when it finally hit several trees. Um…" she stopped and rubbed her head.

"You're doing fine, babe," Blaise encouraged, receiving a small smile.

"I climbed up…I can't tell you how long it took me, but I'd say at least thirty minutes because I had to stop every couple of feet. My head was no longer bleeding, but it hurt really badly. Gypsy stayed with me and a couple of times, she allowed me to grab her as she pulled me forward."

"Tell us about the road when you got to the top. Was it two lane, four lane, gravel, paved blacktopped, have lines painted, straight, curvy...anything you can think of," Marc queried.

"Um...it was two lanes. But there was shoulder space on each side so it wasn't too narrow. I stood there for a while before I started walking downhill. The trucker came fairly soon after that. Um...let's see...it was paved...blacktop and not recently. It had lines painted, but again not recently because they were sort of worn. There were curves and," she looked up suddenly and said, "there were no guardrails. Why would there be no guardrails?"

"There are supposed to be guardrails, but some lesser-used roads are susceptible to them being missing or in disrepair and I don't know how often they're checked," Marc answered.

"What can you tell us about the area around the road?" Jude asked.

"It was heavily wooded. When the trucker picked me up, we drove down the mountain about ten minutes before we passed any buildings."

"Do you remember the buildings?" Patrick asked excitedly.

Scrunching her forehead and then wincing in pain, she added, "An old building. Like it used to be a gas station way back in time. Bob's...or Bill's...or something like that."

Jude immediately began entering in the information and within a few minutes, said, "We may have a location. On State Road 842, part of it cuts near the

Skyline Parkway. It's wooded, curvy, and there's a Rob's Gas & Groceries. Obviously no website, but it could be our place. If we assume the trucker was going about 40 miles per hour down the curvy road, that gives us an approximate place to locate her car."

Grace glanced up at Blaise to see him smiling—grimly. *I wonder if that's a good look or an unhappy look.* He looked down at her, seeing her brow crinkle in confusion.

"Sorry, babe. This is good news. Marc, Jude, and Patrick will head up there and begin a search."

"Would it help to have Gypsy with you? I could go as well."

"No way am I having you out there in the woods," Blaise argued, before conceding, "But a dog is a possibility. I've got a friend with a good tracker dog. It may have been too long and the scent is gone, but I'm willing to take that chance. Can I have your backpack? It's got your scent and Gypsy's scent on it."

She walked from the room to retrieve the bag and Blaise immediately placed a call. By the time she returned, he explained, "It's all arranged. The Saints will take a tracker and his hound with them."

A few minutes later, the trio left, leaving Grace standing in the living room, worrying her bottom lip. As Blaise walked in, he observed her nervousness. Pulling her into his embrace, he kissed the top of her head. "We know what we're doing. We'll find the answers."

"Somehow, I know you will," she replied, her hand resting on his chest, leaning her head back to see his face. "I guess it's just the answers I'm now afraid of more than the unknown."

"I found out more about your parents toda—"

"I want to know," she blurted, her eyes wide and piercing.

Leading her to the sofa once more, he sat on the coffee table with his knees on either side of hers, his body a shield. Taking her hands in his, he said, "I only know the basics…but you were brought up, as you know…an only child, on a small farm. After you left for college, your parents sold the farm and moved to a small house in the suburbs of Richland. A couple of years ago they were out when an ice storm hit and they slid on icy roads and were killed together."

He said no more, observing her carefully for signs of distress. She simply nodded and released a long sigh, but no words were forthcoming.

"I know you feel lost, but I've got something for you." He reached inside of his shirt and pulled out the saint medallion, slipping it over his head. As she watched with questions in her eyes, he then slid the chain over her neck. "This is my Saint Blaise pendant," he said. "St. Blaise was the healer of animals in the fourth century. Legend states that animals would come to him, on their own, and he would heal them. The stories also say that the animals would assist him in his work."

Eyes wide she peered down at the pendant in her hand, as he continued. "I thought it made sense to give this to you. I can't give you back your family, but I want you to know you have me. You and Gypsy came to me...on your own...and she assists you. Somehow it kinda works."

Lifting her gaze, she smiled at him, touched beyond measure how much his words filled her soul. Blinking rapidly to keep the tears at bay, she breathed deeply through her nose before letting it out slowly.

"There's more," Blaise continued, his fingers flipping the silver medallion over. "On the back, Luke has attached a tracer. If you are ever lost again, we can find where you are. The other Saints have given their pendants to their women and the tracers have come in handy. I pray we never have to use it, but I hope you'll wear the necklace for me."

Swallowing hard, she admitted, "I...I don't know what to say."

"Say 'yes' to wearing it. It'll give me peace of mind knowing that I can always find you." Scooting closer, he brought his hands up to her face, cupping her cheeks. "And," he added, "I'd be honored for you to wear my Saint."

Smiling through her tears, she nodded. "Yes, Blaise, I'll gladly wear your Saint. Proudly." Silently, she added, *With all my heart.*

CHAPTER 11

G RACE HELD HER body rigid as the doctor, with a grey, military haircut, examined her forehead. His manner implied gruffness, but she was beginning to see that it was all a bluff. His fingers were gentle as they probed the injury.

"I hear you decided to drive down a mountainside to see what you could find." Dr. Sanderson quipped.

Her lips curved upward in spite of her nervousness. "I…I thought it was the quickest way to see the Blue Ridge Mountains," she joked back.

Blaise sat to the side holding her hand, allowing Grace to squeeze when the probing caused her pain.

Standing back, the doctor snapped off his gloves and sat down on the stool in his examining room. With a twinkle, he said, "Gotta say, you're the prettiest Saint I've ever had the pleasure to work with."

Smiling, she blushed, immediately liking the dour doctor. "So will I live?" she asked, matching his manner.

Laughing, Dr. Sanderson looked over at Blaise and said, "I like her. Wish to hell the rest of you had more of a sense of humor when I'm patching you all up!" Turning his gaze back fondly toward Grace, he patted her knee. "Well, Miss Grace, I'm sure you know that under the right circumstances, you should have had stitches given the size of cut. I'm sure it bled a lot—most head injuries do. With stitches, the two edges of the wound would have been pulled together tightly, therefore the scar tissue forming would have been more of a small line. As it is, you have a wider area for the tissue to fill in, creating a larger scar and, of course, taking longer to heal. It causes no physical problem…just one of vanity."

Biting her lip, she replied, "So I'm stuck with the Frankenstein look, right?"

"Babe," Blaise interrupted, standing to his full height, gazing down at her. "You're beautiful…abso-fuckin'-lutely beautiful."

Shifting her smile between the two men, she nodded resolutely, saying, "Well, it is what it is now."

"You can certainly opt for plastic surgery at some point to lessen the appearance of the scar and I can recommend someone to you if you decide that is something you'd like to pursue."

"Dr. Sanderson, right now, I have no money, no health insurance, and for all intents and purposes, I'm supposed to be dead." Allowing Blaise to assist her off the examining table, she sucked in a deep breath, saying, "I think, for now, I'm good with just being alive. But once all this is sorted, I'd like those recommendations from you...just in case."

Doc's eyes warmed as he smiled down at the brave woman in front of him. Taking her hand in his, he added, "It's been an absolute pleasure meeting you, Ms. Kennedy." Cocking his head in Blaise's direction, he said, "I think you're just perfect for this one." The older doctor's heart skipped a beat as he was gifted with one of her brilliant smiles.

~

AN HOUR LATER, Blaise and Grace, accompanied by Bart and Cam, walked into her apartment. Stepping over the threshold first, the men ascertained no one was there. Turning back, Blaise viewed Grace standing at the edge of the doorframe, uncertainty written clearly on her face.

Saying nothing, he raised his hand toward her, palm up. She eyed it for a second before reaching out and placing her hand in his larger one. He wrapped his fingers around hers gently, not tugging, but allowing her to step inside at her own pace. After only a moment and a deep breath let out slowly, she entered.

Her eyes moved slowly around the space, searching for anything familiar. The living room was on the left, a window overlooking the park nearby. The furniture appeared worn, but clean. Magazines were scattered across the coffee table. *Nothing.*

The kitchen and small area for a dinette table were to the right, divided from the living room by a bar.

Nothing.

Walking on wooden legs, she moved down the hall to the bedroom and bathroom. Peeking into the bathroom, she saw towels, toiletries, and a dirty clothes hamper. *Nothing.*

Going into the bedroom, she halted. Pale yellow walls on three sides and one in green. *My dream. I did remember something about this!* Looking at the furniture brought no memories and she stepped into the walk-in closet, noting her clothes hanging haphazardly. *Nothing familiar.*

Looking across the room, on the other side of the bed she saw a large dog bed on the floor. A flash jolted through her and she gasped. *Gypsy, sleeping on the bed. Me patting the bed each night and she jumping up to sleep with me, once I had given her the command.*

"Yes, yes!" she exclaimed, her eyes opening wide. "I remember Gypsy sleeping here and she would wait until I gave her the signal that it was all right to jump up on the bed with me!"

Crossing the room toward her, Blaise grinned as he hugged her. "That's great, babe. I think it'll all come back eventually."

Still smiling, she felt more at ease looking around. "I was certainly messy, wasn't I?" That thought gave her pause as she slowly shook her head. "Blaise? I don't think I was this messy. I can't explain it, but I haven't left any kind of a mess in the almost month since I lived away from here."

Blaise thought back to the hovel she had lived in and remembered her sweeping up the room, the neat stack of blankets on the floor. "Bart and Cam believe this place was searched. Do you know what someone would be looking for?"

Turning around slowly, Grace allowed the sights to seep into her consciousness. While nothing appeared familiar, it also did not feel as though she were in a strange location. Looking back at the men, she admitted, "There is something here that makes me feel as though I have been here before, while not remembering it exactly. But I don't know what I could have had that anyone would have wanted."

"What about a computer? Laptop? IPad?" Bart asked. "We didn't find anything here."

Scrunching her forehead, she said, "I'd have to have something…I mean, who doesn't?"

Placing a quick call to Luke, Cam asked, "Hey, man. Check her credit cards, bank statements, and internet accounts. We're looking to make sure she had a computer, iPad, something like that, 'cause there's nothing here."

"It could have been in the car," Blaise surmised.

The others nodded and then proceeded to move back to the living area. Grace walked over to carefully look at a few framed pictures on the cabinet holding the flat-screen TV. She picked them up, one at a time, but shook her head. "It's weird," she said.

"What is, babe?"

"I look at these pictures and, while I can't tell you who's in them with me...at the same time, they seem familiar."

"Good, that's good. That may mean that your memory is slowly being triggered."

Cam's phone rang and he took the call from Luke, nodding as he jotted down information. Disconnecting, he reported, "You had an iPhone and a Mac and an iPad. Looks like you were an Apple girl."

"But none of them are here." she said, frustration showing.

"Luke is working to see if he can get a signal from any of them."

"Why don't you get some of your clothes and toiletries together, while the guys finish fingerprinting?"

"I'm not staying here?" she asked.

"You think for one minute I'm letting you stay here?" He glanced over, seeing Bart and Cam grin, and pulled her gently into the bedroom. "Look, Grace. Right now, until we have the mystery solved as to what happened to you, you need protection and I'm giving it. All the way. Twenty-four-seven." Seeing the uncertainty crossing her face again, he asked more softly, "What about that concerns you?"

"I don't want to be a burden, Blaise. I can never repay what all the Saints are doing for me, and you? I have no idea how to ever pay you back for all the help you've given me."

Stepping closer, until his toes met hers, he lifted her

chin with his fingers so that he was able to peer deeply into her warm, tear-filled eyes. "Grace, I admit when I first saw you at the bar, while I was attracted to your beauty, it was your obvious need that brought out my protectiveness. But as we spent time together, I began to look forward to our lunches. Being with you and Gypsy. Getting to know you. I could tell you had secrets…I wanted to have you trust me enough to share your secrets."

"What are you saying?" she whispered, her voice shaking.

"I'm saying that when I'm with you, I feel something. Something I want to explore. And it goes way beyond my wanting to help you…or protect you. I can only hope you feel the same."

A single tear slid down her cheek only to be wiped away by his thumb as his hands caressed her face. She nodded, not trusting her voice.

"I gotta hear it, babe."

"Y…yes," she agreed, a tremulous smile forming on her lips. "At first, I was just desperate enough to take your charity, but then I really wanted to see you each day too. You didn't look at me like you thought I shouldn't be in public without a shower. And then when I saw you with Gypsy and how she liked you, something inside clicked. But…well, I thought maybe it was just my imagination."

"This is no imagination. This is you and me, and our beginning."

Biting her lip, she said, "So what about this place?"

"Right now, you take what you want and we'll leave the rest. The Saints are going to start interviewing the people who knew you and worked with you. But," he emphasized, "we're not telling people that you're alive. Just missing. We don't want to tip off anyone who might have wanted to harm you and assumes you're dead."

"Oh, Blaise, do you really think someone wanted me dead?" she cried, her strength failing her.

Holding her close, he said, "Don't know, sweetheart, but if they did, we'll find them. And then, they'll pay."

STOPPING AT THE ramshackle store, Rob's Gas & Groceries, Marc, Jude, and Patrick walked into the building. The tracker, Nathan, and his bloodhound, Scarlett, stayed in the vehicle. It appeared gas had not been sold at the old store in years, but the inside contained the grocery items a nearby resident might need if they did not want to make the long drive down the mountains into the nearest city.

A teenager sat behind the counter, staring at a TV on a table nearby. "You need some help?" he called out. "We ain't got no gas."

Jude and Patrick grabbed a couple of sodas and chips off the shelves while Marc sauntered to the counter. "This road traveled much?"

"Nah, we don't get much traffic no more. Old man Custis keeps saying he's gonna close the shop, but then there're a few oldsters that live up on the mountain that come here to get some food."

"Besides a few people living around here, is there anything else around?"

"Couple of farms. Other than that, I see some traffic come by, but we close at five p.m. so don't see nobody at night."

"Where's the closest airport? Or even airstrip?"

At that, the teen's eyes widened. "Airport?" Barking out a laugh, he said, "Mister, ain't got no airport around these parts. Not unless you count a crop duster landing strip on an old farmer's field an airport."

Watching the young man continue to chuckle, Marc paid for the items the group picked up and threw a twenty down on the counter, saying, "Thanks for the information."

They walked out, getting back onto the road, leaving behind an open-mouthed teen, fingering the twenty-dollar bill.

"You get anything good?" Jude asked.

"The road isn't traveled much and the area is scarcely populated, so if someone wanted to get rid of someone, this is a good place to do it. Found out there are no airports or airstrips nearby, other than for a crop duster. I still want that checked out, once we find her car."

Leaning forward from the back seat, Patrick put his

arms on the seats in front of him and asked, "What are you thinking?"

"Why would a single woman be driving on this road? She knows no one up here. And she had her dog with her. Not just any pet, but a trained, drug-sniffing dog. If she wasn't up here on business, what the hell was she doing?"

"Okay, I'm going about forty miles an hour and we've been on the road for almost ten minutes. Keep your eyes peeled for any signs that a car went over the edge."

"You can park anywhere and let me and Scarlett out," Nathan said, looking out the window at the woods. "She'll find the scent, if it's still viable."

"Okay, let's see what they can do." Parking on the side of the road, the three Saints got out and began walking along the edge, closest to the ravine, watching in awe as Scarlett immediately began moving along the edge of the road after sniffing a shirt Grace had worn.

"While Nathan and Scarlett are searching, you two keep looking for any sign of a car leaving the road," Marc called out. Splitting up to cover more area, ten minutes later Nathan came through the radio.

"Scarlett's got it."

Marc jogged back to the car and drove the few minutes to where Jude stood by the side of the road. Looking down, they could barely see where Nathan and Patrick stood in their bright orange vests. Marc grabbed his military grade scopes and scanned the area below, trying to locate anything amongst the brambles and trees.

The two men began the climb down the steep hill, but their physical training made the trek easy. Within a few minutes, they came upon Nathan, Scarlett, and Patrick standing next to a dark sedan. The front was crumpled against a wall of trees. The airbags had inflated and now lay flat on the seat, covered with bloodstains. The back left corner of the vehicle was damaged as well.

"Photograph the entire vehicle and scene," Marc ordered, as he made the call to Jack. Disconnecting, he said, "Jack'll call Mitch and the FBI will be coming out here. They'll be able to determine if the car was tampered with." He continued to stand back, observing the vehicle, his mind turning over the possibilities. *The front is smashed into the trees. Why was the back corner hit as well? Unless…* "Hey, Patrick, get close-ups of the back corner that's dented."

Patrick glanced first at Marc and then back to the car, seeing what his more experienced co-worker had noticed. He took pictures of the vehicle and the surrounding area. Jude searched the inside but did not find her purse, cell phone, or computer.

Marc walked over to Nathan, who was squatting next to Scarlett, giving her a rubdown. "You two did it," he praised. "Been a long time since I've seen a bloodhound at work, but damn, she's good."

Mitch had prioritized the report and within two

hours, a group of FBI agents met them at the site. Marc relayed their findings and then stood back, letting the agents do their job. Leaning back against a tree, the large, bearded man crossed his arms over his chest, seemingly at ease in the wilderness. Patrick moved to stand next to him, a glower on his face.

"What's got your boxers in a twist?" Marc asked, eyeing the younger investigator.

"We find her vehicle and begin to process it and then they show up and take over."

Jude grinned, knowing Patrick was about to learn the same lesson he had to learn when working for the Saints.

"You after a medal?" Marc asked sardonically.

"No," Patrick replied, his eyes moving from the agents to his co-worker.

"Then what the fuck does it matter who gets the glory?" Marc pushed off the tree, his height giving him the advantage—one he had over most men. "We work the cases no one else wants…or can solve. And the end goal is that the case gets solved. Period. Got it?"

Nodding, Patrick blushed as he agreed. "You're right. Sorry, man."

Chuckling, Marc said, "No worries, rookie. We've all been there. Done the legwork and let someone come in and take over. But out here? We need them. If her car was tampered with, that's something they can determine." Shrugging, he added, "Although Cam could have, too, if he were here. But this means they can impound the entire car and go over it with a fine-tooth comb. And while they're doing the grunge work...the Saints can be interviewing."

The lead FBI investigator walked over, talking on his cell phone. Disconnecting, he stepped up to Marc. "I just talked to Mitch Evans and he gave me instructions to let you know our preliminary findings."

"Appreciate it," Marc said.

"There are multiple fingerprints on the doors and we'll run those through our database. We are also taking samples of the blood stains to make sure they are of Ms. Kennedy. And one more thing from my lead auto mechanical investigator over there," he nodded toward a man just sliding out from underneath the front of the car. "There are bits of white paint on the area of the back left dent, indicating she may have been run off the road." Looking at the three men standing in front of him, he added, "And gentlemen. There are two bullet holes in the back of her car."

Fucks rang out from all three Saints in unison.

CHAPTER 12

B LAISE CAME IN from feeding the animals when his phone vibrated. Glancing at Grace in the kitchen, he stepped back outside to take the call.

"Marc? Tell me you got something for me," he answered.

"We found it, man. We processed it and Jack called in the FBI. They got out there and will be taking it in. But gotta tell you, there was no purse, no cell phone, no laptop. And on top of that, they confirmed that there's a strong possibility she may have been run off the road and shot at. We'll know more after they go over it in detail but, for now, man, it looks like someone was definitely after your woman."

My woman. As angry as Marc's report made him, hearing Grace referred to as his woman sent an arrow straight to his heart. Closing his eyes, his heart hammered in his chest at the thought of her racing down a dark mountain road being shot at. And then run off. Sucking in a deep breath, he said, "Thanks, Marc. I'll be heading out tomorrow with Monty to interview her last training center."

"You need me to watch over Grace?" Marc offered.

"Appreciate it, but she's going to go with Miriam and Bethany for an initial consultation with the trauma psychologist."

Disconnecting, Blaise attempted to contain his anger as he walked into the house, but as soon as he observed Grace moving about his kitchen fixing dinner with the cats swirling between her legs and Gypsy and Ransom sitting on their haunches, looking up in hopes of a morsel falling their way, he stopped dead in his tracks. *Jesus, she looks so at home here. And here is where I want her to stay.*

The few women he had tried to bring to his house over the past couple of years flew through his mind. Their expressions ranged from disgust over having several animals in the house to irritation over pet fur on the sofa. *And I'd cleaned it!*

Grace shook her hips as she danced to a tune in her head, stirring a pot that by its smell contained spaghetti sauce. Dressed in khaki shorts and a navy tank top, her rich brunette hair pulled up haphazardly on top of her head, her long legs tapped along his kitchen in rhythm to the music. *Beautiful. Fuckin' beautiful. And some son-of-a-bitch tried to kill her.*

She looked up just then, seeing him scowl at her and immediately felt self-conscious.

As soon as he saw the smile fall from her face, he headed around the counter, not stopping until he was directly in front of her, his arms encircling her. "Ignore my mood, babe. I love seeing you in my kitchen."

"So what's got you upset?" she asked. When he did not answer right away, she leaned back, observing the tick in his jaw. Already recognizing his facial expression, she said, "I can only think of one thing that would make you angry. Did the others find something?"

He let out his breath slowly. "Yeah, sweetheart. Your car. The FBI are processing it, but I can tell you that none of your possessions were there. And…" he hesitated, but knew her safety depended on her knowing the fact. "It appears you may have been run off the road. And there's one more thing," he added, his heart heavy. "The back of your car had bullet holes. Someone was shooting at you."

Unsure what her reaction would be, he was prepared for tears, but instead, she jerked out of his arms, stalking across the kitchen.

"You've got to be fuckin' kidding me!" she yelled. Whirling around, she said, "I've spent the past three weeks living homeless, on the streets, with nothing but the clothes on my back and my dog by my side, because someone wanted me dead?"

Red rage poured from her as she said, "Do you know what my life would have been like if you hadn't seen me and taken an interest in me?"

Blaise immediately stalked toward her but she jerked away with her hand up, palm facing him. "Oh, no. I'm pissed. Fucking pissed!" she shouted, pacing away once more. "Lived in fear…lived dirty and hungry. All because of what? And I can't even fucking remember what happened, so the fuckers get away with what they did to me!"

Letting her rant die down, he pulled her back into his embrace. "Grace, I'm so sorry this happened but, babe, let's focus on finding out who was involved and making sure you're safe now." He felt his arms quiver as he continued, "I've got you in my life now and I don't want anything to happen to you."

Feeling his words slide over her, they crept into the cold, lonely places in her heart. Neither spoke for a few minutes, allowing the silence of the evening to soothe their rushing thoughts.

She felt his lips on the top of her head again, loving the feel of those gentle kisses, but wanting more. Leaning her head back, she turned her face upwards. Their eyes bore into each other's, the unspoken question moving between them. With the barest nod of her head and a smile playing about her lips, she gave her answer.

Blaise captured her mouth with his, sealing their fates. His strong, soft lips owned hers in a kiss the morphed from gentle to possessing. She opened her mouth and his tongue invaded, tangling with hers and seeking every crevice. Plunging over and over into her warmth, he tasted the essence of Grace and knew he was ruined for any other woman…and had no desire for anyone other than Grace.

Melting under his kiss, she clung to his arms before sliding them upward to clasp around his neck, uncertain if her legs would hold her up. It did not matter that she had no memory she knew she had never been kissed...owned...like this before. Their bodies melded together, two parts fitting together perfectly.

The long, wet, possessive kiss seemed to last forever, but slowly Blaise eased the kiss into a soft exploring, finishing with small touches of his lips to the corners of her mouth before pulling back.

Both, staring into each other's eyes, breathed heavily as they tried to regain their balance. His straining erection pressed against her stomach. Licking her kiss-swollen lips, she was thankful his arms held her tight as her body quivered in his embrace.

"Wow," he whispered, the kiss having rocked him, never remembering feeling this connected to anyone ever before.

"Yeah, wow," she whispered back, forcing her feet to stay on the ground and not lift up to take his lips again.

Slowly relaxing his arms, he said, "I don't want to let you go, but if I don't, there's no telling where we'd end up." He moved back just enough to ease his erection from her body.

"I know where we'd end up," she said boldly, glancing down at his crotch, wanting to feel him more than her next breath.

"Yeah, I guess I do too," he grinned. "But not now.

I want to make sure you know what's happening. I want it to be the right time."

Loosening her arms, she moved back slightly as well. "I…I'm probably not what you're used to—"

"No, you're not," he said, honestly. "You're perfect."

Cocking her head to the side, she silently questioned his response.

"Perfect for me. A woman who can be at ease in a kitchen with a bunch of animals swirling about her legs. A woman who is strong, self-reliant, yet soft and caring." Chuckling, he added, "A woman who's not afraid of a little pet fur."

Giggling, she pretended to slap his arm, saying, "Wow, you're easy to please. Just looking for a woman who doesn't mind fur on her clothes."

Bending down, kissing her gently once more while giving a squeeze around her waist before letting her go, he said, "Babe, you're perfect in a lot of ways."

"Well, you haven't had my cooking yet, so I guess we'd better give that a try," she said lightly, walking into the kitchen on shaky legs, trying to stop the tingling between her legs. *Damn, but that man can kiss.*

Taking a moment to adjust his straining erection, his eyes followed her ass as she walked in front of him. Willing his dick to behave, he knew it was going to be hard to resist her. *I can't take advantage of a woman who can't remember who she is!*

STANDING IN THE small hallway between the two bedroom doors, Blaise watched as Grace fiddled nervously. He lifted her chin with his fingers, placing a gentle kiss on her lips. She lifted on her toes to take the kiss deeper but he pulled back, keeping his hands on her shoulders. Hating the expression of confusion on her face, he said, "Sweetheart, there's nothing I'd like to do more than make love to you…and make you mine. But you're vulnerable right now, and I can't take advantage of that."

Her lips tingled from where his lips branded hers. "What if I want you to take advantage of me?" she whispered, her voice husky with need.

Raising his head toward the ceiling, looking heavenward for strength, he closed his eyes as though in pain. Sighing heavily, he dropped his head back, piercing her with his gaze. "What would you say if I told you that I was thrilled to learn that you didn't have a man in your former life? That I knew we could move forward…if you wanted to?"

Her lips curved into a shy smile, her chocolate eyes warming. "I'd say that would make me happy as well. I'm not sure I would have wanted to meet up with someone that I had no memory of." Pulling her lips in, gathering her courage, she continued. "And…I now know that gives me a chance to move forward with you…if you wanted to." She grinned as she repeated his words back to her.

Chuckling, he pulled her closer again, kissing the

top of her head. Holding her against his chest, he heard her mumble. "What'd you say, babe?"

Leaning back again, she said, "I know you said that we need to not let whoever may have been after me know I am alive, but will you promise to let me know what you find out about me?"

"Grace, I can't imagine how this is for you...not knowing...and yet finding out things a bit at a time. That's the reason I want us to go slow...it's not fair, pulling your emotions into a relationship right now when you are trying to get your life...and memory...back. But, I promise that whatever the Saints find out, I will tell you. Each step of the way." Holding her gaze for another moment, he added, "You're safe with me, sweetheart." Leaning down, he kissed her gently again and, this time, it was a promise.

Nudging her toward the guest room, he said, "Sleep tight," and grinned as Gypsy, padding on a much-healed paw, followed her mistress.

~

MY HEADLIGHTS PIERCED the darkness as the winding road passed underneath my car. "Hang on, Gypsy. I'm trying to get us out of here." Glancing in the rearview mirror, the faint glow of headlights came into view. "Fuck!" I'd been shot at and had no idea if the person chasing me was the one with the gun. Stepping on the accelerator, I pushed it as fast as I dared to go on the unfamiliar, unlit road. My tires squealed in protest at the speed I was taking some of the curves. The light became brighter and brighter as the following vehicle came closer.

Heart pounding in fear, I stared out of the windshield looking for something…anyone who might help… but the darkness was the only answer. I didn't need to glance at the mirror anymore as the following headlights now illuminated the inside of my car. "Come on, come on," I prayed, pushing my car faster.

The lights moved to the side. "Are they passing me?" I wondered just before the sound of metal crashing into metal rang out.

"Fuck! They hit me!" The steering wheel jerked in my hands as I tried to keep the car on the road. "NO, NO, NO!"

I could not stop the spinning movement and then the nose pointed downward. "Oh, my God, Gypsy!" Down, down, down into the blackness. The bone-jarring movements. The crashing to a stop. Something slamming into my face…

"AUGHHHHHHHHH!"

Blaise, having heard the screaming coming from the guestroom, tossed his covers, running toward Grace. Throwing open her door, the illumination from the hall cast its light across the bed. Gypsy stood on the floor next to Grace, whimpering next to her mistress. Grace was a moving tangle of legs, arms, and bedcovers.

Patting Gypsy's head as he crawled onto the bed, he gathered Grace into his arms. "Wake up, babe. You're safe. You're safe."

Eyes jerking open, panting, she fought against his arms until his voice finally broke through her terror. Gasping, she grabbed him, holding on as her mind came back from the images of crashing down the ravine.

Holding her close, he murmured comfort as one hand cradled her head against his strong heartbeat and the other soothed up and down her back. Slowly, her breathing steadied as her shaking calmed. After several long minutes, he asked, "Do you remember what you were dreaming?"

He felt her nod against his chest, but stayed quiet, allowing her to respond in her own time. Finally, her trembling voice spoke.

"I remember the crash. I remember driving down the road. Someone was chasing me. I could see their headlights getting closer, but it was so dark and the road was so curvy. I remember Gypsy in the back seat."

She remained quiet for another moment, the images still strong in her mind. "I remember the headlights filling my car as they were right behind me. Then my car was darker and I realized they had moved to the side. I thought maybe they were going to pass me."

Shuddering, she clutched his arms tighter. "The other car hit me...they hit me. Oh, God, they wanted to kill me."

"Shhhh," Blaise comforted, gently rocking her back and forth, his arms continuing to envelope her in his embrace.

"I woke up as I was crashing down the mountainside. It was dark. I had no idea where I was going to land. And then…the car slammed into something…that's all I remember."

"Babe, that's good. That's so good. And as your memory comes back, just know that I'm here for you."

She leaned back from his naked chest, grabbing the edge of the sheet and wiping her nose and eyes. As her thoughts settled with the knowledge she was safe in his steady arms she viewed the muscular chest in front of her. Shaking her head, she thought, *I must truly be crazy to be focusing on his gorgeous body when someone tried to kill me.*

"Babe?" he asked. "You okay? Your face is flushed."

Blushing harder, she choked out, "Yeah, yeah. Just trying to make sense of…everything."

Sitting up, she said, "I guess it's a good thing I'm going to the counselor today, isn't it?"

"I think the timing's perfect," Blaise agreed. "Are you going to be able to go back to sleep?"

"Um…sure. Gypsy'll keep me safe."

He hesitated as he started to rise from the bed, then turned back to see her vulnerable face peering up at him. "I could stay…if you wanted." Her smile illuminated the room even more than the light from the hall.

"I'd like that."

Sliding back underneath the covers, straightening them around their bodies, he gathered her in his arms once more. Spooning her back to his front, he pulled her body in tightly, offering his warmth as well as his protection. Kissing the top of her head, he said once again, "Sleep tight," then added, "I've got you now."

With that, she fell into a dreamless sleep.

CHAPTER 13

PULLING UP TO the K-9 dog training facility, near the Marine base north of Richland, Blaise and Chad stepped out of their vehicle. The grounds contained several buildings and a large grassy field to the side. Stepping inside, they moved to the front desk. Pulling out their identification, Blaise said, "We're here to see Douglas Wilkins, concerning a former trainee. He should be expecting us."

Just then, an older, fit man with a military haircut, greying at the temples walked from the back. "Gentlemen, I'm Douglas Wilkins. Welcome to our facility. Come on back."

Receiving visitor badges from the receptionist, they followed him to a small, uncluttered office. As Douglas walked around the desk, he motioned for them to take the seats in front.

"You said in your phone call you're investigating the disappearance of a recent graduate of our program."

"Yes, sir," Blaise began. "Ms. Grace Kennedy has been missing for a couple of weeks."

At this, Douglas' eyebrows shot upward in surprise.

"Grace?" Shock evident on his face, he added, "Missing? No one's seen her? What about her dog? Any sign of her either?"

"No, they're both missing. It was reported by a friend and we're trying to retrace her last known steps."

"I haven't seen Grace or Gypsy since the graduation we had here about six weeks ago. I remember them well. Good reflexes, good instincts."

"Ms. Kennedy or the dog?" Chad quipped.

"Both, both," Douglas enthused. "Both the dog and the handler need to work together as one. Those two were special."

"We've read about your facility. Can you give us some insight into your school and her career aspirations after she graduated?"

"We have some people who come here to train the dogs for other handlers to then take possession of. Some employers have their own dogs and kennels. Others come with their own dogs that have been trained since pups. That was Grace. She came to us with Gypsy and her career goals were heading toward TSA. Some of our trainees go DEA, ATF or police. She and Gypsy trained and excelled with the drug sniffing and she had already interviewed with the TSA. In fact, if memory serves, I think she had already begun the training portion of her career with TSA in Richland."

"What can you tell us about her friends or fellow trainees? Anything about her time here?"

Rubbing his hand over his face, he appeared to

ponder the questions. "Well, can't say that I recall much about her and the other trainees. She got along well with everyone. Nice. Polite. But focused...I'll say that about her. She was really all about the job."

Douglas glanced outside the window overlooking the grassy field, now filled with dogs and their handlers. "Hate like hell, she's missing." Coming out of his musings, he said, "I do remember she used to talk more to Carter Boren and Jocelyn Montez. Now that I think about it, those three hung out more than I saw her with anyone else. Carter was also going to TSA and Jocelyn, I think wanted a job with the local sheriff's office. I know Carter probably felt some competition with Grace."

"Competition?" Chad prodded.

"The Richland International Airport needed another TSA handler and she and Carter were both up for the same job. Now, quite frankly, I think they both would have landed jobs there because the TSA is always adding new positions. But when they left here, she had the position."

"We'll need Carter and Jocelyn's contact information. If you need, we can have the FBI make the formal request, although we are investigating with their authority."

"I understand. The FBI contacted me yesterday to say that I was to cooperate so I've got no problem." He began typing into his computer and pulled up the records on previous students of the program. His printer began to whir, spitting out the information. He leaned over, grabbed it and handed it to Blaise.

"Gentlemen, I wish you success in your search. She was a real nice girl. Smart. Self-reliant. Easy to get along with and had a fucking great relationship with her dog. I hate that something may have happened to her. Any chance you can let me know what you find?"

"We'll keep you apprised of our investigation to the extent that we are able," Blaise answered noncommittally. Standing, he and Chad made their way back to the receptionist desk, turning in their badges.

Walking back to his jeep, Blaise was unaware that eyes followed the pair before making a phone call.

MIRIAM AND BETHANY sat in the waiting room as Grace met inside with the counselor. "I wish we could be with her," Bethany said.

"I know," Miriam agreed. "Somehow, it actually seems harder sitting out here, doesn't it? But I know Dr. Saren will be good for her."

Bethany nodded her agreement, her blue eyes seeking the dark gaze of her friend. "It's hard to believe it was a year ago that I was stalked by a serial killer and met Jack."

The two women, so different in appearance with Bethany's tanned body and blonde hair, blue eyed, girl-next-door look in contrast with Miriam's dark hair, dark eyes, and slightly exotic visage. But having both been rescued by Saints, they formed a bond along with the other women in their group.

Glancing at the clock slowly ticking off the minutes, they sighed, returning to their conversations about pregnancies and babies. Bethany was just showing while Miriam was almost due.

Inside the room, Grace spoke eagerly to the trauma counselor. "I want to remember. I want to know what happened to me. Who I was. Where I was. Where I was going. Who was after me. But I'm so frustrated that it's all just black. Well, until last night's nightmare brought some of it back."

"That isn't uncommon," Dr. Saren said. "Often with temporary amnesia caused by trauma, the person will slowly regain their memory. It may be like turning the pages of a book, where it is revealed a bit at a time. Because you had a head injury as well as what appears to be an emotional trauma, your body and mind are having to heal."

"But I will remember, right? It will come back to me?"

"Everyone is different but, hopefully, yes, you will regain all of your memory. Some people only forget the traumatic event but, in your case, you lost all of yourself—"

"Yes! That's just how it feels," she exclaimed. "I lost all of myself."

"Except Gypsy, right?"

Nodding, Grace agreed. "But I didn't remember

her either. If it hadn't been for the nametag on her neck and the fact that she wouldn't leave me, I wouldn't know she was mine."

"Memory loss is generally due to the brain simply deciding that it is too painful or frightening to remember something. The brain monitors your memories, so to speak."

"What about hypnosis? Can that work?"

"Well, there are some reliable counselors trained in hypnosis that I can suggest if you want to try them. But, it's not like they would snap you into and out of a trance and you would suddenly remember everything."

Huffing in frustration, Grace leaned back in her seat.

"I understand your frustration, Grace," Dr. Saren said. "I would suggest you and I meet a few more times, talk over what you are remembering and then decide if you want to pursue hypnosis."

Agreeing, the two continued the rest of the session, discussing the nightmare and what Grace now remembered.

"When I think about progress," Grace admitted, "I now know that Gypsy was my dog. And we must have been somewhere possibly dangerous or stumbled onto something dangerous. We were followed and I was trying to protect us both when the accident occurred."

"That's so much more than you knew beforehand," Dr. Saren pointed out. "So while that seems small, not only did the event replay in your mind, but the emotions as well. That tells us your brain is beginning to accept that you can handle what happened. I believe that bits and pieces will come back."

Finishing the session, Grace walked back to the waiting room, suddenly exhausted. Bethany and Miriam rushed to her, forming a group hug.

"That's not easy," Grace admitted, to the nods from the other two women.

"That's why I think a trip to Angel's Cupcake Heaven is necessary," pronounced Bethany, quickly supported by Miriam.

Grinning, Grace agreed. "Lead the way, ladies."

Soon the three were ensconced in ACH at a back table, enjoying the fruits of Angel's labors, with her joining them. Dani, Faith, and Sabrina walked into the shop at the same time.

Grace looked up then jerked her gaze to Bethany and Miriam. "You called them, didn't you?"

"Guilty," Bethany admitted. "I know you're used to doing things on your own, but girl…you've got all of us now."

Plopping down, Dani agreed. "Anyway, with half of us pregnant, we don't need much of an excuse for a cupcake!"

Laughing, Grace smiled at the women sitting around the table. Sharing cupcakes. Sharing her difficult day. Sharing her life.

ENTERING THE RICHMOND International Airport, Blaise and Chad were met by Monty. Greeting them, Monty explained before they had a chance to ask. "Got us access to talk to the head of TSA security here, as well as her trainer."

Nodding his appreciation, Blaise led the way toward the TSA office. Bernard Tanner met them at the door. After introductions, they followed him down a long hall, lined with pictures of TSA personnel and their dogs.

The realization slammed into Blaise that Grace could have—should have—been on the wall as well.

Jolted out of his musings, they were escorted to a large, but spartan, conference room.

"Gentlemen," Bernard said. "Got a call from my superior, who'd been directed by the FBI, to assist you, but I wasn't told why."

"We are investigating the disappearance of a woman who was part of the TSA drug handler training program. She had graduated from the Virginia K-9 facility and it is our understanding she was being offered a job with the TSA here at RIA."

His brow crinkled in thought as he said, "Kennedy. Ms. Kennedy?"

Nodding, Blaise agreed. "Grace Kennedy and her dog, Gypsy."

"Yes, I remember her well. Very promising. We were happy to hire her. We had finished the initial processing—she had already been cleared having started that process while still in school. She was assigned to one of our trainers to work until she became a full-fledged employee."

His dissertation stopped, and Blaise prodded him for more. "But what happened?"

A look of confusion crossed his face, and Bernard asked, "Happened? I'm not sure I follow you."

Holding onto his exasperation, Blaise continued. "She's been missing. For a month. What did you do when she didn't show up?"

"Do?" Bernard's face turned red. "We didn't do anything. If she wanted the job, she should have continued to come. Do you know how much money was already spent on her background investigation? Training? When she stopped coming, her direct trainer came to me and I told him we'd move to the next person on our hiring list. We don't have time to coddle someone who gets scared of coming to work or doesn't have the work ethic we require."

Chad shared a quick glance with Monty, knowing Blaise was about to explode, and he stepped in quickly.

"So a potentially excellent new employee, one you sought out, suddenly doesn't show up and no one tried to find out why? Or go to the trouble of reporting her missing to the police?"

"I didn't know she was missing! I just thought she changed her mind. It can happen. Sometimes people think this job is glamorous. But it can be tedious. Stressful. Maybe she just didn't think she wanted to come here anymore," Bernard blustered, trying to defend his position.

The silence hung between the four men, three hanging onto their tempers and one trying to maintain his credibility.

Bernard finally broke the silence first, saying, "I never thought anything untoward happened to her. She was a really nice young woman and very professional. I admit I was surprised when she left us, but it has happened before. I gotta ask, though…why didn't someone in her family contact the police?"

"If you'd bothered to check," Blaise bit out, "she was an only child of deceased parents. New in the area."

A long sigh released from Bernard. "Goddamn." Rubbing his hand over his military cut, dark hair, he shook his head. Looking up, he asked, "So no one knows where she is? Or her dog?"

"That's why we're investigating," Monty stated the obvious. "We need to speak to her trainer."

"Yes, yes, I'll take you to him."

"By the way," Blaise said, as they rose from their chairs, "Can you tell us who got the job that she *vacated*?"

"Why, yes. Another excellent candidate from the same school. Carter Boren."

CHAPTER 14

S TEPPING INTO ANOTHER hall leading into the depths of the baggage area of the RIA, the three men followed Bernard to a large room where luggage was passing through on conveyor belts. Several TSA uniformed men and their dogs were around, all looking up as the impressive group came into the area.

"Preston, need you for a few minutes," Bernard called out to a tall, lanky man who appeared to be overseeing the others.

He walked over, a friendly smiled on his face. Bernard introduced the Saints, adding, "They're here to gather information on Grace Kennedy. Seems she's gone missing."

"Missing?" Preston appeared confused and then surprised. "Missing! Is that why she didn't come back to work?"

Bernard rubbed his chin, blushing slightly. "Yeah, it seems we were premature in thinking she just didn't want the job."

A muscle in Blaise's jaw ticked once more in anger, taking all of his self-control not to blast both men.

"They'd like to talk to you for a few minutes," Bernard continued. As he began to turn away, he hesitated, his eyes on the floor. Finally lifting them, he spoke, regret filling his voice, "I wish you all the luck in the world, gentlemen. I'd hate to think anything happened to her."

Preston lifted his hand, ushering the group away from the noise of the baggage search area. Closing a door behind them, he said, "Sorry, we're stuck in a hall, but I don't have an office down here."

"No problem," Blaise assured him. "What can you tell us about Grace?"

"She was a good handler. Came highly recommended by the K-9 training facility. Bernard and I went there and interviewed her and a couple of others. She was our first choice."

"How long had she been here before she went missing?" Monty inquired, his notebook out, sending the information given straight back to Luke for verification.

"Only about three weeks. She was doing fine. She was a great trainee and so was Gypsy. Those two were perfectly in sync. Most of our handlers are, but gotta say, there was something special about the bond between those two."

Unable to professionally detach himself from the answers, Blaise thought back to seeing Grace and Gypsy in the park. Their movements as one. *She had no family. Few friends. Making her way in life alone. Except for her dog.* Startling, he realized Chad had asked another question and his mind worked to catch up.

"I know that sounds hard as hell but, honestly, we have some TSA handlers that can't handle the job. Granted, they usually come tell us but, well, when she didn't return to work, we just figured she wasn't interested." Sticking his hands in his pockets, his hound-dog eyes looked up. "What have you found? Do you think she's off hurt somewhere? Is her car missing?"

"Why would you say that?" Blaise asked, his voice strident. Chad, barely nudging Blaise, reminded him to maintain his composure. Sucking in a deep breath, Blaise continued, "After all, anything could have happened to her. Perhaps, as you say, she just left for another job."

Licking his lips, Preston swallowed hard. "I don't know. I mean, I don't know what happened. I was just thinking that if she's missing, that sounds like you all think something happened to her."

Noticing that Preston was verbally back peddling, Blaise pierced him with a glare.

"Um, if that's all, I really need to get back in there," Preston said.

"One more thing," Chad stepped in. "Can you tell us if Carter Boren is working today?"

"Um, no. This is his day off. We work twelve-hour shifts, three days on, two days off."

Leaving the flustered trainer, the trio of Saints headed back out as Luke sent them Carter's home address.

As Preston walked back into the baggage area, he noticed Bernard talking to one of the other TSA dog handlers. The two men shared a long stare, neither saying a word.

~

MONTY LEFT THE other two, heading back to consult with Jack and Mitch. "I want to find out what they've got on her car," he said.

"Let me know as soon as they process something on the paint marks from her back bumper," Blaise demanded, gaining a nod from Monty as he headed toward his truck.

The other two drove to Carter's house, discovering he still lived with his parents. Blaise eyed the two cars in the driveway, one white, but saw no damage to either. Ringing the doorbell, they were met with the sounds of barking, followed by a sharp command and the barking stopped.

A woman answered the door, looking up at them, a questioning expression on her face. "Yes, can I help you?"

Standing back, so as not to give a threatening vibe, Chad asked to speak to Carter. She began to speak when the sound of a young man's voice came through. "Mom, I got this." Carter stepped around his mother, giving her a smile, as he gently moved her back from the door.

"I got a call from Preston, saying you'd be coming

by," he explained, amicably. "Come on in."

Curious as to why Preston would have called Carter, Blaise said nothing as he and Chad walked into the small living room. Carter's mom disappeared and returned a minute later with glasses of iced tea on a tray.

"I thought you gentlemen might like some refreshment," she explained, nervously glancing between them.

Thanking her, they noticed she left the room after receiving a pointed stare from Carter. He turned to them, saying, "Sorry. It's kind of embarrassing to be twenty-five and still living at home. But, now, with a steady income from the TSA, I should be able to rent my own place soon."

Nodding, Blaise began, "We are investigating the disappearance of Grace Kennedy and understand that you were close to her when at the K-9 training center."

"Yeah, I guess you could say we were close. The first day of training, I was nervous as hell and just happened to be sitting at a table with the only two women in the class. Grace and Jocelyn Montez. Both nice as could be and I think just as nervous as me. We got to talking and stuck together for most of the training."

"Tell us what you know about Grace," Chad prompted.

"She was super smart…probably the smartest one in the class. She and her dog had a real bond." He smiled as he reminisced. "We didn't hang out after class. She lived close enough to drive but far enough away to have to leave right after class most days."

"Anything personal?"

Crinkling his brow, Carter said, "Not too much, although I know her parents had died and she had no one in her family. We had a little graduation party at a nearby restaurant when we finished the training and most of us had some family with us. She was alone."

"Tell us about the position with the TSA at the Richmond International Airport. We know you were hired at RIA after she did not return. Rather fortuitous for you, wasn't it?"

Startling, Carter immediately sat up straighter. "Wait, you don't think I had anything to do with her disappearance, do you?"

"We're just trying to establish what was going on in her life at the time she went missing," Blaise explained smoothly.

"Listen, it's like any other job. There's gonna be more applicants than jobs and so it's not unusual for us both to be interested in the same place. We, and Jocelyn, were the only local people at the K-9 facility."

"It's our understanding that she was the front-runner for the job and had begun the TSA job at RIA shortly before you graduated."

Nodding his head, still scowling, Carter admitted, "Yeah, I know. And, honestly, when they called to offer me the job, I was surprised. But they said she quit, so I thought 'Lucky me.'"

"Lucky you?" Blaise asked as Chad glanced his way again.

"I didn't know anything bad happened to her. I had no idea she actually disappeared. I just thought maybe she found another job," Carter defended.

"Did you bother to check with her? Try to call her? See if Jocelyn had heard from her?" Chad asked.

"Naw. We didn't see each other after the K-9 class. I just didn't think about it. I'm not ashamed to say, I was thrilled to receive the call." His eyes shifted from them to around the small room. "My goal was to get outta here and into my own place. This job'll make that happen." As an afterthought, he added, "But I never wished her any ill. I hope you find her, safe and sound."

Driving away, the two Saints were quiet for a few minutes, each man deep into their own thoughts. His eyes still on the road, Chad asked, "You okay, man? The investigation is only gonna get more intense, you know."

Sucking in a deep breath before letting it out slowly, Blaise replied, "Yeah, I know. And I'm all right. Sort of." Chuckling, he said, "I guess that didn't sound very convincing, did it?"

Grinning, Chad shook his head. "It's all good. Don't worry about trying to sound convincing to me. You just gotta stay cool while we're interviewing."

"I know," Blaise agreed, "but it's so fuckin' hard to

not want to bash someone's head in for not reporting her missing!" Running his hand through his hair he let out a long sigh. "You should have seen that broken down, abandoned house she was living in, Chad. No heating or cooling. No furniture. No running water or electricity. Just her and Gypsy sleeping on the floor."

Chad grimaced, angry at what the sweet woman had endured. "You can't beat yourself…or anyone else up, Blaise. She's in your life now and that's where you can help her."

"She was freaking out last night and I told her the same thing. We can't turn the clock back but can focus on moving forward."

Chad spared a glance toward his friend. "She it for you?"

A smile replaced the scowl on Blaise's face as his mood lightened just thinking about the beautiful woman back at his house. "Yeah, man. It may sound crazy, but yeah."

Chad, matching Blaise's grin, proclaimed, "Nothing crazy about finding the woman that clicks with your life…or the life of a Saint. I felt that about Dani and wasted too much time before letting her know. Don't make the same mistake I did."

❧

DROPPED BACK OFF at Blaise's house, Grace waived goodbye to Miriam before turning to head inside the house. The symphony of barking met her ears as she walked straight through to the back room. Filling up the buckets the way Blaise showed her, she made the trek to the kennels, Ransom and Gypsy following on her heels. Having learned their names, she greeted each one, taking the time to ruffle their ears and while they gobbled the food, she hosed down their kennels.

Finishing the outdoor animals, she moved to the few cats that were inside. The figure-eights they pranced around her legs ceased as soon as she filled their dishes as well. Hearing a high-pitched mew, she looked over at the tiny kitten. "I didn't forget you, little one." Unable to resist, she opened up the cage and lifted the small animal to her chest. Its claws came out as it hissed.

"Ouch!" she exclaimed. "You've got little talons there."

Stroking the dark fur, the kitten began to purr. "Mmm, you may have sharp claws, but you're just scarcd arcn't you." Continuing to hold it close, she said, "You know? I think Talon is a good name for you."

Feeding the little tigress, she put her back into the cage and moved into the kitchen. Fixing a sandwich, she looked at the clock. *Only two p.m. Ugh. I wonder if Blaise has found out anything more?*

She looked down at the temporary cell phone he gave her and hovered her finger over the keys. *No, stop it. If he had anything I needed to know, he'd call.* Flipping through the channels on the TV, she quickly became bored. Gypsy trotted over, laying her head in Grace's lap, her amber eyes staring at her mistress, whimpering.

Smiling, she stood and said, "Let's go, girl. I'm bored. You're bored. Let's have some fun."

Finding some tennis balls and dog ropes in the feed room, the two of them headed outside, with Ransom plodding along after them, curling up in the shade. Grace and Gypsy began with a simple game of ball toss that soon morphed into her calling out commands. As her training came slamming back into her, Grace gave Gypsy a workout, remembering how they used to play together after getting home from training.

Tossing a ball in the park near my apartment. Her sleeping on the pad next to my bed. Our training! I remember her on a leash, going over concrete walls, wooden crates, plastic pipes. She would sit and bark once when she found something.

Excited, Grace tried to pull up other memories of people she knew, but the only ones that crowded into her mind were of her and Gypsy. *But, thank God, it's a start!*

The crunch of tires on gravel had Gypsy and Ransom barking and Grace jogged around the house to see one of the Saints dropping Blaise off in the front. "BLAISE!" she screamed her greeting.

He stopped halfway out of the truck, the sight of her causing his heart to pound. Her long, dark hair flowing behind her. Her tight jeans making her legs appear long and slender, while fitting her delectable hips perfectly. Her breasts bouncing slightly in the old t-shirt. But it was the expression on her face that rocked him. A wide smile, bright eyes, and unadulterated joy at seeing him.

Without holding back, she ran straight to him, jumping up in his arms as he planted his feet to brace himself.

Laughing at his reception, a woman in his arms, two dogs running circles around their legs, and a couple of cats lounging on the front porch—*what more could I want?*

"Hey, babe," he greeted. "Looks like you had a good day!"

"I remember some things! I remember training with Gypsy and running with her in the park near my apartment! And I remember her sleeping next to my bed in the apartment! That's all, but it's a start and the counselor said more should come with time!" she gushed, capturing his lips with hers, sealing them with a kiss of joy.

His arms tightened around her body, feeling her trembling, but this time with excitement instead of fear. *Thank God!* Her breasts pressed into his chest and he could feel her heat through their jeans. Forgetting Chad's presence, he angled his head, taking the kiss deeper.

Hearing another car door close, she jerked away, a deep red blush rising from her chest to her hairline.

"Oh, I'm sorry!" She wiggled to get down, but Blaise held on tight as he turned his body to where they faced his friend.

"I realize it's too hard to remember all of us, but I'm Chad."

"It's nice to see you again," she said, her wide smile lighting her face as she observed the large man with the dark hair and quiet demeanor.

Chad watched the pair, perfectly aligned as Blaise held her close, with the animals running around, and grinned. It was easy to see that Blaise was right—she was definitely the one.

CHAPTER 15

A S THE SUN moved past the woods in the back, the moon peeked out from the other side. The evening air was slightly cooler as Blaise and Grace sat on the patio, droplets sliding down their beer bottles.

He did not want to interrupt her jubilant mood, but she insisted he tell her every detail of what his investigation had uncovered about her past.

She now sat, contemplating all he had revealed. Taking a deep pull of her beer, she set it down on the wide arm of the Adirondack chair she lounged in. "So, in a nutshell, I'm an only child, orphan, who has a dog I love. I graduated from college, then decided to go to K-9 school and did the training there. Gypsy and I were so good we were the top pick for the TSA at the Richmond International Airport. I had two friends, one was in competition for the same job. I got selected, started the TSA training shortly after I graduated school, had my accident about 3 weeks later and my friend got the job since I didn't show up anymore. No one has heard about me since I disappeared and no one reported me missing."

Blaise listened as she calmly recited the facts as though talking about the weather. "Sweetheart—"

"No, Blaise," she interrupted, finally giving emotion to her words. "Don't give me platitudes about my former life. I just find it hard to think that no one cared."

He scooted his chair so that it was now facing hers, directly in front, and moved his large, muscular body so his long legs pressed on the outside of hers. Taking her hands in his, he pulled her forward so she was forced to be at eye level with him.

"You need to listen to me," he ordered softly, but deliberately. "You were in a state of transition. You only lived in your apartment for a month or two and had already paid for two more months. You hadn't had time to meet neighbors. You graduated from the K-9 school, so they didn't know you were missing. You had only been in the TSA training for three weeks when you left, so you hadn't had time to establish friends there either. Their office is busy, overworked and understaffed, so, unfortunately, you were seen as more of a number than a person. It sucks, but it happens sometimes." He paused for emphasis then continued, "This situation is not on you. Granted, I grew increasingly pissed as the day wore on, but Chad had to remind me that the state of transition hindered your situation."

She grew quiet, mesmerized by his crystal clear, blue eyes not wavering from hers. His hands, fingers laced with hers, were warm and strong. She caught a whiff of his masculine scent, not from cologne but musky and original to him. His words wrapped around her heart, sinking into the loneliness she felt when she attempted to stare into her blank past.

Sighing heavily, she nodded slowly. "You're right. It just made me sound like such a loser when I said it earlier. But I'd like to think that I'm the kind of person that people would miss."

Without skipping a beat, he leaned in further, saying, "Babe, if you were missing from my life for one day, I would miss you more than my next breath. I'd never stop searching for you. I'd circle the globe, just to find you."

This time, his words slammed into her, taking her breath away as he pulled her closer. Leaping from her chair, she landed in his lap, their lips sealing the promises between each other.

Slipping his tongue deep into the warmth of her mouth, he reveled in the heady taste of her, exploring every crevice. The sensations shot straight to her core as her womb convulsed. She squeezed her legs together in an attempt to ease the ache between them.

Sucking his tongue into her mouth, she swallowed his groan, feeling him shift her body over his groin. His erection pressed against her as she wiggled more.

Lifting his hand from her hip, it slid up her side, resting just underneath her breast. She pressed herself further into him, her unspoken acquiescence given. His large hand cupped her breast as his thumb moved over her hardened nipple. This time, he swallowed her moan as her squirming increased.

The pressure of her ass against his cock blasted all other thoughts from his head other than seeking release. Their lips never left each other's as he stood, slipping his hand under her knees as he lifted her in his arms.

Stalking inside, he maneuvered her body so as not to hit her head while he closed and alarmed the back patio door. His head had to turn out of necessity, but she grabbed his cheeks in her palms, forcing his lips back to hers just as he secured the door.

Chuckling through the kiss, he moved to the stairs, taking them two at a time, easily moving with her in his arms. Reaching the upper hall, he hesitated.

Mewling at the loss of his lips, she peered into his eyes questioningly. He let her legs slide down to the floor while keeping her pressed into his chest, his prominent erection against her stomach.

"I need the words, babe. I wanted to wait…thought you needed to wait. I need to know that you want this as much as I do."

"You can't tell?" she smiled.

Grinning in return, he said, "Babe, I can feel your heat searing into me and I'm hanging on by a thread. But I gotta hear you say it. And that you understand this'll be no fuck…but the start of you and me."

Holding his gaze, her heart overflowing with emotion, she lifted her hand to cup his cheek once more. "Blaise, I want you. I think I've wanted you ever since I saw you that night at Chuck's, but especially since the first time I saw you with Gypsy and knew you were special. You were sent for me. You were for me. I want everything about you to be a part of everything about me. I might not remember my past, but I sure as hell know I want you in my future."

Her smile was interrupted by his lips. Sealing their fates. He lifted her and carried her into his bedroom. Looking behind him, he said, "Sorry, y'all. This is just for us," and he kicked the door shut, keeping Gypsy and Ransom outside.

Setting Grace down again, he tossed back the covers before turning back to her eager lips. Soft and pliant, he reveled in her taste. Intoxicated, all rational thought left him as his body yearned to join with hers. Claim her. Possess her.

His hands grasped the bottom of her t-shirt and he pulled it up, tantalizingly slow. When it finally came to her breasts, she lifted her arms up, allowing him to pull it over her head before tossing it to the floor. Bringing her hands down, she repeated the movement on him, adding his polo to the pile.

His gaze lingered on hers as his hands moved to the front clasp of her bra, unsnapping it, allowing her breasts to fall naturally. With a flick of his wrist, the material fell away. His eyes then dropped to her glorious breasts—full mounds with dusty rose nipples.

Already distended, they beckoned his mouth, but he resisted. The desire to have her naked overrode any other pleasure.

Placing his hands on her jean's waistband, he slid the zipper down after unsnapping the button. Her hands mimicked his, unzipping his pants at the same time, although she had to maneuver the zipper over his pressing erection.

Stepping back so that her hands fell from his pants, he hooked his thumbs in her jeans and panties, sliding them to the floor. She rested her hands on his shoulders as he assisted her in stepping out of them.

And there she was…finally, naked. Gloriously naked. His eyes feasted over her perfect form, the scent of her arousal almost unmanning him. As he lifted his gaze back to hers, he smiled. "Perfection," he whispered, winning her grin in return.

Trailing her eyes over his broad shoulders, down his muscular pecs and defined abs, she fought the urge to run her fingers over his stomach. "You appear to be overdressed for the occasion," she said, her mouth dry with anticipation.

A cocky smile on his face, Blaise moved his hands to his pants, pushing them down as well, kicking them to the side to land on the other discarded clothing. Fisting his massive erection, glad to be free, he watched her eyes land on his cock and widen. *Jesus, she's good for my ego!* While he had never had any woman complain…and plenty had wanted a repeat performance...there was something about the way Grace stared at him. Need. Want. Lust. And even awe.

Suddenly the thought hit him—*if she can't remember anything, what if she's a virgin?* One look at her enticing body almost had him convinced she could not possibly be one, but not willing to take a chance, he let his erection go, determined to seduce her slowly.

Stepping forward until her breasts touched his chest and his erection prodded her stomach, he tipped her head up and once more plundered her mouth. Long, slow, wet kisses made his head spin and he hoped it had the same effect on her.

The tingling between her legs had her seeking relief as she squeezed them together. Lost in his lips on hers, she barely realized he maneuvered her to the bed, laying her back on the soft mattress, following her down. His body pressed into hers but he propped his weight up on his arms. *How did he do that without ending the kiss*, she wondered, but the sensations slamming through her ceased all thoughts.

Caressing her breasts, he kissed his way from her lips to the pulse point on her neck, nipping as he went. Marking her, he continued his path to the tops of her mounds, moving from one breast to the other until finally latching onto a distended nipple. Licking the areola, he then pulled it into his mouth, sucking deeply.

The electricity jolted straight to her womb causing her hips to involuntarily lift against his, desperate to ease her longings. Chuckling as he felt her movements, he slid his hand down as he moved slightly to the side. His fingers found their prize, her slick folds welcoming him. Easing first one finger and then two, he scissored them deep inside, eliciting more moans from her parted lips.

The scent of her sex combined with the sounds she was making in the back of her throat undid him. Sliding down her body further, he pushed her legs apart as his tongue lapped up her savory juices. Her hips bucked and he placed a large hand on her stomach to keep her steady. Thrusting his tongue inside, he moved his hand up toward her breast, tweaking her sensitive nipple.

Lost in a sea of sensations, she lifted her gaze and kept her eyes on his head between her legs. With a nip on her clit, she jumped again as her orgasm rocketed her into orbit. Slamming her head back onto the mattress she allowed her body to float into space until it slowly came down.

Finally able to lift her head again, she saw his lazy smile as he licked her arousal off his lips.

"Aren't you the cocky one," she barely managed to say, still overwhelmed from her orgasm.

Crawling over her body, his erection straining and eager, he said, "Babe, I'll show you cocky when my dick is buried to the hilt inside of this gorgeous, soaked pussy."

His words turned her on more than she thought she

could be. "You're going to kill me with an overdose of orgasms, aren't you?"

"What a way to go," he murmured, grabbing the condom from where he had tossed it on the bed. Ripping the package, he rolled it over his erection. Leaning back down, his lips met hers again. Reaching down to center the swollen head of his cock at her entrance, he slipped inside slowly. Deeper and deeper, he stretched her inner walls, happy to see no signs of discomfort from her.

Pushing all the way, balls to her ass, he groaned as her tight sex grabbed his dick and held on. He felt her arms wind their way around his neck as her legs circled his hips, opening her up even wider. Settling his hips securely, he moved out in slow agony before plunging in again.

She felt his rhythm increase as he thrust harder and harder. The delicious friction soon had her moaning, desiring nothing more than to orgasm to relieve the need.

Continuing to rock her body, Blaise was lost in the euphoria as his balls tightened and his lower back muscles contracted. *Please come again...I can't last!* "I am," she gasped and he realized he spoke his thoughts out loud.

Just then she cried out his name as her second orgasm exploded. Hearing his name on Grace's lips was all it took for him to grind himself deep inside, pulsating until every drop was drained.

He fell on top of her, barely managing to roll slightly to the side before crushing her. Unable to move further he lay, half on her, his heart pounding erratically. *Never, fuckin' hell, have I ever felt like that before.* Not speaking, he continued to pant, hoping sweet words were not needed at the moment, unsure he had the breath to speak.

She lay, his heavy weight comfortably pressing on her side, her heart pounding. Her arms still wrapped tightly around his, her hand slowly stroking his shoulder. Closing her eyes, she reveled in the feeling of their sweat-slicked bodies together.

After several long minutes, the comfortable silence only broken by their breathing as it became steadier, he lifted his head and peered into her eyes. Their warm sparkle met his gaze.

"You okay, sweetheart? I didn't hurt you, did I?"

Shaking her head slowly, she moved her hand to cup his cheek. "I don't think it would even be possible for you to hurt me," she replied honestly.

Grinning, he kissed her lips before saying, "I'll be right back." He left the bed reluctantly, striding into the bathroom to dispose of the condom.

She watched his magnificent ass as it moved away from her, but as he swaggered back into the room, she decided it was the front view that would win the prize. His walk was sure and confident.

Leaning up on her elbows, she suddenly wondered what was expected. *Do I go back to the guestroom? Does he want me to stay here? What should I—*

"Grace," his gentle voice interrupted. "I can hear the rush of your thoughts." He opened the door, allowing Gypsy and Ransom to come trotting into the room. "Floor," he commanded and the two obediently curled up on the rug. Sliding back onto the mattress, Blaise pulled the covers over their cooling bodies.

"I want you here. With me. All night. And every night from now on," he confessed, as his arms pulled Grace in tightly.

Kissing her lips softly, he tucked her in and for the first time in as long as she could remember, she fell asleep instantly.

CHAPTER 16

"*GRACE! IF YOU bring home one more stray, we aren't gonna have any room left in the house,*" *dad called out as I walked into the den, my arms full of two little kittens.*

Mom walked in from the kitchen. "Dinner's ready, you two—Oh Lordy, child, what is in your hands?"

"Mr. Fields said they were in the alley at the back of his grocery store and in the garbage. Mom, we can't let them eat garbage."

"Grace Marie Kennedy, you would have the whole house filled with animals if you could." Mom walked over, taking one of the kittens out of my hand, cuddling it close to her chest. "Well, I suppose you can let them grow a little before finding new homes for them."

Grinning, I hurried into the laundry room, grabbing an old towel from the hamper. Placing the kittens on the soft material, I turned around and almost ran into my dad.

He held a box out for me, his lips curving into a knowing smile. "Figured you'd need this, Gracie."

Grabbing the box from his hands, I gave him a quick hug before turning back to my task. Placing the box on the floor, I scooped up the towel with the purring kittens and set them inside. "Now you're warm and safe," I told them, jumping up to get some food. By the time I was in the kitchen, mom was holding out some food for me.

"Hurry up and feed them so you can come to dinner."

I did as I was told and in no time, tucked my legs under the table for the blessing. My father's rich voice carried as he prayed. Tonight, he blessed the food and our family as always, then added, "And God bless our Grace, as she cares for your creatures."

Holding on to my giggles, my fingers drifted along the fur of my dog, Max. Feeling his soft tongue lick my hand, I hoped momma didn't see or she'd make me go wash my hands again.

As I lifted my eyes after the blessing…

The table floated away…as another scene drifted in.

The German Shepherd puppies bounded over, tumbling over each other to claim the visitor. I knelt down, my arms wide as I accepted the bundles of fur crawling onto my lap.

"Oh, my gosh, they're gorgeous," I laughed, falling backward on the grass and allowing the puppies to crawl over me.

The K-9 breeder smiled down at me and said, "Well, just like I promised, you get the pick of the litter. Any one of these pups will make a good K-9 dog for you."

"How will I ever pick?"

Sure that I would never be able to choose which puppy to buy, I sat cross-legged on the grass, watching the dogs *carefully. One furry bundle of energy kept coming over to me, sniffing first me and then sniffing over to where my purse was sitting on the ground about ten feet away and back again. Finally, the puppy plopped herself down next to me, her brown eyes staring at me as she cocked her head to the side while her brothers and sisters continued to tumble.*

Scooping the small dog up, I knew. Somehow, I knew she was the one. She picked me. Looking up at the breeder, I grinned. "This is it. She's the one."

"You got a name picked out," he asked, as we walked back to his house.

I thought...my parents are gone, college is over, I'm working in law enforcement but want to move into a new career as a dog handler. I have an apartment, but know I'll move when she's old enough for us to work for something like the TSA...I live like a gypsy. And she'll now be with me as we train together. "Gypsy," I answered. "Her name is Gypsy."

The farm began to fade away as dark trees came into view...

"Oh, Jesus, I have to get out of here! I have to go!" My car was hurling down the twisty mountain road, taking the curves too fast. "Gypsy, hang on, girl!"

The black night closed in on all sides with only my headlights beaming ahead...and the two yellow globes of the headlights following far behind...getting closer and closer.

The crash of metal. The loss of control. The downward

plunge. "Aughhhhhh!"

"Grace, Grace. Wake up! Come on baby, wake up for me. Breathe, baby, breathe."

She stopped thrashing as she felt the pressure of a heavy thigh covering her legs and hands rolling her toward a large, muscular body. The already familiar scent of Blaise filled her senses.

Panting, her throat raw from crying out, she blinked awake, orienting back to his bedroom. *Oh, God. A dream. A nightmare.*

Blaise muttered soft, nonsensical words of comfort for a few minutes, holding her body tightly to his. His hand smoothed her hair back from her sweaty brow, kissing her forehead. Her body slowly stopped shivering, her heartbeat steadying. Rolling over, he turned on the lamp by the bed.

"I'm okay," she whispered into his chest, her arms tightening around him as his warmth and the light chased away the last of the dreams. "I was dreaming."

"You've been twitching for a while now, but I wasn't sure if I should try to wake you or not. I'm sorry, babe. Next time, I'll wake you up."

Leaning back so she could gaze into his concerned eyes, she shook her head. "No, no, it was good. At least to start with. Blaise," she gasped, "I remember my parents. I dreamed about a time when I brought home two kittens and, just now, I realize that was a memory."

He listened to the nervousness in her voice and

questioned, "Do you remember everything or just those times?"

He loosened his grip and she sat up, rubbing her hands over her face, sucking in great gulps of air. Her mind seemed a jumble of memories flooding back, but she attempted a smile. "I remember...I had a dog named Gunner. I remember hunting Easter eggs in the backyard and one of our dogs kept finding them first. Dad used to say that I should train dogs to hunt for things."

Curling her legs up under her, her quivering voice stronger, "I remember happy times. It's like an old movie is playing in my head."

Blaise chuckled but did not get a word in before she continued in a rush, as though if she did not speak her thoughts, they would all go away.

"I remember my bedroom when I was little was green and yellow and that was why I painted my bedroom those same colors when I rented my apartment." Her eyes, bright with tears, searched his once more. Grabbing his face with her hands, she whispered, "I remember...some things. But, Blaise...I can't remember my parents dying."

Her smile dropped and he instantly regretted her excitement being replaced with sadness. "It doesn't matter," he rushed. "It'll come back. This is just a start. You're safe now."

Continuing to sit quietly for a few more minutes, she shook her head, wincing in pain. "I also can't remember the night of the accident…other than the accident itself. I…I…can't pull that up in my mind."

"It'll come back, babe."

"But what if it doesn't?"

"Well, if you remember some events in your life up to the accident night, then that's really good. That means you're claiming your life back. Just leave that night to us Saints. We'll find out what happened."

Tossing back the covers, Blaise swung his long legs over the side and stalked to the bathroom. Grace heard running water and watched as he came back to her, a glass of water in his hand.

"Here, drink this. You've been sweating and talking so much, you must be parched."

She took it gratefully, downing the entire glass before handing it back to him. Looking up, she said, "Maybe I should go to the guest bedroom. I don't think I can go back to sleep. My mind is racing." He set the glass on the nightstand then climbed into the bed after tossing some pillows against the headboard. Leaning back, he settled her into his arms, comfortably.

"You stay with me, sweetheart. Do you want to keep talking? About whatever comes to your mind."

Relaxing, she said, "I don't know what to say. When I think of my childhood, I now remember so many things…they come to me in flashes." Twisting her head up, her eyes capturing his, she added, "It feels so good to remember my parents…what they looked like. How they talked."

His arm tightened in a gentle squeeze but he kept silent, allowing her to speak freely. Her voice, stronger and steadier now, continued to relate the memories she could recover.

Yawning widely, she snuggled deeper into his arms. He listened as she began to yawn more and more between her reflections until she finally grew quiet and he felt her body sink into his. Sliding down, bringing her with him, he once more tucked her into his embrace as he listened to her steady breathing. Sleep had claimed her once more and he wanted to be there if more dreams or nightmares crept into her slumber.

Thrilled she now had many memories back, his mind turned over to the night of the accident. *What happened? Where were you? And who tried to kill you?* Remembering his vow of earlier, he closed his eyes. *We'll find out what happened.*

THE SAINTS SAT around the conference table the next morning reporting on their investigations as Mitch listened in.

"So, your feelings about Carter Boren?" Jack prompted after Blaise and Chad reviewed their interview.

"He's got the motive. He's competitive and envious of her skill with Gypsy. Grace was getting the job he wanted and the employment would get him out of his mother's house and on his own. Means? I didn't see any dents in the front of the two cars in the driveway but that doesn't mean that he wasn't involved. He may have had repairs done."

"I'll check to see what his car registrations are and what work he's had done…if he put it on a credit card or made an insurance claim," Luke volunteered, turning to his bank of computers.

"What about opportunity?" Marc asked. "She was not near anything else, so the question still comes down to why was she on that road."

"What other impressions did you get yesterday?" Jude asked.

Chad shook his head, saying, "Everyone had great things to say about Grace, but not one of them did a thing about her being missing…if they even knew. Douglas Wilkins from the K-9 Training Facility gave us info about her relationship with Carter and Jocelyn when they were there. Grace had already graduated by then, so he had no further contact. It would be unlikely for him to be involved. I was less impressed by Bernard Tanner and Preston Solter, from the RIA TSA office."

"Neither of them seem to give a fuck that she just stopped coming to work," Blaise growled. "Both talked about what a good trainee she was and how they were glad to get her. But when she stopped coming, they just made the assumption she was no longer interested in the job."

"So they hired Carter?" Bart asked, his face registering his incredulity. "Without checking to see what happened to Grace? That makes no fuckin' sense!"

"They claim that some of their trainees quickly learn the job isn't very glamorous and the long twelve hour shifts are not what they want," Chad said. "They're also understaffed and overworked, so they claim, and that was another reason they just jumped to the next person on the list."

"Carter," Marc stated, shaking his head while muttering.

Mitch added, "I've been in contact with my TSA counterpart in DC, Carin Torgensen, and she is ready for us to continue this investigation with their approval. She's not happy with what we've uncovered and wants us to find out how they lost a valuable drug dog handler and now know that an attempt was made on her life."

"We need you to interview Jocelyn today," Jack ordered, nodding to Blaise. "Take Chad with you again. Luke, you continue to follow up on those that have been met with already. Mitch, see if you can get a rush on the damage to her car that was from the other automobile hitting her. Marc, I want you and Blaise to go back up on the mountain and see what you can find."

"So what are we looking for specifically?" Marc asked.

"She didn't just wander up on that road leading to nowhere," Jack explained. "She would have been there for a reason and my guess is that if we find that reason, we'll find who tried to kill her."

CHAPTER 17

SITTING IN DR. Saren's office the next day, Grace relived the night before. "I'm so glad you could see me today! I woke with such fear, but the things started coming back to me. Then I tried so hard to remember about my childhood. Does this mean it's gone forever?"

"No, no," Dr. Saren assured. "Repressed memories can easily come back in bits and pieces. It's usually not like TV where someone wakes up and suddenly their entire memory is back."

Sighing heavily, she looked down at her hands, tightly squeezed together in her lap. At the counselor's prompting, she admitted, "I remember so many good things about when I was growing up. But I don't remember my parents' deaths. Blaise said he could find out all the details."

"Do you want him to?"

"I…I'm not sure. Right now, it just feels good to remember pleasant times."

"Then I think you should write down all of the things you remember from your childhood and save the sadder occurrences for later. You may recall them on your own or maybe from another dream. Or you may decide to let him find out and tell you. But it needs to be on your time."

The counselor peered at Grace for several long, silent minutes. "What else is on your mind?"

Lifting her gaze, she admitted, "I'm kind of lost." A small giggle escaped, and she added, "I guess that sounds pretty dumb coming from someone who can't remember hardly anything. What I mean is that I want to do something. But what? I know Gypsy and I trained as a drug dog and handler, but," shrugging, "I don't remember that right now."

"What do you want to do?"

"Something. Anything. I've been at Blaise's house for a few days and help with his rescue animals. But that doesn't take long. He doesn't want me out much because we don't know who was after me."

"And you're bored?"

"God, yes!"

"You said that you had made some friends…a few former clients of mine." Seeing Grace's nod, Dr. Saren suggested, "Then why don't you spend time with them. It's fine to want your memories back, but you don't want to waste time not building a new life."

"I do like spending time with them. I can't really go into the city right now, but one of them has a place in the country. Maybe Gypsy and I could visit and enjoy some time there."

"I think that makes perfect sense."

Standing to leave, Grace hesitated at the door. Turning back, she asked, "Do you think my memories will come back at night?"

"At night, your mind is relaxed and that is often when we have our clearest thoughts. So, yes, your memories could come from your dreams. Are you afraid to sleep? Afraid of the nightmares?"

Grace thought of the man who held her through the night, first with his body worshiping hers and then in care when he soothed her fears. Her lips curved into a slight smile as she shook her head. "No…no, I'm not afraid anymore."

ARRIVING AT THE Albert County Sheriff's office, Blaise and Chad walked in out of the summer heat into the cool interior. Mitch had contacted the office, preparing the Sheriff for the Saints' visit.

Showing no surprise to be greeted by Sherriff Antonio Montez, shaking hands, he offered a friendly greeting and escorted them back to a small conference room.

"Gentlemen, I understand you want to talk to Deputy Jocelyn Montez, my daughter. I've radioed for her to come in and she should be here shortly."

Blaise expected to be questioned as to the reason for their visit, but the Sheriff was completely professional. Declining the offer of coffee, they exchanged pleasantries until Jocelyn entered the room.

Petite, with ebony hair sleeked back in a tight bun, the uniformed deputy confidently walked in, immediately shaking their hands. The Sheriff nodded at the assembly and left the room, closing the door behind him.

Jocelyn turned her dark eyes toward the men and cocked her head to the side. "How may I help you?"

"We're investigating the disappearance of Grace Kennedy—"

"WHAT?" she cried out, her eyes large, confusion filling her face. "Disappearance? What do you mean…I mean…she's—"

"Deputy Montez, she's been reported missing and we're talking to those that were close to her."

Dropping all semblance of composure, her eyes filled with tears as she blinked several times in an attempt to keep them at bay. Taking a ragged breath, she said, "Please tell me what you know and how I can help."

"Why don't you tell us about your relationship with Ms. Kennedy first."

Nodding, she drew in a fortifying breath before beginning. "We met at the K-9 Training Facility. We were the only two females and kind of bonded immediately over that initially. But then we became friends. There was another trainee, Carter Boren, and the three of us formed a tight group there."

"And after graduation from the K-9 program?"

At that, she winced. "We stayed in touch…but we

were both so busy. God, that sounds terrible, doesn't it? I talked to her about six weeks ago, just as she was moving closer to her job. But, I'm ashamed to admit that I haven't talked to her since then." Thinking for a moment, she said, "No, it was sooner than that. She had just worked for the RIA TSA for about a week and it was my birthday. She couldn't come to the party, but called that night."

Chad, jotting everything down, asked, "How did she sound?"

Smiling, Jocelyn said, "Great. Just great. She was loving the airport trainee work and was expecting to finish on schedule and become a full-fledged TSA employee there."

"Did you know that Carter now has her old job?"

A flash of disgust crossed her face, but she quickly replaced it with a professional demeanor. "No, no. I had no idea. Carter and I...haven't talked much after K-9 graduation. Well, actually not at all."

"Can you tell us why?"

Sighing heavily, Jocelyn turned her head, staring out of the window for a moment. Finally, she turned back to the two men and said, "It's rather embarrassing. I never even told Grace what happened. After the graduation party, we were fairly intoxicated." Sitting up straighter, looking them in the eye, she said, "Carter and I spent the night together. It was truly a one-night stand. We both knew it. But we did go out the next morning for breakfast and he was such an...ass. He talked about Grace the whole time. How she got the job at RIA because she was a female. How he really needed the money and she could still live off her parents' insurance money." Shaking her head in disgust, she said, "I was angry with myself that I had even slept with him and irritated that I thought we were such friends while in training. Anyway, after that, I never called and he didn't either."

Offering a gentle nod, Chad thanked her for her candor.

"So," she said, after taking another deep breath, "Grace is missing and he has her job. Damn." Lifting her gaze, she implored, "What can you tell me about her?"

"Nothing right now," Blaise lied smoothly, not willing to have anyone know she was alive and well. "We had a report from her apartment manager and we're now investigating."

"Gypsy? Her dog?" Jocelyn asked, eyes widening again. "Is she missing too?" Seeing Blaise's nod, she said, "She would never leave her dog. They must be together."

"Can I ask about your work here?" Chad queried.

With a self-deprecating chuckle, she said, "Nepotism is alive and well, I suppose. My dad's been the Sheriff of this county for the last two terms. He wanted me to come and join the K-9 team here and," offering a little shrug, "it is home. But I do work part time at the Charlestown airport. It's a small airport, so they use me sometimes to fill in."

Finishing the interview, they all stood, Blaise lifting his hand to shake hers. "We'll find out what happened to her," he promised, seeing despair cross her face.

"Please keep me informed," she begged. Gaining their acquiescence, the three headed out of the conference room and toward the front door.

Blaise noticed the Sheriff eyeing them from behind the counter, offering his goodbye as well.

As he walked through the front door, he glanced behind him, seeing daughter and father deep in conversation.

BLAISE PICKED MARC up at his house. Marc's property was very similar to Blaise's—plenty of wooded acres. But Marc had built his house from the ground up. A two-story log cabin, much smaller than Jack's, it had been his project for over a year. He had help with the log building on the outside, but most of the inside had been finished with his own two hands. It was rustic but comfortable—just like Marc himself.

While Blaise drove, Marc said, "I've had Luke give me whatever he could about the area and topography. There's a small private airstrip on one of the farms, but it has no hangars, just an old outbuilding as the office. From what I can tell, it houses only crop dusters. I've checked with a few of my pilot buddies who've flown over that area, but so far nothing that would indicate a place where Grace would have gone or why."

Blaise maneuvered the snaky curves going up the old two-lane road, noting the drop off on the other side. "I can't believe she had to speed down this road in the dark," he bit out, his voice dark with anger.

"Do you want to know where she went over the side?" Marc asked cautiously.

"No." A pause. "Yes," he said, heaving a sigh.

"We'll watch for it on the way back down."

Thirty minutes later, the road leveled out, meandering through farmland and woods. A few houses dotted along the sides, but most were placed back from the road. After a few more miles, they noticed a crop dusting plane land behind a grove of trees.

"You in the mood to check it out?" Blaise asked.

"Hell, yeah," Marc agreed, eager to see what the tiny airstrip consisted of.

Turning off the road onto a gravel drive that went for a mile through a wooded area, they came to a clearing. An older barn sat next to a small wooden building. The dust was still billowing behind the old plane that taxied toward the barn.

Parking next to the building, the two men got out and walked toward the pilot, who looked at them, surprise on his face. He sauntered over to them, wiping his face with an old, faded, red bandana.

"Can I help y'all?" he called out.

Marc easily took charge of the conversation as he moved toward the plane. "Sorry to bother you, but we were driving by and noticed your crop duster. I told my co-worker I had to stop and take a look."

The man crinkled his brow as he twisted around to follow Marc's progress over to his old plane before turning his gaze back to Blaise.

Marc patted the side of the plane as he looked it over. "My grandpa used to fly a Boeing Stearman PT-17. First plane I ever went up in."

The man's grey bushy eyebrows lifted as a smile split his face. "Yeah, yeah, I remember those. I bought an old used one and flew it for a few years."

"My dad bought a 1980 Piper Brave—"

"No, kiddin'? One of them yellow ones?"

Marc laughed and nodded. "And that was the first plane I ever flew." Sticking out his hand, he said, "Marc Jenkins. And this is my friend, Blaise Hanssen."

"Bob Davison," the older man said, shaking their hands. "Well, I don't get many visitors up here, but you're welcome to come into the barn and sit a spell. I've got some cold water and beer in a little ice chest I brought from home this morning."

Blaise, taking his cue from Marc, followed the man as he led them to the ancient barn. Settling down on a couple of rickety wooden chairs, that Blaise was afraid would not hold his weight, he took the proffered beer.

The conversation immediately crackled with the excitement of two pilots, finding a love of old planes. Blaise hid his grin, knowing Marc was working up to his questions.

"Are there any other airstrips around?"

"Well, I think I'm the only crop duster around here. Not many people use the old ways anymore. Sometimes, I see some planes flying kind of low, but they might come out of the Charlestown airport."

Blaise and Marc handed their bottles back to the old man as they stood. He grasped Marc's hand and said, "You ever want to take a trip down memory lane, son, you just come on up and we'll go up in that old girl out there."

"I just might take you up on that, sir," Marc laughed as they left the barn.

Back in the car, Blaise glanced over to Marc. "What do you think?"

"On the surface, just an old farmer who, years ago, started doing his own crop dusting and keeps it up."

"And below the surface?"

Marc shook his head. "Don't know. Something flashed in his eyes when I asked about other airstrips." Shaking his head again, he said, "But, then, I might be looking for something that's just not there."

"At this point, to keep Grace safe, I'm willing to follow up on everything," Blaise vowed.

CHAPTER 18

GRACE SMILED AT Bethany as they turned down the lane where the large wooden sign proclaimed **Mountville Cabins Rental and Wedding Venue**.

"Oh, this is lovely!" Grace exclaimed as the house came into view.

"This was the house my grandparents built and lived in their whole lives. They lived upstairs and the registration lobby and guest recreation hall were downstairs. There are ten cabins they built that circle around the little lake over there."

"And you lived here for a while too?"

"Yep. My grandmother kept the cabins after my grandfather died and, when she began having health problems, I quit my marketing job in Richland and moved here." She continued to drive, saying, "I'll take you on the grand tour so you can see the place."

Bethany pointed out the small, but neat, A-frame cabins that were spaced around the lake. When they came to a place with a bench and flowers planted around, she said, "There used to be a cabin there, but Jack had it torn down and a garden planted instead."

"I have a feeling there's a story behind that?" Grace asked gently.

The pretty blond looked her way, her braid flipping from her shoulder to her back. "There was a man who used to stay there all the time. He was a serial killer and, well, before he was caught, he took me as well."

Sucking in her breath, Grace's face showed surprise and heartfelt sympathy. "I am so sorry," she gushed.

Shrugging slightly, Bethany said, "All's well that ends well. And now you can see why Dr. Saren is my therapist also!"

Stunned into silence, Grace did not know what to say. Bethany took pity on her and said, "So do you want to hear about how I met Jack?"

"Absolutely!"

Laughing as she parked the truck by the pier leading out over the lake, Bethany admitted, "It was definitely a serendipitous meeting! Gram, who was already suffering from Alzheimer's, wandered off and got onto Jack's super-duper secret property. He and the others came charging out of the woods, encircling us."

Grace, entranced with the story, rushed out of the vehicle to make sure she did not miss any of it. Gypsy, excited, jumped down with her.

"Gram thought he was someone from her past. Jack thought we were intruders. The other men seemed confused. And I was just pissed." Bethany's blue eyes met Grace's chocolate ones, as she admitted, "Well, pissed...and turned on!"

Laughing, Grace nodded as she said, "When I first saw Blaise, I ran away. I wasn't sure who he was or why he wanted to help, but I was not at all ready to take a chance. I was afraid of everybody and everything."

The two women walked out on the dock and sat on the end. Gypsy trotted faithfully by her side until Grace let her run. "Go girl, chase some squirrels." The dog took off, enjoying the summer day and the chance to run in the woods.

Leaning back with their faces to the sun and their weight resting on their arms behind them, "This feels so good," Grace moaned. "How nice for you to have been able to spend your childhood vacations here."

"It was good, although Gramps always put me to work." Laughing again, she said, "But that was good. It made it easier when I came to here to live."

"So tell me about the other women," Grace requested, then clarified, "The other Saints' women. Did they all meet under odd circumstances?"

"Oh yeah. Well, you know Miriam and Cam's story…how he was sent to Mexico to rescue her when she was kidnapped while working as a Red Cross nurse. Faith has a special gift. She sometimes gets visions and helped the Saints on a case. She and Bart hated each other at first."

Thinking of how protective the large, handsome, blond was over his petite fiancé, Grace was surprised to find out they did not like each other at first.

"In fact, the women'll be out later. Bart and Faith's

wedding will take place here in a couple of weeks."

Smiling, Grace allowed the warmth of the sun to penetrate as she listened to Bethany talk about the Saints and their women.

"Sabrina is Bart's cousin and her fiance, Jude, was medically discharged from the SEALs and became a Saint. Angel and Monty met when she was involved in a case the Saints were working on. Dani and Chad were old friends when they both worked for the ATF, sort of lost touch and finally found their way back to each other. And that just leaves Evie. Her fiancé is Angel's brother, Patrick. Like Jude, when he left the military, they moved here so he could work as a Saint also."

"Wow," Grace said, looking over at Bethany, whose face was turned to the sun as well. "That's quite a group!"

"Yeah, I'd like to think that I got things started for them all." Seeing Grace's gaze turn to her, head cocked to the side expectantly, she explained, "Jack didn't think his world would allow for a relationship. But when we got together and made it work, I think the other men realized it could happen to them as well. But," she added, meeting Grace's gaze, "It takes a special woman to be with a Saint."

Grace dropped her eyes, moving them back to the sunlight glistening over the water. Hearing Bethany giggle, she looked over.

"Honey, you're just like us and you're perfect for Blaise!"

The acceptance warmed Grace as much as the sun. Before she had a chance to reply, the sound of other vehicles pulling into the gravel nearby had both women looking up.

Soon, the sound of all of the Saints' women's voices filled the air as they finalized the plans for Bart and Faith's wedding. Grace hovered on the outside of the group for a few minutes, feeling like an interloper, until the others quickly pulled her into the fold.

Remembering the counselor's words...*It's fine to want your memories back, but you don't want to waste time not building a new life*...she knew it was time to move forward, embracing the new Grace.

BETHANY DROPPED GRACE off at Blaise's house and offered to come in and wait for him to get home.

Smiling her appreciation, Grace declined. "Thank you, but I'm good. I need to take care of the animals and get dinner started."

"You know," Bethany said softly, placing her hand on Grace's arm. "Blaise would never expect you to work just to be here."

Sucking her lips in, Grace ducked her head. "I know. But I want to stay busy and I love the animals." Giving a wistful sigh, she added, "I owe him so much..."

"Sweetie, from the look I've seen on Blaise's face lately, I'd say he knows he's the lucky one to have you in his life."

Laughing, Grace leaned over and hugged her new friend. "Thank you...for everything."

With that, she hopped out of the old truck and called for Gypsy. Twenty minutes later, Blaise crunched up the gravel driveway stopping as soon as he cleared the trees. The vision of Grace in his kitchen last night had his heart pounding, but the sight of her and Gypsy trekking around the kennels as she fed the barking dogs made his breath catch in his throat, rocking his whole world.

Stepping on the accelerator, he drove straight to the front of the house, barely getting out before she greeted him as she did last night—jumping straight into his arms. One arm under her ass and the other holding the back of her head as her lips slammed into his. Tongues tangling, the greeting flared into an inferno.

Gypsy began barking and jumping on them with Ransom joining the fray, both dogs enjoying a chance to frolic. Throwing her head back, Grace giggled. "I'm sorry! It's hard to keep kissing when she's seeking attention."

Laughing, he hefted her as a signal to put her legs down and then set her feet on the ground. "You must have had a good day," he commented, happy to see her smile.

"I did. I had Bethany take me to the counselor again to let her know about the dreams."

Dropping his smile as he carefully peered into her

face, he searched for signs of distress. Seeing none, he asked tentatively, "And…did she help?"

Nodding quickly, she answered, "Yeah. She said that at night when I'm relaxed is when my memories may come back. She also said it seems that now that I feel safer, I'm starting to remember the happy times in my life." Shrugging slightly while scrunching her nose in distaste, she admitted, "But the memories that I am frightened of, may take longer. My mind is shutting out whatever tragedy occurred."

"We'll get there, babe, I promise."

Throwing his arm around her, they walked into the house with the dogs trotting at their heels. As they sat at the counter, side by side, eating dinner, he noticed her pushing her food around her plate.

"What else is on your mind?"

Jerking her head around, she asked, "What makes you think something is on my mind?"

" 'Cause if you smush your peas any more, you're just going to have pea soup on your plate."

Glancing back down, she realized her dinner was somewhat messy. "Oh."

Chuckling, he added, "You got something to say to me besides 'oh'?"

Huffing, she responded, "I'm not crazy about peas."

"Then why did you fix them, sweetheart?"

"They were in your cabinet, so I figured you liked them."

Turning on his stool so that he was facing her, he maneuvered her legs around so that her knees were captured between his as he took her hands in his. Leaning over slightly so that they were at eye level, he said, "Grace, first of all, you don't have to cook for me. You don't have to clean, feed the animals, or anything. You're not here to do anything except be safe and heal. Second of all, can we end the conversation about peas and you tell me what you really have on your mind?"

Biting her lip, she replied, "I was wondering...well, I would do it myself but I don't have a car...or a driver's license—"

"Come on, babe," he softly prodded.

"Well, for starters...since I now remember my parents, I'd like to go back to my apartment to get more things...just until I move back there, that is," she rushed to add.

His eyebrows lowered as he said, "Move back? You can't move back now. If someone is still looking for you, that's the first place they'd look." He did not add that he wanted her here in his house, afraid of overwhelming her. "We can go back to get some of your things to make you more comfortable here."

"That's the problem," she admitted, her gaze dropping to where he clasped her hands in his larger, stronger ones. "I'm very comfortable here."

Lifting her chin with his fingers, he smiled. "Grace, I told you last night that this was the beginning of you and me. I want you very comfortable here." Seeing a shy smile curve her lips, he continued, "You said, 'for starters'," he reminded. "What else can I do for you?"

"I'd like to visit my parents' gravesites. I didn't at first, but after a nice day with the other women, listening to the wedding plans, getting ready for babies...I decided that I don't want to be afraid of learning about the past. I don't remember quite everything about my parents, but I'm ready to learn more."

"Are you sure?" he asked, his voice laced with concern.

Nodding quickly, she said, "Yes. I mean, it's all well and good to remember the happy times in my life, but I need to remember everything. Opening myself to the pain of losing my parents, might enable me to be ready to open myself to learning about the night I was attacked."

He had to admit her reasoning was logical and, as much as he wanted to protect her from sadness, as well as hurt, it was the right thing to do. "Okay, sweetheart. I've already had Luke pull up your parents' information and we can go tomorrow. Both to your apartment and to the cemetery. I'll leave work early and we'll go after lunch."

Heaving a huge sigh of relief, she tucked a dark strand of hair behind her ear and glanced back down at her plate. "Um...do you think we can skip the rest of dinner and go straight to the dessert?"

Leaning over, he placed a kiss on the corner of her

mouth. "You're the only dessert I'm interested in."

She heard the desire in his low voice, shooting straight to her core. Her nipples hardened and she squeezed her legs together.

His hands slid down her legs, gently pulling her knees apart as he stood, stepping into her space. His crotch nestled against her heat as he kissed her again, this time sealing his lips firmly over hers. Thrusting his tongue into her warmth, he plundered her mouth. Angling for better access, he deepened the kiss, the taste of her intoxicating.

Grace felt lightheaded as their tongues danced, tangling around each other's, his scent filling her nostrils. *Swooning. I'm fucking swooning.* He was more than any romance book hero as he bent her back in his arms, his mouth leaving hers only to kiss a trail down to the edge of her shirt and then back again.

Her crotch pressed against his swollen erection, causing him to consider the possibility that his zipper was leaving a permanent impression. Stepping back, he gazed into her face...her moist, kiss-swollen lips barely parted, mussed hair and chocolate eyes now melting. Throwing caution to the wind, he held her face in his hands, smoothing his thumbs over her flushed cheeks and confessed, "Grace, I want you here with me. Not just for your safety, but for you. And what we're becoming."

Her warm gaze never left his as she whispered breathlessly, "And what are we becoming?"

"Us," he replied, leaning forward to seal his vow over her lips. Bending, he slid his arm under her knees and stood, easily lifting her in his embrace. Striding to the stairs, he carried her up, this time not stopping in the hall, but heading directly to his bedroom.

Seeing acceptance in her smile, he kicked the door shut before laying her on the bed. And showing her what becoming an "us" meant to him.

WHY WON'T THE knocking stop? Finally waking to realize someone was at the door, I stumbled to answer the incessant banging. As my sleep-filled eyes focused, I saw the two policemen standing outside, the icy rain pelting the walk behind them. No! I know why they're here. They step in…and then rock my world. Mom? Dad? Noooo!

Then blackness falls all around…and I am now in a grassy field and sunshine beams.

"Grace! You and Gypsy take section C! I've got the section over here," called out Carter, giving instructions as we maneuvered through the drug-dog training course. He had Beaumont with him, his beautiful dog.

"Where's Jocelyn?" I asked, knowing we were supposed to cover the area completely.

"I see her over at section A with Torch."

Gypsy and I worked together, her skill at sniffing out the drugs unparalleled. "Good girl," I praised. We finished our section and moved over to Carter's, helping him finish the last part of his course. I noticed a flash of a glare, but he quickly hid it, knowing we were being judged as a team right now. I can't help it if he was slower, I thought. Finished with our two sections, we jogged over to section A, just as Jocelyn was completing hers. The three of us made our way quickly back and had the fastest time of any team. Gypsy, Beaumont, and Torch pranced by our sides as though knowing they had completed all the tasks.

Congratulating ourselves, we high-fived after giving our dogs their rewards.

The clouds in the sky settled down to the ground as the world became foggy and the voices more distant...

The bar was crowded, which I hated, but I knew that a graduation celebration was expected. I liked the people and the dogs in the class, but really only became close to Carter and Jocelyn. Coming back from the ladies' room, I heard Jocelyn on the phone with her parents. I could tell from her excited comments, they were offering their congratulations, sharing her pride. Carter was busy texting when I approached. His eyes held mine for an instant, guilt flashing through.

"I'm sorry, Grace," he said. "I was just texting my parents." He shot a look toward Jocelyn. "I know everyone is...well..."

"Carter, it's fine. You should be excited about talking to your parents." Shrugging, I added, "It's no one's fault that my parents have passed. They would've been happy for me."

He walked over, giving me a sideways hug. "I'm glad

we got to know each other, Grace, even if I'm jealous of your new job!"

"I heard they would be hiring more soon, so keep your fingers crossed."

"Don't worry! I'll do more than rely on luck to get the job I want."

Unsure what he meant, I didn't have time to ask when Jocelyn bounced over. The three of us group-hugged, then went back to the rest of the party, the beers flowing.

The bar began filling with fog but I wasn't afraid. It's so hard to see everyone. Carter…Jocelyn…where are you?

Jerking awake, she felt the bed shift as Blaise leaned over, grabbing the water bottle. Taking a long drink after he handed it to her, she settled back in against his chest.

"You want to talk about it?"

"I remembered Carter and Jocelyn…it's the first time that I've remembered someone from my recent past," she whispered into the dark, her hand absent-mindedly running over his tight stomach muscles.

"We were at the training and then, after we gradu-ated, we had a celebration. I remember that I wished my parents could have been there." Her tortured gaze jerked to his and she whispered, "And I dreamed of the night the police came to my house to tell me they had died in a car crash."

They lay with their bodies pressed together as he smoothed her hair back from her face, offering quiet reassurances.

"My memories are coming back more and more," she confessed. "Sometimes, I'll be sitting, doing nothing in particular, and something will slam into me. It's as though a movie reel is playing in my head."

"This is good, Grace. This means you are more and more ready to accept what happened that night."

She nodded against his chest. "I think you're right. The memories are very real now. I remember most of my childhood and now the training with Gypsy. Nothing beyond that, but…"

"What, babe?"

"I feel like I know me…know who I am. But I still don't know what happened to me. Why someone would want to kill me. I want my life back, Blaise."

"We'll get there, I promise," he vowed. "Together…we'll get there."

CHAPTER 19

GRACE STRETCHED IN the bed, the morning light pouring through the window. Never one to lie about in bed in the mornings, she reveled in the delicious feelings leftover from the night before.

As Blaise had worshiped her body, she discovered that she enjoyed pleasing him as well. Moving as one, they made love long into the early morning hours before finally falling asleep in each other's arms. Her mind roamed back to the words he promised as the moon moved across the night sky.

"I need you to understand what we are," he whispered into my ear as his body rocked into mine. "I want you, Grace Kennedy. And not because I'm protecting you. But because I can't imagine my life without you in it."

My neck arched back, meeting his thrusts, but fear broke through the lust. "What if when I remember everything, you won't feel the same?" I whispered to the ceiling, afraid to gaze into his face.

"Babe, look at me," he ordered and I had no choice—I immediately followed his command and held his eyes.

"I pull into the driveway and see you in the yard play-

207

ing with the animals and my heart soars. I see you in my house and know that this place is now a home with you in it. I'm falling, babe, and have no intention of letting you go. I only hope you want the same thing."

My throat threatened to close as tears stung my eyes. One slid down to the mattress but he captured the next on with his lips. "I may not know everything about me," I managed to choke out, "but I know I want you in my life as well. If you'll have me as I am, I'm yours."

Lifting his head to look down at me, a broad grin split his face, turning handsome into breath-haltingly gorgeous. "You're all I want...or need," he replied before returning his lips to mine as we both plunged over the precipice.

Gypsy jumped up on the bed, startling Grace from her musings. "Hey girl," she greeted. Looking over at the clock, she saw it was already eight a.m. "Oh, my God, I never sleep this late!" she exclaimed tossing the covers. A piece of paper floated to the ground. Bending to pick it up, she read,

Hey babe, I wanted you to sleep in so I snuck out to work. Already fed the animals so don't let them lie to you and try to get another breakfast. I'll come home early and we'll make our trips out. Love, Blaise

She read the note several times, grinning more with each reading. *Love. He signed it Love.* Even if he did not mean it now, he had made it very clear last night that he was falling. Sucking in a deep breath, she glanced down at the expectant faces of Gypsy and Ransom. "Are you two lying to me, just to get another breakfast?" she joked.

Jogging down the stairs, still clad in only panties and Blaise's t-shirt, she headed into the kitchen, placing a pod into the coffee maker and grabbing a slice of bread for the toaster. Feeling calmer than she had in a long time, she breathed deeply again, letting the memories of the night and the sunshine pouring in the windows warm her soul.

Deciding to bond more with Talon, she walked to the back room and gently picked up the small, purring kitten. Talon tried to hiss when she saw the dogs at Grace's feet, but she cuddled her closely, offering her protection.

Walking back to the front of the house, she carried Talon in one hand against her chest, had a piece of toast sticking out of her mouth and reached for her coffee cup on the counter, when a noise had her whirling around.

Two wide-eyed, open-mouthed women stood in the kitchen. Jumping in fright, Grace dropped her cup back onto the counter, coffee sloshing out over the side. Gypsy growled, placing herself protectively in front of Grace as Ransom began wildly barking. Talon, scared by the noise, used her claws to try to climb up Grace's neck, causing Grace to howl in pain.

Backing up while trying to dislodge the angry kitten, she tripped over Ransom and ended up on her ass on the floor, bare legs flying upward. Talon ran to the back room, leaving Grace with red, bleeding claw marks on her neck as she tried to scramble up. Managing to stand, albeit awkwardly, she shushed Ransom but remained behind Gypsy's protective stance.

"Who are you?" she asked, her mind whirling. The younger, statuesque woman was breathtakingly beautiful. Long, blonde hair flowed about her shoulders and her sky-blue eyes stared back at Grace, laughter dancing about her lips. The older woman was also a beauty, similar to the younger woman.

The younger woman grinned widely, as she spoke, "I'm Bayley...Blaise's sister." Before Grace had a chance to speak, Bayley continued, "And this is our mother, Barbara."

As the women's eyes trailed down Grace, from the top of her sex-messed hair to the t-shirt that was obviously Blaise's, to her naked legs which only a moment ago had been prominently stuck up in the air, she processed the introduction. *Oh, my God! His sister...and his mother!*

Before she could speak, the front door slammed open and Blaise stalked in, halting as he viewed the scene in front of him, before turning his angry eyes to his family.

"I...I..." glancing down, Grace said, "Quiet, Gypsy." The dog immediately came out of protective, growling stance and sat. Determined to make the best of the awkward situation, she tried to plaster a smile on her face as she stepped forward and said, "Hello, I'm Grace. I...I apologize. I seem to have made a mess," she blurted out, noticing the spilled coffee on the counter and the toast on the floor. Her eyes searched Blaise's, uncertain of his anger.

He crossed the space in two steps, tilting her head gently, saying "Babe, what the fuck happened to your neck?"

"Uh...I had Talon in my...uh...arms...I guess I...startled and she got scared," Grace babbled, feeling like an idiot. Blushing bight red, she wrapped her arms tightly around her waist. She lifted her gaze to his and mouthed, *I'm sorry!*

Furious, Blaise turned toward his family and barked, "Bayley, why don't you keep your phone on? I got your text saying you were stopping by and tried to call you back to say not to come!"

Bayley fumbled in her purse and looked up, her face a mixture of mirth and regret. Her eyes sought Grace's and she said, "I'm so sorry we startled you."

Barbara stepped around her son and moved to Grace, her hand out. "My dear, please don't be embarrassed. Bayley and I are the ones at fault. It is very nice to meet you and I do apologize that we frightened you." Her eyes dropped to the bleeding scratches on Grace's neck before lifting to her forehead. Smiling genuinely, she continued, "But it is so refreshing to see someone at my son's house besides another stray he's picked up."

Jerking back at Barbara's words, Grace's face crimsoned even more. "Ex...excuse me," she said before turning to rush up the stairs, taking them two at a time. Running into the hall bathroom, she closed the door, sliding down, leaning her back against it. Resting her face in her hands, she could feel the heat from her blush. After a moment, she pushed herself up and looked into the mirror. Dark eyes, with yesterday's mascara smudged underneath. Tousled hair. The scar on her forehead, still red and jagged. *And let's not forget the cat scratches marring her pale neck.* Her gaze dropped to Blaise's t-shirt, her nipples prominently showing through the thin material. *Oh, my God. What an impression I made. Hell, I look like a stray, so why does it matter?* Grabbing a washcloth, she gently cleaned the scratches, hoping the rest of the household would magically disappear before she had to leave the safety of the bathroom.

Downstairs, Barbara's eyes widened as she searched her son's angry visage. "Oh, Blaise, what did I say? I was shocked to see her here, but so glad you have someone in your life. I wanted to make her less embarrassed."

Dropping his chin to his chest, his hands resting on his lean hips, he said, "Jesus, mom. I know you've got no idea what's happening, but this could not have been more fuc—, messed up. You two need to leave. Let me go take care of Grace and I'll call you later."

Barbara placed her hand on her son's arm, stilling

him momentarily. "She's important to you. I can see it. At first, I was mortified thinking we had walked in on a...um...well, um...pickup, I suppose would be the right word. But I can see she's different."

Meeting his mother's eyes, he nodded. "Yeah, mom, she's different. And we've been making progress, but I have a feeling this may have just set things back. So you and sis need to go—"

"Nope," Bayley pronounced, stepping forward next to her mom, watching her brother. "We made this mess and we'll clean it up. So you go take care of your woman, and y'all come back down and let's meet properly." Seeing him about to refuse, she softened her command, "Blaise, if this woman is going to be in your life then mom and I want to meet her properly. And if we don't do it soon, the embarrassment will be the only thing Grace remembers. So let's give her a chance to meet us without the embarrassment."

Without agreeing, Blaise turned and headed up the stairs. At the bathroom door, he knocked, softly saying, "Babe, let me in. Let me check on you."

"I'm fine," her voice called through the door. "I'm just washing my face."

"Let me in," he repeated, "I want to check your scratches."

"Blaise, I'm fine. It's not as though I haven't had worse cuts...that much should be obvious by my face."

He heard the defensive tone in her voice and cringed. "Honey, they feel really bad and you've got no idea how fuckin' sorry I am about this. I just need to—"

The bathroom door opened and he almost fell forward from leaning on it. Straightening himself, he looked at Grace, seeing a mixture of anger, embarrassment, and doubt on her face. The first he could deal with, the second would pass in time, but the third emotion shot straight to his heart.

"Sweetheart, I'm so fuckin' sorry," he repeated. "You should feel safe in my house...I promised you that, and I know they scared you and I'm taking their key today so they'll never do that again. And I know you're mortified to be seen like you'd been loved well all night long..." he put his hands on her shoulders and gently pulled her forward before continuing, "but I did love you all night long and I'm proud as fuck you're still in my t-shirt." He felt her body melt into his slightly, and took a fortifying breath.

"And, the sight of doubt on your face kills me." He felt her stiffen again and tightened his hold, pressing her against his heartbeat. "You are no stray. Not to me."

Sighing heavily, she slowly encircled his waist with her arms. "Maybe that's not so bad," she finally said. Before he had a chance to refute her claim, she lifted her gaze to his, explaining, "For people like you and me...a stray isn't a bad thing. It's just a creature that needs love and hopes someone special will find them. That was me...and you're the someone special."

Placing his hands on either side of her face, he

kissed her as his heart pounded out his love for the woman in his arms. *You're perfect…fuckin' perfect for me.*

Finally remembering his mom and sister downstairs, he pulled back reluctantly. "They still want to meet you formally," he said, worried about her reaction.

Standing straight, she grimaced for only a second before pronouncing, "Then I guess we'd better stop kissing and let me get ready."

Fifteen minutes later, her hair combed, simple makeup applied, dressed in jeans and a pink tank top, she followed Blaise down the stairs and into the living room. Bayley and Barbara were sitting on the sofa, both jumping up as soon as they laid eyes on Grace.

Before she was able to move, Barbara noted her son's arm around Grace's shoulders—as protective as the dog had been earlier. Smiling, she stepped up to Grace and held out her hand. "My dear, please accept my and Bayley's apology for our untimely entrance this morning. You have nothing to be embarrassed about…it was entirely our fault for not ringing the bell first. You must think the worst of us."

Barbara's hand held hers gently and Grace felt the sincerity of the kind words. Returning the smile, she said, "If you can forgive my undignified introduction to you as I tripped over the dogs and had a cat claw its way up my body, then I can certainly forgive your entrance. Perhaps we can start over."

"Oh, I would so appreciate that!" Barbara exclaimed, shooting her son an approving glance. "Hello, my name is Barbara Hanssen and I'm Blaise's mother."

Bayley, jumping into the group, piped up, "And I'm Blaise's sister, Bayley."

Laughing, Grace shook their hands, saying, "It's nice to meet you. I'm Grace Kennedy. I'm...uh..." suddenly realizing she had no idea how to introduce herself, she floundered.

Stepping in easily, Blaise answered for her. "Mom, Bayley, this is Grace...my girlfriend."

Bayley' blue eyes sparkled just as Grace could have sworn Barbara's twinkled. Before she had time to think on that too hard, Blaise ushered them into the living room, while Bayley headed to the kitchen.

"Well, my son has kept you a secret, but I can tell you that I'm thrilled to meet you," Barbara said.

"We haven't been...I mean, I haven't really been...um," Grace stammered, her gaze jumping between Blaise and his mother.

Once more, Blaise came to her rescue. "We haven't been together too long, so there was no reason to introduce her to the family yet." His arm tightened around her shoulders as he grinned down at her. "But, I wanted to rectify that situation, so as awkward as this was, I'm glad you get a chance to meet each other."

Just then, Bayley came back from the kitchen with a plate of toast slathered with butter and jam and carrying another cup of coffee. Handing them to

Grace, she said, "Here, we totally interrupted your breakfast and I didn't want you to go hungry."

Grinning at the blonde beauty, Grace accepted the plate.

"So how did you meet my brother? He's not exactly Mr. Sociable out here with all his animals."

Grace hesitated, deciding to let Blaise answer for her. His eyes searched hers as he whispered softly. "We can trust them, Grace, but only if you're comfortable." Nodding her acquiescence, glad for his lead, she smiled in return.

"I met Grace when she was having some difficulties," he began. "She'd had an accident and subsequently lost her memory."

Bayley and Barbara's eyes widened in surprise, clearly not expecting such a dramatic answer.

"Oh, my dear, how horrible," Barbara gushed.

Grace noticed Barbara's eyes moving to her forehead and she nodded. "Yes, that's where I got this," she said, fingering the puckered skin gently. "I'm afraid I treated it myself and so, while it is healing, I have a rather large scar to contend with."

"Nothing mars your beauty, babe," Blaise said, leaning over to place a kiss right next to her scar.

Grace faced Blaise's family and added, "So you see, I am like the strays he has found…only this time, I'm a human stray."

Blushing deeply, Barbara leaned forward, grasping Grace's hands once more. "I have bungled this entire meeting, haven't I? I'm so sorry I made such a statement."

"Mrs. Hanssen, it's fine. Really. I accept what happened to me and we're working to piece my past back together, so it's all good. After all, a stray is when you find something worth protecting so much you bring it to your home."

"Brother dear, you'd better keep this one!" Bayley laughed, before turning her eyes back to Grace. "Girl, I think you and I are going to be good friends!"

The awkwardness of the morning sliding away, Grace grinned. *Maybe, just maybe…this day will be a good one after all.*

~

SEVERAL HOURS LATER, Grace walked through the Midlands Memorial Gardens, a bouquet of pink mums clutched in one hand, Blaise's fingers linked with her other hand.

"I can't remember their death, but I remember that mom loved pink mums," she said, as they wandered through the gravesites.

They made their way to the site, the double headstone carved with entwining roses and vines. Kneeling, she placed the flowers in the middle of the marble then bowed her head while placing one hand flat on the surface.

Blaise stood back, far enough to offer privacy and yet close enough to provide comfort. Wrapped in the warm blanket of the summer sun, Grace sat for several minutes listening to the sound of birds in the nearby trees. Finally sighing, she lifted her head as her hand slid down to trace the words on the gravestone.

Martha Graham Kennedy and Thomas Carl Kennedy
Together in life...together in heaven

As she glanced at their birth and death dates, she sighed as she thought about their deaths. "They died on the same day...together. I remember being told by the police about their deaths, but I don't remember details." She twisted around to look at him, observing his face registering sadness, not surprise. "Do you know?"

Nodding, he knelt beside her. "Babe, I found out everything I could about you when we were first learning who you were."

He watched her carefully as she digested this information, relieved when anger did not present itself. Only resignation in her slumped shoulders. "Do you want to know?"

She met his gaze and said, "Yes. The counselor said that my most traumatic memories may be the last to come back to me. Was it...particularly traumatic?"

"I think the sudden, unexpected death of any parent would be traumatic, sweetheart. You can tell by the dates that it was over two years ago, so at least you were an adult. They were killed in a car accident. Icy road and they…" he hesitated, searching her face to keep his pulse on her emotions, "slid off the road and down a ravine."

"Just like me," she said, eyes wide.

"No, baby," he corrected. "You didn't die that night."

Sucking in a breath through her nose before letting it out slowly, she nodded. Turning back to the tombstone, she said, "Right now, I can't remember the horror or the aftermath…but I remember how happy they were together."

With her hands in his, Blaise stood, gently pulling her up with him. Kissing the top of her head as his arms encircled her, he added, "Then just keep remembering that, sweetheart. Hold on to those good memories as we make new ones together."

Arm in arm, they left the cemetery and headed over to her apartment. This time, stepping inside, she felt more at home. Smiling, she walked over to the family pictures on the wall, now recognizing the young girl and her parents. Blaise stood back, his smile equaling hers as he watched her move about the room. Tossing her dark hair over her shoulder, she bent to look at the books on the shelves below the TV. He walked over and said, "Babe, as I'm standing here, I realize what a change this is for you. You've just remembered some of your past and I'm taking you from this."

Smiling, she shrugged. "It's not like I haven't had a lot of change in the past month." She glanced around, adding, "And, while I like this place, from what you tell me, I only lived here about a month before my accident anyway, so it's not like I would have a lot of memories built up with this place."

Kissing her forehead as he pulled her into his embrace, he asked, "What would you like me to pack up, babe?"

Looking around she said, "I guess more of my clothes, books, and any personal items, such as pictures."

For the next hour, they worked side by side, laughing at old photos of her as a child, most pictures of her with her own menagerie of animals. "Wow, we've packed most of my stuff, except for the furniture and kitchen items."

"We'll figure out what to do with everything later," he said. "You're paid for awhile so we don't have to rush."

Walking out, locking the door behind them, Grace took a look around, but nothing seemed overly familiar, while not feeling completely foreign either. Following Blaise to his truck, she smiled. *None of this was in my life-plan, but here's to the next step!*

CHAPTER 20

B LAISE STARED AT the video-conference with Mitch and the Saints, his jaw tight as he listened to what the FBI's investigation was proving.

"Ms. Kennedy's car definitely sustained an impact on the left bumper and back side that would not have occurred when it came to a halt against the trees. The lab was able to determine from paint chip fragments, she was hit by a Range Rover, color match was Fuji White."

A few whistles were heard around the table, as Bart exclaimed, "Kind of pricey vehicle for some farmer to have, isn't it?"

"After the fiasco with the ATF a couple of months ago, I lit a fire underneath my counterparts at a few of the other agencies that have a presence down here. I've since found out that the DEA is looking into drug cartels using some of the obscure farmland around the state as landing strips for moving their drugs. Cam, I hate to even mention this, but it looks like the Sinaloan Cartel has a presence."

"Fuckin' hell," Cam exploded, the memories of

fighting the Mexican cartel to rescue Miriam from their clutches still fresh in his mind. "Those ruthless bastards'll stop at nothing."

"So what are you saying?" Blaise bit out. "That they are the ones who were after Grace?"

"We don't know. We have no evidence of that at all, but I wanted you to be aware of what you might be up against. I know you've checked on that mountain, and the Saints never back down. I just need you to be aware of the possibility of what's there. I don't suppose she remembers why she was on the road?"

"No, not the reason...just that she was there." Blaise looked at Mitch and then at Jack. "I want to go back up there to see what we can find."

"I'm working on the satellite images of the area," Luke added. "Got lots of farmers' fields that could be used, but so far I don't have an image of someone flying in." He slurped a sip before setting his coffee cup down, sloshing a bit over the side. "Damn," he said, grabbing a tissue to dab at the spill.

The men chuckled as Bart said, "You need to pull back on the caffeine, man. That hard stuff you slam down will kill you."

Shooting him a glare, Luke proclaimed, "Yeah, well, I've already been cutting back. I've only had one cup and it's fuckin' decaf. I think that's why I'm shaky!"

"Caffeine withdrawal alert," Chad quipped. "Better get the lock down room ready."

The air lightened for a moment as the men smiled for the first time since the meeting began. Jack never held them back when they released some tension, but it only took a moment for the seriousness of the situation to settle over the group once more.

"Okay," Luke began again, "here's what's weird, and, Mitch, maybe you can shed some light on this."

Alert, the Saints gave Luke their full attention. "I'm locked into some satellites and can see basically what the CIA can see—"

"Jesus, don't tell me your illegal shit," Mitch bit out.

"Hey, man, I worked for the CIA...hell, I developed some of these programs for them," Luke protested.

"Yes, but that little clause you signed as an employee that said...oh, hell, just keep going and I'll pretend I don't know where you get all your intel!"

The Saints chuckled under their breaths, as Luke continued. "Every single time the satellites get to a certain point, there's a blip." He paused, looking around the table in expectation. Everyone's blank faces stared at him. Lifting his arms up for emphasis, "Don't you get it? A blip?"

The stares continued, now with expressions of confusion. Blaise growled, "Luke, we don't get it! What the fuck do you mean by a blip?"

"Oh, yeah, right," he muttered. "Well, the image simply disappears for just a moment. Now, normally, that wouldn't mean too much…it could be atmospheric problems, equipment failure, human error—"

Blaise, anxious to get on with the explanation, huffed. "Why are you concerned about the blip? What does it mean?"

"Because it happens over the same part of the area every time. Every. Single. Time."

"Okay," Jack acknowledged. "Why do you think that is happening and how big of an area are we talking about?"

"I know I call it a blip, but the area is large enough that I don't think a simple drive by will let us know what's going on. And the why? My best guess is that whoever is down there doesn't want to be seen and has a way to interfere with the signal."

"Goddamn drug cartels!" Cam burst out again, slapping his hand down on the table.

Mitch nodded and said, "Okay, I'm going to my superiors at the FBI and also the DEA to see what they know about this."

"Is there any way we can scope it out on the ground?" Jude asked, "Like we did looking for Grace's car?"

Luke shook his head and said, "I think it would be too hard. Might not be off a main road."

"Why don't we take a plane?" Marc asked, a gleam in his eye.

"You want to take your Cessna up and scout the area?" Jack asked.

"I was thinking of something that wouldn't draw any attention if it flew lower," Marc answered, grinning at Blaise.

"Cropduster?" Blaise asked.

"We could go back and see if that farmer would let us take his up. Pay his gas and give him some money to rent it. I bet he'd be good with that."

Monty grinned, saying, "You can fly lower and don't need a flight plan. Brilliant."

Marc added, "We get up in that man's plane and no one around will think anything about it. It'll give us a chance to scout out the area."

The men grinned, the idea of the mission moving forward re-energizing the group. Jack said, "Marc, you're on point with that. Take Patrick with you. He's been with the Army Corps of Engineers and has the training to scope out areas and how to mark an aviator map. Once complete, report to us so we can plan a little nighttime recognizance if needed."

~

"WHY DON'T YOU and Gypsy come to visit my grandmother with me today?" Bethany asked Grace.

"Doesn't she live in an assisted living facility?"

"Yes. Well, actually she lives in the section for residents with memory care problems, like Alzheimer's."

Twisting a lock of hair around her fingers, Grace pondered the offer. "I'd love to, but I'm not sure about bringing Gypsy. She's perfectly trained, but she's a big dog. What if the residents are afraid of her?"

"I know she's not a companion dog, but I think the residents would love her."

Grinning, Grace relished the thought of getting out with Bethany today. Blaise did not mind her being out, as long as she was with someone he trusted, but she hated to impose on her new friends. Looking at the hopeful expression on Bethany's face, she agreed, "Then, we'd love to!"

Dressed in white capris with a robin's-egg blue, sleeveless blouse, Grace walked into the facility with Gypsy, leashed, at her side. Bethany, comfortable in the summer sun with khaki shorts and a navy t-shirt, led the way.

The elderly residents immediately looked up from their chairs or wheelchairs and watched the trio as they passed by. Making their way to a covered outdoor patio where ceiling fans rotated in a slow movement, circulating the air to keep the residents cool, Bethany walked toward an older woman sitting on a cushioned seat.

"Gram, I brought you a visitor today," Bethany greeted and introduced Grace. Ann's eyes immediately latched onto the dog, sitting obediently at Grace's feet.

"Dog," Ann pronounced. "Pretty dog. Pet."

"Yes, you can pet her, Mrs. Bridwell," Grace said, moving closer and directing Gypsy to sit quietly.

Ann's thin hand moved slowly toward the dog, not out of fear, but all of her movements were now slower. She placed her hand on Gypsy's head and began to pat her fur.

"You can rub her, Gram." Bethany took her grandmother's hand and moved it down the dog's back.

Grace watched carefully, proud of Gypsy's training and obedience. Looking up, she noticed that several others were gathering around.

"Hey girls," Miriam called out from behind.

Whirling around, Grace smiled widely. "I forgot you worked here as a nurse."

"The residents were all curious about Ann's new friends," Miriam laughed, assisting a man with a walker to come closer to the dog.

Miriam, Bethany, and Grace finally decided to have the residents sit in a large circle and Grace walked Gypsy around to them. Each one petted the large, patient dog and several smiled or conversed, something many of them had difficulty doing on their own.

"I don't suppose I could convince you to bring Gypsy around to us more often, could I?" Miriam asked, her expression full of hope.

"Really?" Grace asked. "You'd like us to come back?"

"Absolutely," Miriam and Bethany said at the same time.

"I'll be going on maternity leave soon, but I'd love to know the residents were getting good visits in while I'll be gone. I plan on bringing the baby out when I can so they can be reminded of little ones, as well."

Ease spread through Grace's mind as she recognized

what their words meant to her. For weeks she had felt in limbo—discovering she and Gypsy had been a working pair gave her a clue into her past, but no longer performing those tasks left her adrift. Squatting next to her dog, she leaned her face into Gypsy's neck and whispered, "What do you think, girl? Could we make some other people happy?"

A sharp bark was her reply and, as Grace stood, her smile lighting her face, she had her answer.

~

BLAISE FELT GRACE jerk and braced himself. He had come to learn that jerks were only the beginning of her dreams, which sometimes led into nightmares. She slowly remembered more of her childhood and even adulthood, but so far they stopped after the time she and Gypsy trained for K-9 work. He glanced at the clock on the nightstand—two a.m. Then his eyes landed on the pictures next to the clock, a grin on his face. One frame held a picture of Grace and her parents, brought back from her apartment. The other, a photograph of Grace smiling widely at the camera, kneeling by Gypsy, the K-9 graduation certificate in her hand.

He had encouraged her to put her things in his house wherever she wanted, hoping the more she integrated into his world, the more at home she would feel. At first hesitant, she had slowly added her small touches and the two pictures on the nightstand were a start.

As she jerked again, he tightened his arms around her. Fighting the urge to wake her, he knew her memories often came back in her dreams. It chewed at his protective nature, but he allowed her to sleep, vowing to assist her through the memories as they came when she awoke.

Fast asleep in his arms, Grace was unaware of Blaise's musings as her dreams crept up slowly on her.

"Why doesn't he like me?" I wondered. "Maybe it's my imagination."

Just then, Preston yelled again, "Come on, Grace. You and Gypsy have to work faster. This isn't just a training exercise anymore. You've got to keep up with the baggage that's coming down the conveyor. No, no, you missed one!"

I glance over at the others around and notice they are not working as fast as Preston is pushing me. "Come on, Gypsy, don't let him rattle you. We got this."

I turn and look at the conveyor belt, filled with suitcases and packages, and they keep moving past us...more and more...faster and faster. Never ending.

The conveyor turns into a long hall that appears to have no end. Gypsy and I are walking down the hall. The doors on either side pass in slow motion and my limbs feel heavy. I hear voices from behind one of the doors.

"She can't keep up."

"She's fine, it's you who don't want her here."

"I had someone else in mind who would be a better fit."

"Get over it. I want her here and here is where she'll stay."

"Sounds like you've got some kind of agenda."

"Just do your job and stay out of my business. She's the one we need."

I try to hear more of the voices but they fade away as the hall lengthens and I begin to run, Gypsy staying at my side. Then, suddenly, the hall drops off and we can't stop, so we fall into the black...

"Grace, wake up, sweetheart," Blaise called, gently shaking her shoulders. His attempt to let her keep sleeping was overridden by his desire to not have her scared. The beginnings of thrashing had him waking her.

She blinked her eyes open, once more finding Blaise's concerned gaze on her face. Breathing deeply, she blurted, "I'm sorry—"

"Babe, you never have to say you're sorry." He watched as she licked her dry lips and he leaned over, nabbing the water bottle now kept on the nightstand. Satisfied when she gulped down half of the bottle, he replaced it before asking, "Do you remember anything?"

Rolling to face him, she slowed her breathing. As much as she hated the nightmares, she loved lying in bed, close to the man who now held her heart. Breathing deeply, she nodded. "I remember the airport...or what seemed like the airport. My dreams are a bit muddled."

Allowing the quiet of the night to flow over her, she closed her eyes for a moment, the remembrances seen again. "Someone named Preston was yelling at me and I kept thinking that the others weren't working as hard as Gypsy and I. He didn't like me and I felt that very strongly."

Preston? Blaise's jaw grew tight as he thought of her TSA trainer. *The little shit…acted like she was wonderful to my face.* Suddenly, he felt her hand over his cheek and he refocused on her again.

"What's wrong?" she asked, concern etched on her face.

"Nothing, babe. Sorry, this is about you, not me. Go ahead."

"Well, the next thing I remember was being in a long hall, hearing voices argue. They were arguing about a woman, I assume me. I couldn't see them, but one wanted me gone…probably this Preston person, and the other one wanted to keep me. But I have no idea who they were, other than being Preston's boss."

Preston and Bernard…interesting, he thought. *So not everything was perfect in the RIA TSA.*

"That's all I remember," she added, her voice full of regret.

Cupping her face with his large hand, he smiled. "Sweetheart, that's amazing. Honestly, you're starting to remember things that were unpleasant which could mean that your mind is beginning to accept what might have happened that night." Holding her gaze, he added, "We'll figure it out, babe. I promise."

CHAPTER 21

L EANING FORWARD, SHE rested her head on his chest, her hand absentmindedly moving across his tight abs. Her fingers wreaked havoc with his attempt to quiet his erection. She appeared lost in thought, while his dick ached to answer the call of the wild.

Her fingers now moved with more purpose as they continued to trail across his tight stomach, following the sprinkling of hair leading down the muscular V toward his straining cock. Slipping her fingers around his girth, he groaned, having lost the battle to remain unaffected.

Before he knew what was happening, she curled up, moved to her knees, and took him in her mouth. Sliding his length into her warmth, she swirled her tongue around the tip before moving him in and out. Too large for her to take all of him in, she fisted the bottom of his shaft while sucking.

"Oh, Jesus," he moaned, his hands fisting first in the sheet next to her before traveling to her hair. The silky darkness bunched in his hands as the dangling strands teased his thighs.

Digging small crescents with her fingernails into his thigh, she held on as she concentrated on pleasuring him; and from the satin tightness of his cock, she succeeded. Sparing a glance up to his face, she watched as his head pressed against the pillow, the veins in his neck standing out. Her lips curved around his erection, smiling her delight.

Blaise, awash in sensations, felt his balls tighten and, as much as he wanted to come in her mouth, the desire to come in her pussy was stronger. With effort, he pushed himself up just far enough to grab her shoulders to pull her up.

Staring at him, her lust-induced face turned into one of confusion. "What are yo—"

"As much as I love your mouth, babe, I wanna come, buried balls deep inside of you."

His words sent a jolt straight to her sex as she clenched her legs together, instinctively providing pressure on her clit.

With a smirk on his face, he executed a quick twist, rolling her under him as his knees moved her legs apart. Rolling on a condom, he groaned, "We need to get you on birth control as soon as you're ready."

"I'll go tomorrow," she rushed, earning his wide grin.

"Got no argument here," he chuckled, the tip of his straining cock teasing her slick opening. Pushing in an inch, he added, "I want to feel this…and this…" As he slowly stretched her tight, accepting walls, he continued to whisper in her ear, "I want to claim every inch of you...every wet, delicious inch."

Shivering at the sound of his seductive voice by her ear, she welcomed the feel of his thick cock, throwing her legs around his narrow waist, pulling him closer. Her desire matched her need to be connected to him.

His movements began slowly then increased in tempo as he lost himself in the sensations surrounding his cock. Her walls pulled against him with every outward motion and welcomed him with every thrust. Her nipples pebbled against his chest, the soft mounds of her breasts pressed tightly.

His lips found the sensitive spot where her neck met her shoulders and he sucked, marking her. Feeling the nip of his teeth on her pulse sent convulsions through her core and she grasped him closer. His trail of wet, open mouth kisses continued down her shoulder, where he nipped again before dragging his lips down her breasts.

Latching around a hardened nipple, he pulled it deeply into his mouth, swirling his tongue around the tight flesh. Letting go with a pop, he blew his breath across the bud, watching her shiver in delight.

Body on fire, Grace felt every nerve-ending tingle in anticipation and desire. Her senses were heightened as he played her body perfectly. Where he nipped, her neck still felt the slight sting of his bite. Her nipples, distended and hardened, tingled from his sucking. As his hand slid down her waist, her stomach quivered with his fingers gripping her hip. But most of all, where they were connected held her attention.

As he continued to thrust, she felt every movement as her inner walls reveled in the electricity that bolted outward. Her legs ached from clinging to him so tightly, but her desire to join with him as closely as she could, had them trembling. She could feel the orgasm nearing as her core pulsed. Crying out his name, she threw her head back against the pillow, her sex convulsing around his dick.

"Look at me," he ordered, and watched in satisfaction as she tilted her head forward and her eyes jerked open. "I want to watch you come."

As her body shuddered in ecstasy, her orgasm washing over her, a slow grin curved her lips as she held his gaze. He continued to grind against her clit as he thrust several more times before his neck tightened, the muscles cording as he powered through his own orgasm, emptying deep inside her body. Moving in and out, he continued until drained. Falling forward, he crashed half on her body, half on the mattress.

She welcomed his weight, the feel of his heaviness on top of her, his cock still nestled between her legs. Smoothing her hands over the muscles of his shoulders and down his back, noting the hard planes melding into the dips and curves.

Their breath ragged, hearts drumming wildly, both lay, neither speaking...only reveling in the fading physical sensations and heightened emotions.

With his head still pressed into the pillow, she whispered into the night, "You don't have to say anything back...and I know this might not be what you want to hear...but I've fallen for you, Blaise Hanssen."

His head lifted from the pillow and he pierced her with his blue-eyed gaze, not saying anything.

RUSHING ON, BEFORE she lost her nerve, she continued, "I know I haven't remembered everything, but I've recalled enough to know who I am...and what I feel...and what I want."

His voice, rough with longing, asked, "And what do you want?"

Holding his gaze, she breathed, "You. I want you."

Slamming his mouth down to hers, he captured her lips as well as her words. Thrusting his tongue between her lips, he plundered her mouth, relishing each curve, ridge, and the taste of Grace. She matched his ardor, her tongue parrying with his. This kiss was different...this felt like being claimed.

As the hard, wet kiss slowed, ending in soft nibbling around the corners of her lips, she grinned. "So my confession didn't scare you away?"

He leaned over her, his forearms holding his weight off her chest, as his hips still rested between her legs. Framing her face with his hands as his thumbs caressed her cheeks, he smiled a long, slow, sexy smile. "Grace, your words pierced my heart. I started falling for you weeks ago, but now…I'm a goner. I want you too."

Pulling him down, she kissed him deeply, hanging on to his shoulders as they allowed their passions to take over. Much later, she curled up in his arms, drifting away into a peaceful sleep.

～

"I WANT TO check on Preston Solter," Blaise announced the next morning to Luke. The others, listening in, waited to see what he had to say.

"Grace dreamed again last night and, this time, she remembered him yelling at her, forcing her to work harder and faster than the others, all the while berating her. She then remembered overhearing a conversation between him and someone else behind a closed door, discussing her. He wanted to get rid of her but the other person wanted her there. My guess is the other person was Bernard."

Luke nodded, then asked, "You want emails, finances, texts…the usual?"

"Yeah, grab whatever you can about this guy. She wakes up, shaking in fear with this guy's name on her lips, and I want to know what the fuck he was doing."

"His comments to us were that she was a great asset," Chad mentioned, his eyes flashing anger. "The fucker must have been lying through his teeth."

Blaise met Chad's glare with one of his own, nodding his head.

"Anyone else?" Jack asked.

Sucking in a deep breath, Blaise admitted, "I don't know. Her memories are coming back, first with pleasant childhood remembrances of her parents and her pets. Then more recent ones of her apartment and early training at the K-9 program. She remembers Carter and Jocelyn, but nothing amiss. She remembers the accident but not why she was on that road or why someone was after her."

"What I can't figure out is why she was there anyway," Patrick said. "Even if Mitch is right and DEA suspects there may be drug activity in a remote area, why on earth was she there at night?"

"She doesn't strike me as the type to just wander around in the middle of the night and that would lead me to believe she must have been up there with a purpose. But what?" Bart said, leaning his large body back in his chair, rubbing the scruff on his chin.

"How would she have heard about the possibility of a drug cartel in the mountains?" Marc asked. "Work? And if so, why not tell her supervisors?"

"Unless, she suspected the supervisors themselves," Cam replied, before looking down at his phone. Excusing himself, he walked away from the table to take the call. Before anyone had a chance to speak, they all turned their heads as he said, "When? You called the doctor? Meet you there."

Turning back, his face registered shock mixed with fear, an expression that none of his friends had ever seen from the big man.

Already on his feet, Bart said, "I'll drive."

Nodding, Cam quickly responded, "Miriam's having some cramping so she's heading to the hospital."

"I'll call your parents," Jude piped up, stepping away from the table as well.

As Cam stalked toward the door, he halted as Jack's hand landed on his shoulder. "We've got your back, Cam…and her's too. Good thoughts going your way, man."

Picking up his house intercom, Jack called Bethany. "Babe, Cam's heading out to the hospital. Miriam's having cramping. Check on what they need from you. Love you."

Nodding, Bart and Cam left the room and a moment later Jude walked back, his hair standing on end from his hand raking through it. "I don't speak Spanish, so I don't know what the hell his mom was screaming about, but at least when I called Miriam's folks, her dad got on the phone so I could give him the info."

The men chuckled as the tension was relieved before turning back to Luke. Jack said, "Okay, let's dish out assignments and work the problem. Luke, dig up everything you can today on Preston and Bernard. Marc, you and Patrick head to the farmer to see if you can coerce a flight out of him. And Blaise?"

"I'm heading back to interview some of the others who worked with Grace…who may have some insight into the reasons Preston's lying to us."

"Good. Take Chad with you again," Jack ordered. "Monty, you stay in touch with Mitch. I don't want us stumbling into some kind of sting operation that the DEA might have going on." Catching the nods of those around the table, Jack finished, saying, "I'll keep you posted on Cam and Miriam."

With *thanks* ringing in the air, the Saints dispersed.

SITTING IN THE break room of the RIA TSA area, Blaise and Chad sat with three uniformed men. The youngest appeared to be in his mid-twenties and the other two, in their forties.

"Gentlemen, as you've been told, we're investigating the disappearance of Grace Kennedy. We've spoken to Bernie and Preston, but since we are still trying to develop leads, we're expanding our interviews to anyone who might be able to shine a light on the situation."

The youngest, Jim, bobbed his head agreeably while his knee bouncing shook the table. Dan blinked several times as curiosity settled on his face, and veiled distrust emanated from Luis as he sat stiffly.

"What can you tell us about her? Anything could be helpful."

"She was real nice," Jim said, his head continuing to bobble, reminding Chad of a bobble-head dog his grandmother had in the back seat of her old car.

"You'd think every pair of tits was nice if the girl

smiled at you," Luis retorted, gaining Blaise's attention.

"Do you think she acted inappropriately?" he asked, his voice belying the desire to land his fist in the man's face.

Startled, Luis backtracked, "No, no. She was always professional. I just meant that Jim here had a bit of a crush."

"She was nice," Jim insisted. "She sure as hell made the job more enjoyable than listening to you squabble every day."

Chad smoothly interjected, "Tell us how she got on with the staff here," directing his question to Dan.

"She'd only been here a few weeks, but was easy to get along with," he replied. "She was a hard worker and, gotta say, she and her dog were naturals at picking up what we do here."

Nodding his agreement, Luis added, "Sometimes it takes rookies a while to work well with their dogs, even though they've trained together. She and Gypsy made a good team."

"Would you say she was pulling her weight in the training or was she slacking?"

At that, a look passed between the three men causing Blaise and Chad to take notice.

"You want to elaborate that point for us?" Blaise's tone indicated it was a demand and not a question.

"Yeah, she pulled her weight," Jim expounded. "She did everything Preston asked, but he rode her ass."

"Jim!" barked Luis.

Sharply turning toward the older man, Chad prompted, "You got a reason why Jim should hold his opinion back?"

"Yeah," Luis said, his face contorted. "It's not our place to talk about a superior. He woulda had his reasons for what he said or did."

"So you're admitting he rode her harder than the rest of you?"

"She was a rookie. We all went through it," Luis bit back.

"So, in your opinion, Preston was just treating her like the rookie she was," Blaise restated.

"I never got treated like that," Jim admitted, glaring at Luis. "I think it was because she was a female."

"That's fucked," Luis fought back. "It's not like we haven't had women handlers here before."

"None as pretty as she was," Jim declared. "I think that's why Preston was so hard on her. As though her looks made her less professional and more of a target for him."

"I don't know about that," Dan finally interjected. "Bernie was glad to get her, but I think Preston just had someone else in mind for the job."

"You mean Carter?" Blaise clarified.

"They've been friends for years, so yeah, I think that he was pulling for Carter."

Friends? Preston never mentioned that when we interviewed him, Blaise thought angrily. Fighting to keep the irritation out of his voice, he clarified, "So the best person gets the job, but Preston, for personal vendetta reasons, tries to set Ms. Kennedy up for failure."

"Well, when you put it like that, it sounds bad," Dan said, his face scrunched in thought. "I just think he was harder on her because she was a rookie and it was going to make her a better handler."

"And when she disappeared?" Chad prompted.

Catching the quick glance between the three, Luis was the first to speak. "We just assumed she wasn't happy anymore and found a new job."

After a few more minutes, it appeared Blaise and Chad had squeezed out of the men what they could and the uniformed trio walked out of the room. Deciding to head down the hall to speak to Bernie again, they halted when Jim suddenly poked his head back into the room. Looking behind him suspiciously, he quickly said, "Preston was an ass to her...more so than just being a rookie. But you need to know that when Grace stopped coming, we were told that she had decided to change jobs, so none of us ever speculated on why she wasn't here."

"Who told you that?" Blaise demanded, piercing the young man with his glare.

"Preston." Ducking back into the hall, Jim disappeared, leaving Blaise and Chad staring in his wake.

CHAPTER 22

PRESTON ENTERED THE room, this time, his snapping gaze landing on Blaise. "Look, I've told you all I know about Ms. Kennedy. I've got work I need to do."

"Won't take long," Blaise remarked, his irritation hidden behind a casual stance. "But it seems as though you haven't been entirely truthful with us. So, until you decide to answer our questions completely, you'll keep meeting with us."

Preston's expression morphed into irritation as he slid into a seat. Clamping his mouth shut, he glared down at his hands.

"You withheld that the person who took over Ms. Kennedy's position, Carter Boren, is a close friend of yours."

"So?" Preston asked defensively, throwing his hands up in the air. "She was gone and Carter was the next one in line. My being friends with him had no bearing on her leaving."

"What about how you treated her? It seems you rode her harder than the other rookies," Chad prodded.

Grimacing, Preston shook his head. "I did ride her hard. I ride all the rookies hard. It gives us a chance to see if they've got what it takes to do the job under the time pressure we work with."

"You saying you weren't harder on her than others?"

"Nope. At least I didn't think so."

"Then you want to explain why you told the others that she left because she found a new job?" Blaise bit out.

Preston, now visibly nervous, ducked his head, studying his hands once again. Heaving a sigh, he said, "Look, we lose some people...the hours are long and the work can be backbreaking. We are standing almost our entire shift and we have to be on point all the time. We miss one bag, one suspicious bag, and a plane full of people can die." He lifted his gaze back to Blaise and Chad. "I wasn't sure she was up to the challenge, so yes, I rode her hard and even tried to get Bernard to let her go. But she was making it. She and her dog met every task."

Rubbing his hand over his face, he continued, "I was surprised when she didn't come in. HR made a couple of cursory calls to her house but we don't have the luxury of sitting around waiting to see if someone is going to phone in. After a few no-show days, Bernie went to the next person on the training list. Yes, it was a friend of mine and I was glad to be able to work with him. But as to what I told the others...well, I felt kind of guilty."

"Guilty?" Chad asked, leaning forward. "You want to explain that?"

"I felt bad thinking she had left because I rode her hard. I was afraid that someone might report me for overstepping my training bounds with her." Giving an embarrassed shrug, he admitted, "So I told them she had taken another job."

The Saints sat for a moment, both stewing over Preston's confession before he interrupted their thoughts.

"So, are we done here? I've really got to get back to work." Obtaining their nods, he hustled out of the room.

"What do you think?" Chad asked as they drove away from the airport.

Shaking his head, Blaise admitted, "I don't get an angry vibe from him, but then he hasn't been forthcoming with us, so it makes me wonder if there is more to him than we have found out." Pulling out his phone, he called Luke. "Hey, man. I want you to dig into the finances of Bernard Tanner and Preston Solter. I want to know if it looks like they have unexplained jumps in their income."

Looking back at Chad, he said, "I've been thinking about the possible drug cartels flying in and out of the farmer fields in obscure areas. Who might know about them? Who might be paid hush money? Anything to tie in what happened to Grace."

"OH, GIRLS, YOU don't have to stay here," Miriam protested as she smiled at the group surrounding her bed, "but I love your company." The doctor told her and Cam that her cramps were false labor but she should stay close to home. Cam immediately pronounced that she was to stay in bed, which Miriam objected to. The compromise had been that when he was out, she would have someone with her. Between her mom and sisters, Cam's mom and his sisters, her house was clean and food was cooked.

The Saints' women piled in Miriam's bedroom, munching on cupcakes and catching up on the news. Dani moved awkwardly, trying to give her baby room to stretch. "This one'll be coming next," she declared.

Laughing, Miriam added, "If mine doesn't come soon, your baby might come first!" Looking over at Grace, she said, "I heard you made another trip to the assisted living home."

Nodding, while trying not to choke on the large bite of cupcake in her mouth, Grace smiled. Swallowing, she replied, "Yes, Gypsy and I went this morning. I think the residents really enjoyed her."

"Have you thought about what you want to do?" Faith asked softly.

Licking more frosting from her lips, Grace shook her head. "I know Gypsy and I trained for TSA, and from all indications, we were good at what we were doing, but…" her voice trailed off.

"Are you afraid you won't remember what to do?" Dani asked.

"Well, for now, Blaise doesn't want me out and about too much. As they investigate, they aren't telling anyone that I've been found. That helps keep me safe from whoever might have been trying to kill me. So I couldn't go back to a very public job. At least not now."

"Do you want to?" Sabrina pressed, crossing her legs as she shifted on the floor.

Scrunching her face in thought, Grace looked around at the expressions of the women with her. *All friendly. All concerned.* "You know, right now, that life isn't what I want. I'm happy with Blaise and his menagerie. I'm happy visiting the Assisted Living home. And I'm happy making new friends."

"Yay!" cried Bethany and Angel at the same time, giggling.

"It will come to you," Faith added. "Whatever you want to do...are destined to do...it will come back. And it may take you in a completely different direction than what you assumed would be your future."

Smiling at her new friends, Grace relaxed, popping another bite of confection into her mouth.

"I AIN'T NEVER had anyone want to go up in my duster," Bob said, taking off his worn, dirty ball cap and wiping the sweat from his brow.

"I'd like to take a trip down memory lane and I've convinced my friend that this is the only way to see the countryside," Marc said easily. "We'd be more than happy to pay for your gas and to rent the plane for an hour."

Bob looked down at his scuffed boots for a moment then looked up. "You don't gotta rent 'er from me, but I'll take a little somethin' for the gas."

Grinning, Marc shook hands again, palming a hundred dollar bill into Bob's hand. The older man met his grin and they walked over to the crop duster. Blaise stayed on the ground with Bob as Marc hefted himself up into the plane.

Fifteen minutes later, with the front propeller rotating, Marc and Patrick were airborne. Patrick sat behind Marc but easily peered out of the windows as the vista passed below them. The fields, each a slightly different hue of green, peaked out between the thick groves of trees covering the mountainsides. Curves of asphalt snaked between the fields and disappeared into the forests. Cedars and pines shared the space with hickory, elm, and oaks.

"What are we looking for?" Patrick asked, looking down at a few houses dotting the mountainsides.

"See if you find a field that looks as long as Bob's...one that might be cleared off enough to have a small plane land on it, or has an outbuilding nearby. Or perhaps one that ends in the woods. That'd be a good place to hide incoming planes."

On the drive up to Bob's farm, they had discussed how the cartels were using private airstrips to transport drugs around the country…

"MITCH SAID THAT they sometimes fly straight into these small airstrips because they aren't regulated. Other times, they manage to get larger amounts into the country and then move the shipments of drugs around using the small, private airstrips."

Blaise wondered what could have led Grace up the mountain the night she and Gypsy crashed. *What did she know? What did she suspect? What was she doing up here at night? And who the fuck was after her?*

"Thinking about Grace?"

"Yeah," Blaise sighed. "I keep wondering why she was up here that night and who was after her. We're only checking out the area because she was with the TSA. Maybe there's something we don't know about her and something she doesn't remember. Maybe we're all wrong about—"

"You know how we investigate," Marc interrupted. "We sift through the evidence, piece by piece. You're right…we have no idea why she was up here and we may be on a wild goose chase now. But at least we'll know more than we did before we came. Up in the air, we can check out Luke's blip."

NOW, UP IN the air while still flying low, Patrick and Marc carefully perused the ground below them as the plane hummed along while Blaise waited impatiently on the ground.

"You doing okay up there?" Patrick asked.

Marc chuckled and said, "Just like riding a bike. I remember my dad teaching me how to fly. God, I thought it was the greatest feeling ever."

Before Marc could reminisce anymore, Patrick called his attention. "Look down there—on the right side. There's a small field where a strip of dirt is showing between the crops and runs straight into the woods."

"You may have something," Marc said, excitedly. Checking his coordinates, he flew over one more time. "Look over there," he pointed. "The road goes by the other side of the woods and it looks likes there's a lane going from the road toward the fields."

Armed with newer information, Marc turned the plane back toward Bob's field. Landing several minutes later, he taxied to the old barn. Alighting from the plane, Marc and Patrick walked over to Blaise and Bob, who were waiting for them, beers in hand.

After sitting for a few minutes, talking about the flight and planes in general, Bob eyed the two men speculatively. "You weren't really just up there reminiscing your childhood, were you?"

Marc pinned the old farmer with his sharp gaze for a moment. Grinning, he said, "What can you tell us about the farm up the road about ten miles? The lane is on the left of the road and disappears into trees before coming out to a field that appears to have a cleared off strip running right through the middle of the corn-field."

Bob leaned back in his rickety chair, pushing the brim of his ball cap up slightly as a slow grin formed on his face, deepening the weather-worn creases. "Figured you musta had a reason for going up. I seen that field. Owned by another farmer. Joe Savine. Never had much dealings with him...seen him around a bit. I ain't seen planes landing there, but I seen that strip when I was up. Sometimes I fly over and ask if anyone needs my dusting service. He didn't want any, so I don't fly over there anymore. But just because I ain't seen anyone land...doesn't mean I ain't seen them fly over." He pierced Marc, Patrick, and then Blaise with his stare, measuring them.

Grinning, he said, "You gonna tell me what you're looking for?"

Blaise was the first to speak. "A woman was chased and run off the mountain road not too far from here about a month ago. We think she may have seen something that someone did not want her to see. And then they went after her."

At his blunt explanation, Bob's smile dropped from his face, his grey eyes flashing in anger. "Ain't got nothin' against Joe, but since he moved to the farm about four years ago, he ain't never done anything to try to fit in with his neighbors. Ain't unfriendly...just not friendly, and that ain't the way we live 'round here."

The three men sat quietly for a few minutes, then Bob said, "You need me, or my plane, again, you come on by. You can take her up whenever you need...and I'll even have a beer waiting for you."

"We appreciate it," Blaise said, standing with Marc and shaking the old man's hand.

"We'll let you know about the plane," Marc added, "but I can guarantee we'll take you up on the beer."

Nodding, the Saints headed back down the mountain, more questions than answers still swirling.

CHAPTER 23

B ART EXCLAIMED HIS greeting as he jogged up the front steps to Jack and Bethany's home. Entering, he found the group anxiously awaiting his arrival.

"It's a beautiful little girl, and both she and Miriam are fine. Cam's fuckin'over the moon!"

The group erupted into cheers, as Bethany's hand went to her small baby bump, meeting Jack's hand already there. Smiling up at him, she said, "I'll get the girls over later, but I have a feeling Cam and Miriam's large families are filling up the hospital room now."

The Saints then followed Jack down into the conference room, where strategy planning ensued. Listening to Marc's description of the obscure airfield, they decided a nighttime reconnaissance was needed.

"I'll go, of course," Bart proclaimed, "but my partner is out of commission for a bit."

"I want in on this," Blaise said, his eyes catching Jack's. "I want to be able to see, first hand, what Grace might have been dealing with."

The other Saints shifted their gazes between Blaise and Jack, as they sat at the conference table.

"There's no evidence at this time that Grace was anywhere near that field," Jack stated calmly.

"I know that," Blaise admitted. "But something sent her up the mountain. She has no friends there, no reason to be there. But she's a trained TSA dog handler and she went with her drug-dog. There's a strong possibility that there is a connection."

"I should go as well," Marc added. "I'm the only one with flight and aircraft experience. I can tell if the field has been used for flying and how recently."

Jack acquiesced. "Alright. Tonight, Bart, Blaise, and Marc will go pay a visit to Joe Savine's property."

"I don't want Grace alone," Blaise said. Before he could continue, the other Saints quickly volunteered their protection.

Nodding his appreciation, he looked up as Jack proclaimed, "She'll stay here tonight. Bethany would love the company and I have the most protected area."

Grace's safety decided, they continued their plans.

THE JEEP SILENTLY held to the curves of the mountain road, the headlights providing the only illumination. Having not been on the road at night, Blaise was once more assaulted with images of Grace having to hurtle down the road to escape whatever was after her.

Passing by Bob's farm, they continued along the road, Marc following a map he had produced based on their air reconnaissance. Calling out from the back seat, he said to Bart, "About another seven miles on this road, then look for a dirt drive on the left."

The miles churned in silence as the three men peered out of the windshield, watching for the drive. Over ten minutes had passed before Bart called out, "Got it."

He pulled the jeep to the right-hand side of the road, turning around and tucking it slightly into a grove of trees for camouflage and for easier escape if they needed. Getting out, they donned night-vision goggles, as well as arming themselves. With a nod, Bart crossed the road with Blaise and Marc following.

Keeping to the edge of the wooded drive, they followed it for half a mile before seeing a small house in a clearing. A single light burned over the front door, but otherwise, the house was cloaked in darkness. The trio continued at the edge of the woods, circling around toward the back of the clearing. A few old, ramshackle outbuildings stood around as dark as the house.

Directly behind the clearing, another path led off through the woods. Once more, staying to the edge, they made their way toward the field. A large barn that had been built, it's structure much newer than the old house, stood in the woods. Just enough trees had been cleared for the building and its roof was covered in tree limbs.

"Someone wants the barn hidden from the air or satellites," Marc whispered. A wide dirt road came directly from between the cornrows in the field to the front of the barn. The three squatted silently, assessing the area.

"If this is used as a transport area for illegal drugs, they may have sensors or security around," Bart warned. A small red light, on the side of the barn, blinked in the darkness. "Bingo," he exclaimed. "They do have security."

"Can you deal with it?" Blaise asked.

"With these goggles on, you can't see the glare I'm sending your way," Bart joked. "Of course I can take care of it."

He stealthily moved forward as the others stayed back. Bart moved out of their line of vision and within two minutes, the red light went dark. Grinning as they got the go ahead, Blaise and Marc moved forward toward the barn.

Slipping around the side that Bart had taken, they met up with him near the front door. "There are no ground floor windows and only this wide door here. As you can see, it's wide enough for a small plane."

"What do you suggest?" Blaise asked. He was an expert in many areas but bowed to Bart's SEAL training.

"I'm climbing the closest tree and getting in that way. There is a window on the east side, close to the woods."

Keeping watch, Marc and Blaise observed as Bart skillfully hefted his large body up the tree, moving out onto a branch that overhung the barn. It appeared the window was not locked and within minutes, Bart was inside. Soon the wide front door swung open, just enough to allow Blaise and Marc to pass through.

Continuing to use their goggles, they perused the large barn, built more like an airplane hangar than a farming barn. The structure did not have a loft; instead, the space rose to the vaulted ceiling. A separate room was in the back and, upon first glance, it appeared to be an office. Stepping inside, Blaise could see a metal desk containing a laptop and printer, along with a filing cabinet in the corner. Maps lined the walls but there was no other furniture or identifying evidence of its owners.

"I'll check the computer," Blaise said, sending Luke a text to alert him to be on standby. Gaining the go-ahead, he inserted the special drive into the computer and while Luke was obtaining the information, Blaise snapped pictures of the maps along the walls. Five minutes later, Luke notified him that he was finished and Blaise pulled out the drive then quickly dusted for fingerprints on the laptop, desk, and chair. Moving to the maps, he fingerprinted the corners where the thumbtacks were as well as the light switch. Lastly, he dusted the doorknob before cleaning the dust residue off all areas.

Re-entering the barn, he stalked over to where Marc and Bart had entered the storage area. Remnants of cardboard boxes and wooden crates scattered the floor, but otherwise, the room was empty.

"Should have brought Gypsy with us," Blaise said, thinking of the dog's training sniffing for drugs.

"Would she have worked for anyone besides Grace?" Marc asked.

"I think she would've worked for me," Blaise replied, continuing to snap pictures.

The trio walked back to the hangar, Marc immediately circling the small plane. "It's a Cessna 205s," he remarked. "Can carry weight and its high wings are perfect for landing on dirt roads. But no way this came from Mexico. This must be what they use once in the country going from small airstrip to airstrip. Otherwise, it'd be detected."

"So they get the drugs into the country, then have them shipped out with these little planes?" Blaise asked.

"That'd be my guess," Marc said. "Get pics and we'll get this to Mitch and his DEA contacts as well."

Blaise stood unmoving for a moment, uncharacteristically lost in thought. Marc and Bart shared a glance, before moving over to their friend.

"Whatever happened to Grace that night...we'll figure it out. And we'll eliminate the threat to her," Bart vowed.

Blaise jolted, nodding before moving around the plane, taking pictures, while Marc and Bart began fingerprinting the aircraft.

Once outside they saw another smaller outbuilding and moved in to investigate. Inside, they found an elaborate setup of mechanical equipment. Marc said,

"Don't know exactly what I'm looking at, but I have an idea this is where the satellite interrupters are located. Goddamn cartels have a fuck ton of money to keep the DEA from figuring out shit!"

Retreating, they made their way back to their vehicle, pulling their goggles off once inside. Heading back down the mountain road, Blaise's mind churned with the possibilities. Even though they had no proof that Grace was involved in the Savine farm at all, his gut told him she had stumbled upon it and then had to flee for her life. *But what made her come up here at all? What made her come searching that night?*

~

LATER THAT NIGHT, Blaise held Grace tighter than normal. She slept, but he found no rest. Earlier, when he picked her up at Jack's, he filled his boss in on what they found and turned the pictures and thumb drive over to Luke, who would process them in the morning.

Grace's greeting smile did nothing to ease his worry, but he covered it as much as he could. It appeared she and Bethany had fun and he did not want to spoil it for her. *After spending weeks living like she did, I'm not about to bring her down.* Even when she questioned him on the way home, he kept his responses noncommittal.

Now, hours later, he wanted answers. He wanted to know why she drove up the mountain that night…and what she found when she got there.

His attention jolted as he felt her twitch. *Here they*

come, he thought, recognizing the beginnings of her dream remembrances. Some nights she would wake, remembering good times with friends or her family. Other nights, the terrors of the accident would jar her awake, sweating and shaking. *What is tonight going to be, babe?* He readied himself for whatever would come.

"Noooooo!" Grace screamed out into the night, sitting up quickly, her hands in front of her.

Before Blaise could act, she vaulted from her side of the bed. Gypsy, reacting to her mistress' distress, barked as she rushed to her. Instinctively, Grace grabbed the large dog, pulling it close, each attempting to protect the other. Ransom, not to be left out, moved to the couple, tangling in Blaise's legs as he tried to get to Grace.

"Goddamnit!" he shouted, tripping over the dogs before pulling Grace into his arms, sitting down on her side of the bed. Forcing his heartbeat to slow, he pressed her into his lap, tucking her head under his chin, his arms enveloping her shaking body. Glancing at the dogs, noticing Gypsy's concerned eyes, he calmly said, "It's okay, Gypsy. I've got her. Shhh."

The large dogs quieted immediately, lying down at his feet. Gypsy appeared content, but her sharp eyes stayed pinned on her mistress.

Grace's breathing slowly steadied as she felt Blaise's arms holding her tightly. The horror of her dream stayed with her as she fought to keep tears from falling. After several long minutes of silence, she finally whispered, "A gun. He pointed a gun at me."

These words were not what Blaise expected and his blood boiled at the thought of what she was saying. "Babe. Sweetheart, I need you to tell me what you dreamed. I want you to go into as much detail as possible."

She lifted her head up quickly, bumping his chin, as she held his gaze. Licking her lips, she opened and closed her mouth several times but no words came out. Blaise twisted his body around, snagging the water bottle on the nightstand. She took it gratefully, swigging deeply, allowing the cool liquid to soothe her parched throat. Nodding, she handed it back to him and he replaced it on the nightstand.

Scooting backward, Blaise settled against the pillows piled up on the headboard and arranged her across his lap again, still holding her closely. "Babe, I don't want you to push these memories away. As much as they frighten you, I want you to describe them to me."

Sucking in a huge breath, she said, "I was...I don't know where...but it was dark. And there were lots of trees around."

His mind jumped to the Savine farm, but he did not want to lead her thoughts, so he asked carefully, "Like a park? Like where we used to meet?"

"No, no. Not like that at all. The trees were thick...like woods. You know, with lots of undergrowth and brambles around. It was dark...nighttime."

"Do you remember why you were there?"

Her forehead scrunched as she closed her eyes in thought. "Following...or maybe looking. It seems like I was moving with a purpose, but I...I don't know what that purpose was."

"Okay, okay. This is good," he encouraged.

"Gypsy was with me. She was very quiet...we both were. We were following a wide path through the trees...it wasn't paved. There was...a large building in front of us, but we didn't go to it."

"Do you remember seeing anyone or anything there? What did the building look like?"

Shaking her head slowly, she admitted, "No. I know we got closer, but there is just a black hole where the building was."

She's blanking out something...something that must be too difficult for her to come to grips with. "You're doing great, Grace. Keep remembering."

She leaned up, holding his gaze. "There's a hole there. I don't remember anything else about the building. But then there was a man and he had a gun. I saw him first before he saw me. I grabbed Gypsy and we started back through the woods the way we came. Then he was chasing me. He yelled for me to stop but we didn't." She bolted up from his chest, panting, "He fired at us. I remember him firing at us. I got back to the car and we jumped in. He ran out into the road after us and fired. But we were ahead of him. That's when the headlights came into my rearview mirror and I knew we were being chased." She lifted her dark eyes, filled with fear, to his once more and said, "Then I woke up."

The two lay tangled together as Blaise encircled her body with his warmth. His heart pounded as much as hers, now sure that she had been at the farm. *Her description is too similar to what I saw tonight.*

"Don't worry, babe. You're getting close to your mind accepting what happened. That's why your dreams are closer and closer to the truth. And I promise the Saints will find out who's behind this." *And I vow to keep you safe, always.*

CHAPTER 24

G RACE, ENSCONCED IN Jack and Bethany's living room, settled on the sofa staring out at the Saints. Everyone was there, other than Cam, who had not left Miriam and their daughter's side.

Grace had just relayed her latest dream remembrance to them and Marc, as well as Bart, agreed it seemed to be at the Savine farm. Luke set a laptop down on the coffee table facing her and began scrolling through the pictures that had been taken the night before.

Staring, she concentrated as hard as she could, knowing how much easier their job would be if she could identify what she was looking at with her memories. Picture after picture showed dark woods, a dirt road, and a barn. *My dream could have taken place here...or the reality is that these pictures appear generic...why, oh, why, can't I pull it all together?*

She lifted her gaze, tucking her hair behind her ear, her expression one of regret, and said, "It could have been here...but I can't be sure. I can't say that there is anything completely recognizable."

"That's okay, Grace," Jack said. "The pressure is not on you to remember or identify, but on us to solve your mystery."

Luke said, "Now, I'm going to show you pictures of the man who owns the property and see if he looks familiar." The screen filled with a picture of Joe Savine.

She closely inspected the middle-aged man with black hair and dark eyes. He was completely unremarkable. Shaking her head slowly, she said, "I can't say if I've ever seen him. In my memory, I just see the gun in his hand. There was light coming from behind him, keeping his face in shadows, but reflecting off the metal of the gun." She thought for a second and added, "In fact, since the only thing he shouted was for me to 'stop', I can't even tell you if he had an accent."

Flopping back on the sofa seat, her frustration grew so that she was barely aware Blaise put his arm around her.

"Don't be upset, Grace," he cautioned. "None of this is your fault. We're piecing it together, bit by bit. Just focus on how much progress you've made."

As the Saints talked amongst themselves, she stared out of the large window for a few minutes. The Blue Ridge Mountains in the background had seemed calming, but now they seemed to be holding a secret. *Something led me up there. And then someone chased me back down...not wanting me to live to tell about it.*

Turning suddenly, she sought Blaise's eyes and moved toward him. Resting her hands on his chest, she said, "I'm tired of hiding. I want to get back out and let people know I'm alive. That could flush out whoever wanted me dead."

Seeing him about to protest, she gently placed her fingers on his lips. "I'm not talking about taking an ad out in the paper that says 'here I am'; just not hiding anymore. And another thing," she rushed on, seeing him lift his eyebrow, her finger still on his lips. "I want to start gaining my old life back. I want to visit the K-9 training grounds with Gypsy and visit with Carter and Jocelyn. Hell, I even want to go back to the Richmond Airport!"

The silence in the room was only broken with Blaise's heavy sigh. After a moment, he nodded slowly, his blue eyes piercing hers. "I know, babe. I guess after what all you went through, I wanted to keep you wrapped up, safe from anyone who wanted to hurt you. But I know you can't keep your existence hidden anymore."

The others were nodding their agreement and Jack said, "I think it would be a good idea for you to be escorted as you go back and discover your old life."

Blaise jerked his head around, "Oh, hell yeah." Looking back at her, he said, "Wherever you want to go, I'll take you."

"Well, tonight's a good time to start," Jack said. "We're all meeting at Chuck's for a drink and some wings. The other women'll be there."

Nodding, she smiled. "I'd like that. I haven't been

back there since Blaise first saw me. I'd like to go back to where we first met...even if our meeting wasn't exactly amicable."

Blaise returned her grin. "All right...Chuck's it is."

The gathering broke up as Bethany and Grace left to visit Miriam and the Saints moved their meeting downstairs in the conference room.

GATHERING AT CHUCK'S Bar and Grille that evening, the Saints and their women toasted to Cam and Miriam's baby. Next came a lifted glass to missions solved, old friends, new friends, and the women they loved. It did not take long for the group to become boisterous with laughter.

Grace looked around at the interior of the bar. She remembered the last time she was here, sitting on the end stool, hoping no one noticed her munching on the peanuts. Her gaze moved back to the gruff looking man behind the bar. *He was the one here before. The one who made sure the peanut bowl was filled and then brought over the plate of wings for me. He knew I couldn't pay, but served me anyway.* Her lips curved into a slight smile, thinking of his kindness. She noticed him looking at her when she came in with Blaise and his only acknowledgment had been a head jerk. *But that movement conveyed exactly what I needed—acceptance and nonjudgment.*

Blaise glanced down at Grace, noting as her dark

eyes took in the familiar setting. Dressed in faded jeans that hugged her curves and an emerald green tank top, she appeared far different than with the baggy clothes she was wearing when he had met her. Her hair, now glistening under the bar lights, flowed down her back. Her face, not hidden behind a hood, was breathtaking. Porcelain skin. A slightly upturned nose. Warm, chocolate eyes. Her makeup was subtle, with just a hint of blush and a dash of lipgloss. As she turned toward him, he realized her expression was pensive.

"What's wrong, babe? Are you all right?" His voice was laced with concern and he was ready to whisk her out of the bar if the memory of being here when her circumstances were dire, was more than she could take.

Startling, she looked up, her face no longer somber. "Oh, I'm fine, Blaise. Really." Seeing the doubt on his face, she explained, "It was a little weird at first, to look over at the bar and remember what I looked like…and felt like, the last time I was in here. But," she placed her hand on his chest, "everyone here was nice and you…honey, this is where I met you."

Grinning, he was about to kiss her when they were interrupted by a call from across the bar. "It's about time you all got in here to celebrate the first Saint baby!"

Sauntering over, Trudi greeted the gathering with smiles and hugs. Stopping at Grace, she cocked her head to the side, saying, "Lordy girl, you clean up good!"

Blushing, Grace was not sure how to take the bold woman but before she could ponder the overpowering woman's words, she was pulled into a warm embrace.

"I kicked myself four ways to Sunday," Trudi whispered in Grace's ear, still holding her tight. "I should have made sure you had all the food you needed that night."

Pulling back just enough to look into the kind eyes filling with tears, Grace said, "It's not your fault. I was skittish, to say the least, and definitely didn't trust anyone. But you gave me food and for that, I am truly grateful."

Trudi, blinking her heavily mascaraed eyes, said, "You remember what happened to you?"

"Some...but not all," Grace replied truthfully, then watched in surprise as the tiny dynamo in front of her whirled around to the Saints sitting at the table.

"What the hell is wrong with you people? Sittin' here, braggin' about how good you are! What are you gonna do about this one and who the hell hurt her?"

The table grew quiet before the chuckles began. Blaise, not sure which was bigger—Trudi's hair, heart or her temper—stood quickly, seeing the concern in Grace's eyes as he pulled her close, said, "Simmer down, Trudi. We've got her covered."

Leaning back, Trudi's gaze focused on Blaise's arm tucking Grace in protectively—and possessively. Her face quickly morphed into a knowing grin. "So that's the way of it. Well, Praise the Lord. 'Bout time you found a good woman…one who's not afraid of a little cat fur!" With that, she turned and high-heeled back to the bar, getting another round.

Several hours later, as the gathering dispersed, Blaise asked, "Did you have a good time?"

"Absolutely! This was just what I needed—a chance to get out with new friends and feel normal again. Not worrying about what I can remember or how long it will take to get all of my memory back."

Looking down, her smile under the slight illumination coming from the bar lit his world. "Come on, babe. Let's go home."

As they drove out of the parking lot, a person stepped out of the shadows, their eyes following the taillights. Pulling out their phone, they placed a call. "She's fuckin' alive. I couldn't believe the rumor, but she is. Sounds like she doesn't remember what happened. And sounds like she's living with some security type guy. Yeah. Yeah. I know. This time, the job needs to be done right and no fuck ups."

TWO DAYS LATER, Blaise drove into the driveway of the K-9 training facility. Gypsy jumped around in the back seat, but Grace nervously peeked out the window. Blaise remained quiet, allowing Grace to explore at her own pace.

Finally alighting from the vehicle, she glanced up at Blaise, clutching Gypsy's leash tightly in her clenched fist. Instead of walking toward the building, she followed Gypsy to the side where the training fields were located. Standing back, he watched as the two wandered aimlessly at first and then with more direction. Gypsy recognized the fields and Grace began calling out commands to the responsive dog.

Smiling, he realized Grace remembered the K-9 training center as she moved as one with Gypsy. Noise from behind had him turning quickly. Douglas Wilkins had come through the side door and Blaise caught his look of incredulity as he stared at the two on the field.

"She's okay," the older man said, a smile on his face. Turning toward Blaise, he continued, "When you came by to say she was missing, I was worried. I even called over to the RIA TSA and talked to Bernard."

"Yes, she had an accident, but is now fully recovered," Blaise lied smoothly, his eyes assessing Douglas' manner. The man appeared pleased to see Grace, but Blaise took nothing for granted.

Just then, Gypsy came trotting over, eager to greet Douglas, who immediately bent down to rub the dog.

"Hey girl, good to see you again," he effused, gaining a bark of approval.

Grace approached more slowly, a shy smile on her face. "Mr. Wilkins," she greeted, her gaze jumping between her former teacher and Blaise.

Standing, Douglas stuck his hand out and, as she took it, he said, "Glad to see you're all right."

She noticed as his eyes landed on her forehead and

she self-consciously reached up to touch the scar. "I'm fine. I was in an accident and had to take time to recover. Gypsy and I wanted to visit our old training ground today. I hope you don't mind."

Shaking his head, he answered, "No, no. Not at all. I saw you running her through the paces from my window. You two look good." He stared off into the distance for a moment before pinning her with his gaze. "An accident? I'm real sorry to hear about that."

"I'm fine now, but had to…um…take some time off of work."

"Well, I'm sure the TSA will be glad to get you back on the job," he added. "They were keen to get their hands on you."

"Thank you…um…have you heard from Carter or Jocelyn since graduation?"

With his hands on his hips, he shook his head once more. "No, not either of them. Last I heard, Jocelyn was with her dad's sheriff's department and I'm not sure where Carter ended up."

Not knowing what else to say, she glanced at Blaise, who stepped up to shake Douglas' hand. "Nice to see you again, Mr. Wilkins," he said, effectively ending the conversation.

As they walked back to the car, Gypsy still excitedly jumping around, they missed the piercing gaze of the K-9 Director as he made his way back into the building. Watching them pull out of the parking lot, he placed a call.

"OH, MY GOD!" Jocelyn screamed when she saw Grace standing in the front lobby of the Albert County Sheriff's Office.

Grace was relieved she had Blaise at her back when the other woman nearly knocked her over in her enthusiastic embrace.

Laughing, the two women hugged as Jocelyn peppered her with questions. "What happened to you? Were you really missing or just off on a romantic adventure?" As Jocelyn leaned back, her eyes moved to the scar on Grace's forehead and her demeanor immediately changed. "Oh, I'm sorry, sweetie. What happened?"

"I had a car accident and had to recuperate for a while."

Jocelyn's eyes widened as she held fast to Grace's hands. "You were alone, weren't you? In the hospital alone?"

"Um…it was okay," Grace stumbled, hating to lie to her friend, but not knowing what Blaise wanted her to say.

"We found her and she's well now," he stepped in, easily explaining without giving anything away.

"Thank God," Jocelyn grinned. Her expression morphed into disgust as she stepped back and said, "And that snake, Carter, got your job, didn't he?"

"Um…"

"After your detective friend here," she continued,

nodding toward Blaise, "came to see me, I called the Richland Airport just to check. I found out you were no longer working there, but he was."

"I wouldn't call him a snake," Grace said, her shoulder lifting slightly. "I wasn't there and they needed someone." Cocking her head to the side, she added, "I thought you two were friends."

Blushing slightly Jocelyn heaved a sigh. "Well…to be honest…we had a falling out. I…we went out one night, drank too much and…"

"Really?" Grace asked, surprised.

"Yeah, really. Then I did the walk of shame and he was such an ass the next day. He started trash talking you and Gypsy and how you only got the RIA job because you were a woman. Such a whiner! I walked away and never looked back."

Wanting to get the conversation off of her, Grace looked around at the neat, orderly Sheriff's office. "So, how's working here?"

Jocelyn shrugged, saying, "It's okay. I know they needed a dog and handler 'cause even small counties now have problems with drugs. Mostly I check out some of the places the teens hang out, hoping to catch some dealers." Smiling, she added, "It's not very exciting, but it pays the bills. I do get to work at the Charlestown Airport. I'm kind of on call there. I get called in when their regular person is out sick or something. It's not very exciting either since it's such a small airport, but it keeps me on my toes."

After a few more minutes of catching up, Grace hugged Jocelyn goodbye with promises to get together soon. As Blaise and she drove away, he observed her carefully. "What are you thinking, babe?"

"At first, I was afraid to try to step back into my life…afraid my memories wouldn't connect to what was real. But the K-9 training field, Mr. Wilkins, Jocelyn…all are just as I remembered."

"So what next?" he asked carefully.

Pursing her lips, she gazed up at him. "I don't know. I wanted to see everyone and that included the airport and Carter, but now I'm not so sure."

"You don't have to do anything you don't want to. We'll do this at your pace," he assured. "If you don't want to ever step foot in the RIA again, that's good too."

Sighing, she said, "Maybe tomorrow. I think I'd just like to go home now."

Blaise grinned as he turned the SUV around, her words warming his heart. *Home. She called our place home.*

CHAPTER 25

THE BARKING OF dogs greeted Blaise and Grace as they pulled up. She rushed out of his vehicle, crying, "Oh, poor babies. We were gone so long!"

Shaking his head, Blaise replied, "Hate to tell you, but they've been left all day before you came along. They're used to it."

She hustled into the back room, immediately going to the food bins. Scooping what she could, Blaise took over, carrying out the heavy containers. While he fed, she grabbed the hose to clean the kennels. Working side by side, he could not keep the smile off his face. *She's perfect. Fuckin' perfect.*

"What would you do when you were gone overnight?" she asked, interrupting his thoughts.

"Huh? Oh, I've got a neighbor down the road. She comes over and takes care of them."

Grace was quiet for a moment before speaking. "Is she…pretty? This neighbor who comes over?"

Blaise stopped what he was doing and turned around, the almost empty container of food in his hand. "Uh, yeah…gorgeous actually."

A flash of jealousy shot through her eyes, as she continued to hose out the kennel. "Does she still come around?"

"Whenever I need her," he replied, beginning to chuckle, then realized he needed to stop the joke. "To be honest, she's beautiful, but would have been more my type about forty years ago. And I don't think her husband would want me checking her out."

"You...you..." she sputtered, glaring at his grinning face. Looking down at the hose, still running with water, in her hand, she met his grin.

"Oh, no you don't," he warned. "Don't even think about it!"

"Think about what?" she asked, her voice sugary sweet, as she turned the hose on him.

Blaise dropped the empty canister, and raced toward the spray of water, getting soaked in the process. Gypsy and Ransom jumped around in the water, barking at their owners.

Screeching, Grace tried to run but her feet became tangled in a mixture of dogs and the hose. Just has she was about to face plant onto the ground, Blaise snagged her waist and, rolling as they fell together, he managed to land first with her safely on top of him.

"Uff," they both groaned at the same time.

Gazing down at his face, water droplets still falling from his blond hair to the ground below, she smiled. His blue eyes twinkled as they gazed back at her. Her heart pounded, staring at his handsome face, realizing he was it for her. Lying protectively on top of him, she said, "You saved me…once more, you saved me."

"If a good dousing is what I get when you're a little jealous, remind me not to make you really mad," he grinned. Sitting up, he tucked his legs under him to stand, his arms still around her.

She glanced down at his shirt, wet and slightly muddy, as the dogs continued to bark in excitement. "I'm sorry I got a little jealous. For someone like you, I can imagine that you'd have women knocking down your door to be with you."

Laughing, he bent over, kissing the top of her head. "Just to get it out there, babe, there are no other women in my life. No one wanted to take a chance on a man who lives out in the country, surrounded by animals."

Standing up straight, she smiled as her dark brown eyes met his gaze. "Well, then the loss is for them…and is my gain!"

They quickly finished the kennel feeds and cleaning, then headed to the house to take care of the inside animals. Talon, mewling at the indignity of being in a cage, poked his paws out to grab their attention.

"Can he come out soon?" she asked.

"Actually, he can come out now. He's had a quarantine time and is now up to date on his shots."

Cooing, she opened the cage, cuddling the kitten in her arms. "I remember the last time you were out and we got surprised, little one. You nearly clawed me to death!" Putting him down on the floor, she giggled as Talon hissed and spit at Gypsy and Ransom sniffing her over.

"Don't worry about them," Blaise said. "They'll learn to get along."

Turning back to him, she said, "You need a shower…and your clothes need to be washed. If you take them off, I'll throw them into the washing machine now."

Lifting an eyebrow, he quipped, "You just want to get me naked."

Blushing, she agreed. "Well, yeah, I do!"

"I'll get naked if you will," he said, stalking over to her, stopping only when his body was pressed against hers.

Leaning her head way back to hold his heated gaze, she breathed, "Oh, yeah…"

Within a flash his lips were on hers, shooting straight to white hot.

Her fingers went to his shirt, fumbling as she tried to undo the buttons without losing his lips. The height difference was not a big deal, but right now, the forward angle of his body to continue the kiss made it difficult to get to his buttons. Abandoning that effort, she grabbed his belt instead.

Unbuckling it was easy but her fingers once more fumbled, trying to unzip his pants over his prominent erection.

Blaise wrapped his arms around her waist and hefted her in his arms, making the lip-lock easier to maintain while he stalked to the front of the house. Turning the corner at the bottom of the stairs, she finally managed to unbutton his shirt and attempted to pull it over his head. Laying her down on the stairs, he pressed his swollen cock against her heat underneath him as he reached behind him, grabbing his polo and jerking it over his head. Tossing it to the side, it landed on the floor by the front door.

She managed to scoot up two stairs while grabbing the bottom of her shirt as well, pulling it over her head, throwing it up the stairs behind her. With his cock desperate to maintain contact with her body, he crawled up until it rested against her jean-clad sex once more.

Grace grabbed his face, pulling it toward her as she thrust her tongue into his mouth, drinking him in. His tongue dueled with hers, vying for dominance.

Lifting his hips, he slid his hands between their bodies as he struggled with her jeans, but the wet fabric proved difficult. She pushed on his shoulders for a second, creating enough space that she was able to scoot a few more steps upwards. Unbuttoning her jeans, she shimmied out of the wet pants, leaving them where they lay.

While she continued to scoot up a few more steps, he divested himself of his socks and then jeans as well. A few more steps and her bra and his boxers joined the trail of clothing from front hall to the top of the stairs.

With only one more piece of clothing left, she grinned mischievously before whirling around and attempting to escape. With a large hand reaching out, he snagged her panties, dragging them down her legs as she dissolved into giggles.

Now, both completely naked, they lay on the top step, panting. His eyes dilated with lust as she spread her legs wide, looping them on his shoulders. With a grin, he kissed her belly before sending a trail of kisses down to the prize he sought.

With the scent of her arousal in the air, he dove in, licking and sucking until she thought she would go mad with desire. Her hands reached down, gaining purchase in his hair, loving the feel of it through her fingers.

Lost in his own world of desire, Blaise tongued her slick folds, nipping on her swollen clit. His awareness was heightened; he felt her calves on his shoulders, her fingers running through his hair. Her taste, unique, filled his nostrils with her scent and his tongue with its warmth.

Her hips bucked upward and she knew her orgasm was close. Grinning, while still sucking, he reached one large hand up and gently tweaked her distended nipple. With a huge jolt, she came in his mouth, cries of his name on her lips.

As she slowly relaxed, he continued his trail of kisses from her sex upward over her belly and to her breasts. Giving each one attention, he moved to kiss her neck before sucking on her pulse point. Sliding his nose up by her ear, he whispered endearments as his body, tight with need lay over hers.

Finally kissing her lips, she tasted her juices on his tongue. Grabbing his shoulders, she dug her fingernails into his skin, pulling him in closer.

"Come on, babe," he finally said, knowing she could not possibly be comfortable on the top step. Standing, he scooped her limp, and sated, body into his massive arms and carried her to the bedroom. Laying her on the center of the bed, he was surprised when she moved faster and rolled so that she was on top.

Grinning, she kept her eyes on his as she shimmied down his body until she was seated on his legs. Leaning forward, she took his cock into her mouth, her moist lips surrounding his girth.

Fuckin' hell! I'm gonna come right now! Trying to keep his eyes on her mouth as it moved up and down his shaft, he finally gave up, throwing his head back against the mattress. Staring at the ceiling, he wondered how he had ever managed to find a woman just right for him. That was the last coherent thought he had as her tongue and mouth continued to work their magic.

Moving on instinct, Grace pumped the bottom of his cock with her hand as her mouth continued to suck, swirl, and trace her tongue around his sensitive rim. She heard his groan and smiled around his erection, memorizing the taste of him.

"God, I'm gonna come." When he could tell she

was continuing, he battled the decision to either come in her warm mouth or buried balls deep inside her pussy. The latter won out. Grabbing her by her shoulders, he pulled her upward until her sex was directly over his cock. "Please, babe. I want in."

"Whatever you say, honey," she panted, reaching between her legs and grasping his dick in her hand, placing its tip at her opening. Sliding down, inch by inch, she kept her hands on his chest as she accommodated his impressive girth. The slow friction only made her want more and as soon as he was fully seated, she rose up on her knees before moving back down again. Over and over until she was panting.

Blaise reached his hands up, cupping each bouncing breast, tweaking the nipples. Watching her face as she bit her lip, her eyes closed in concentration, he felt her sex begin to tighten around him. As she whimpered, he slid one hand own to press on her clit, eliciting the response they both wanted.

Throwing her head back, she screamed his name again as her pussy clenched and the orgasm sent electric shocks throughout her limbs.

Knowing she was exhausted, he took over, lifting her hips slightly with his hands as he began to piston upward. In a minute, the friction sent him spiraling into his own orgasm, groaning as he pumped until he was empty.

She fell onto his chest, her head on his shoulder, legs tangled. His large hands roamed up and down her back from her neck to her ass. The lazy movement, plus the two orgasms, had her relaxed and sated. Several long minutes later, she managed to lift her head, her hair plastered to her sweaty forehead, and looked down at him. His sky-blue eyes held hers as their hearts pounded together.

"You interested in a shower, big boy?" she teased.

"With you? Hell yeah."

Grinning, the two moved from the bed and into the master bathroom. A few minutes later, as the warm water sluiced over their bodies, they made love once more.

BAYLEY AND BARBARA stepped inside the front foyer as Bayley slipped the key into her purse. Barbara said, "Did you call this time?"

"Yes," Bayley said, quickly amending, "But he didn't answer. I just wanted to say goodbye since I've got to go out of town tomorrow."

Barbara's eyes widened. "He didn't answer? Bayley Hanssen! We shouldn't be here if your brother doesn't kno—"

The words halted in her throat as the two women noted the man's shirt on the floor with the woman's shirt a few feet further. Socks, men's jeans and then women's jeans continued up the stairs. A bra and panties mingled with boxers near the top.

The women could hear water running from the

shower. Mother and daughter cast wide-eyed looks at each other, as they both tiptoed backward toward the front door, Bayley grinning wildly.

"Bayley, that's it. Tomorrow, give your brother his key back," Barbara whispered as they stepped out onto the front porch.

Sucking in a deep breath of air, Blaise's mom, red with embarrassment, looked at her still grinning daughter. "Thank God Grace doesn't know we're here or she'd be mortified once again."

"Mom, I can't help but grin. He didn't catch us and, face it, doesn't it feel good to know that he's *with a good woman?*" Bayley asked, winking at her mom.

Rolling her eyes at her daughter as they drove back down the driveway, Barbara smiled secretly. *Yes, I am glad my son is with someone so good.* Breathing a sigh of relief as they made it back to the road, she vowed, *No more impromptu visits!*

CHAPTER 26

STANDING ON HIS front porch the next morning, Blaise sipped his cup of coffee, barely hearing Grace padding outside in bare feet to encircle him with her arms.

"How'd you sleep, babe?"

"Mmmm," she grinned, looking up at him. "With the workout you gave me, I slept like a baby."

Bending to kiss her sweet lips, he barely touched her before his phone buzzed. Glancing at the screen before answering, he said, "Hey mom."

Grace headed to the kitchen to give him some privacy, shooing the cats away as she walked. Resorting to giving them some food, she then bent to rub Gypsy's fur. "Hey, girl," she said, staring into her dog's warm eyes. Looking up as Blaise came back in, she asked, "Is everything all right?"

"Yeah," he said. "Bayley is flying out today to go on a business trip and mom wanted to know if I could take her."

"Sure we can," Grace offered.

"You want to go too?" he asked.

"Honey, I'm not going to fall apart just because I see an airport. I used to work at one, you know," she teased.

Stepping closer he put his hands on her shoulders and bent to look into her eyes. "I know you say you're ready to get out there and face your past, even face the unknown, but you don't have to do it all at once. Yesterday was big for you,"

Nodding slowly, she smiled softly. "Thank you," she whispered as she leaned forward, resting her head on his chest. "I certainly wouldn't be ready today to go meet Carter and the group in Richland, but the small Charlestown airport should be easy. If I do it today, then I'll be ready to tackle the much larger airport...maybe tomorrow."

"You're ready to jump into this feet first, aren't you?" his voice rumbled in her hair.

"I think I've remembered all I can from dreams...and nightmares. I think getting out will stir more memories. At least solidify the ones I have, like the training center and seeing Mr. Wilkins." She squeezed her arms around his waist, then continued. "Being with you has given me strength...and courage, to face the rest of what happened to me."

"Grace, I'm telling you straight up...you're the bravest person I know."

With his arms enveloping her, the two stood for several silent minutes in the kitchen, bodies pressed together, hearts beating as one.

~

LAUGHTER RANG OUT in the SUV as Grace listened to a few embarrassing childhood stories about Blaise. She was quickly finding that Bayley had very little filter when it came to making fun of her brother. The drive was soon over and the three walked into the mid-sized airport. Giving Bayley a hug, Grace stood back to give the siblings a chance for a private goodbye. Wandering over to a row of small shops, she found herself next to the security line. Watching as people moved through the security she stared at the TSA agents, in their dark blue uniforms, herding the travelers.

A blinding flash bolted through her mind, painful and searing. Grabbing the wall next to her, she blinked rapidly. An image blasted to the forefront of her mind.

Leaving the locker room, I check the mirror first to make sure my dark TSA uniform is perfect. Lifting my gaze to my face in the reflection, I take a deep cleansing breath. "I got this," I say out loud. Glancing down to Gypsy, sitting obediently at my side, I grin. "Come on, girl. Let's do it."

Stepping out of the locker room, we walk down the hall, passing through several doors, ending in one of the large luggage bays. Preston is already scowling at me. Wondering why, Gypsy and I hustle over to him. He begins barking orders and without hesitation, Gypsy and I perform.

The baggage carousel is loaded with every size and

shape of luggage, but she and I work as we've been trained. Preston continues to bark orders as the carousel begins to fade...

Blinking rapidly as the Charlestown airport came back into view, Grace clung to the wall. *I remember the Richland Airport. Being here has triggered more memories.* Closing her eyes again, she willed her memories to continue, but nothing came.

"Grace, Grace," Blaise called, his hands grabbing her shoulders. "What happened? Are you okay?"

Blushing, she opened her eyes, glancing around in embarrassment, hoping no one was watching her fall apart.

Searching his face, she steadied her breathing. "Yes, I'm fine. I just had a flashback. It was triggered seeing the people move through the security lines."

Pulling her in close, he held the back of her head to his strong chest, saying, "Can you tell me?"

"I remember my first day at the airport in Richland. I remember seeing Preston as he yelled out his commands to Gypsy and me. I had on the same uniform as these TSA agents. I remember feeling really proud, kinda nervous, and sure that Gypsy and I could do the job."

"Come on, Grace. Let's get you out of here," Blaise ordered gently, tucking her underneath his arm, guiding her away from the wall.

Afraid she had made a spectacle of herself, she glanced around once more, stumbling as her eyes landed on a man staring at her. Dark hair. Dark suit. No smile. Just staring.

Blaise steadied her as his concerned gaze drop to her. Making their way out into the bright Virginia sunshine, she breathed deeply.

"Better?" he asked, leading her to his SUV.

Nodding, she forced a smile, but the eyes of the man from the airport continued to bore into her mind. *He seemed familiar. I think...I think I've seen him before. But...I can't remember.*

As they pulled out of the parking lot, the suited man stood on the sidewalk outside the taxi line and placed a call.

"I've seen her. She was not fuckin' killed. I thought someone went to the car and checked. She saw me...looked right at me, but didn't seem to recognize me. No, no. I'm not taking a fuckin' chance that she won't remember where she saw me. I want her taken care of...permanently this time."

~

BLAISE SAT AT the Saints' conference table, listening to Luke's report and growing more frustrated by the minute.

Finally, he blurted, "So we've got no identifiable fingerprints from the plane, the barn or office, nor from Grace's apartment. And Mitch is telling us there are no other prints on Grace's car other than hers."

Luke glanced at the others before continuing. "I've

been running the finances of everyone on the list Grace provided, from the K-9 training center to her co-workers at the TSA, and, so far, I don't see anything odd at all. No large deposits, or withdrawals. No new accounts that I can find. Nothing suspicious at all."

Throwing himself back heavily in his chair, Blaise ran his hand over his face. "So, right now, we still got nothing. We've got no fuckin' idea why she was on that mountain, although we can suspect that it had some-thing to do with the Savine operation. The FBI's got nothing new on her car."

Mitch, on video-conference, replied, "We know what kind of vehicle hit her but have found no garage in a fifty-mile radius that claims any body work has been done on a vehicle fitting that type."

"What made her go up that mountain?" Marc asked, pondering out loud.

"Okay, men," Jack said. "Brainstorm any reasons you can think of."

"She found something at the RIA."

"She'd have reported it there."

"She was meeting someone."

"At night? With Gypsy? There's no indication any-one on that road knew her."

"Maybe she discovered something on her job. Gyp-sy reacted, but didn't find it."

At that, the others grew thoughtful. Looking over at Blaise, Jude added, "Grace remembered feeling pressure at work. Maybe she and Gypsy noticed something but, as a TSA trainee, missed it…or wasn't sure."

Blaise, unconvinced, sighed heavily. "I guess it's possible. But what did she notice?"

"Noticed an address? Followed someone?"

Monty, the quiet Saint, spoke up after listening to everyone's suppositions. "We're going about this backward." Gaining everyone's attention, he explained, "While we can't be certain, we can make a good assumption that her being on the mountain road had something to do with the Savine property and the fact that it's more than likely a private drug running airstrip."

He looked at Blaise and said, "We can still look at who she was with at RIA but, at the same time, we can look deeper into what's happening on the mountain. Then we might tie it back to her."

"I'll get back with DEA and see if there is anything they can do to assist us," Mitch promised.

"Can they get some dogs up there?" Patrick asked.

Shaking his head, Mitch said, "Not without probable cause or a search warrant."

"Hell, if Grace knew this, she'd probably volunteer to take Gypsy up there," Blaise moaned, "but I'll be damned if I would let her anywhere near it!"

The others nodded their agreement. Marc, leaning his forearms on the table, speculated, "It's got to be a connection between the Savine operation and her job at the Richland Airport. My money's on Carter…or

Preston."

Luke responded, "I'll dig deeper into the two of them."

Looking over at Blaise, Jack asked, "Has she been back to RIA?"

He shook his head, answering, "She wants to go tomorrow. I'll take her and be right there to see the reactions of the group when she walks in."

SITTING IN THE counselor's office, Grace turned to look out the window overlooking a park. The same park Blaise had found her in.

"What are you thinking?" Ms. Saren asked, after allowing Grace several minutes of silence to pull her thoughts together.

Glancing at the kind counselor, Grace smiled. "I was thinking back to when Blaise found me...right there in that park."

"How does that make you feel?"

"I suppose it should make me upset thinking about how horrible my life had become after the accident."

"There's no right or wrong way to feel. You can own whatever feeling you're having."

Nodding slowly, Grace continued to smile. "Well then, it actually makes me happy. I don't know what I did to deserve someone like Blaise. I've asked him what made him notice me. At first, I felt like one of the strays he picks up."

"And now?" Ms. Saren prompted.

"Now I just feel that we were meant to be together. We...just seem to fit." Her smile faded slightly as she turned her gaze back to the counselor.

"Well, he certainly seems to have helped you a great deal. I'll admit I was a little worried at first that you were confusing a feeling of safety and being cared for with love."

Grace's eyes grew wide as she blushed. "I haven't said I love him...well, not yet. I admit that's what I feel and I assure you, it's not just a rescue reaction. But...well...he hasn't said anything and I'm not about to be the first." Giving a little shrug, she added, "I'm willing to just see where we go." Wanting to change the topic, she blurted, "What do you think of my memory from the airport?"

"It's hard to say, but I'd guess that your mind is more ready to accept whatever happened that night."

"I know Blaise is investigating...I can feel his frustration that he doesn't know what happened to me yet."

"Your mind may open up and allow you to discover the truth before he does."

Nodding again, Grace responded, "I thought about that. I think, at first, I just wanted to know who I was and it was okay that he tried to figure out what happened to me. But, now that I remember me... and my past... I'm ready to remember what happened. I just wish that I could flip a switch and have it turn on, like a light."

"You know it doesn't happen that way, but take heart, Grace. From what I can see, your mind is healing and what you seek may be just around the corner."

CHAPTER 27

S TEPPING THROUGH THE doorway, Grace looked at the long familiar hall in front of her. "I remember this."

Blaise, his arm protectively around her, glanced down. Her face was slightly pale but, other than that, she appeared eager. A door opened and Bernard walked out, his eyes sharply falling on the pair.

"Grace? Good God, it's nice to see you!" Hustling toward them, the creases in his face deepened as he broke into a smile. Sticking his hand out, he grasped hers firmly. Eyeing Blaise, he added, "I see you found her."

Blaise smiled, although he intently studied the man in front of him. Bernard appeared genuine, but he had not forgotten how quickly Grace was replaced—or that no one reported her missing.

Grace noticed Bernie's eyes move to her forehead. *Is this scar always going to be what people notice first about me?* Forcing self-pity out of her mind, she returned his smile. "Yes, I've been found. I was in an accident and was recovering."

"An accident?" Bernie said, his eyebrows lifting in apparent surprise. "But...but...you should have called us...let us know."

"I was unaware of my surroundings for several weeks," she replied, using the response she and Blaise had determined would be the best.

"Oh, I am sorry," the older man said. He appeared to be wrestling with a decision as he rubbed his chin in thought. "We didn't know. So, uh...your position was re-filled. But, under the circumstances, I can speak to HR and see when we can take you back on."

"We'll see," she agreed noncommittally, glancing up at Blaise, smiling at his warm gaze meeting hers. "I'd like to go in and see everyone, if possible. Just to say hello."

"Sure, sure. Of course," Bernie nodded hesitantly, turning slowly. "I believe you know Carter Boren. He...he was hired after you...um...left."

Looking up, she saw the blush cross her former boss' face and almost felt sorry for him. *At least I would if Blaise didn't have me thinking of everyone as a possible suspect in wanting me harmed.*

She remembered their conversation on the way to the airport—one she knew they needed but one she also hated.

"Grace, what you have to realize is that there is a very real possibility that someone you know was involved in whatever happened to you that night. You know you were driving back down the mountain with someone after you

and they bumped your car with theirs."

"Yes, but I have no idea who or why," she huffed, the frustration still high.

"That is what we are trying to find out. We're working with the FBI and DEA now that we suspect drug runners on the private airstrip up there. We're working on the assumption that you were there with Gypsy for some reason."

Incredulous, she glared over. "You know, Blaise, I might not be able to remember that night, but I know enough to realize that I'm a smart person. Why the hell would I take a drug-dog, at night, just to pay a social call to drug-runners?"

He sighed heavily and she knew her sarcasm was misplaced.

"I'm sorry, Blaise. It's just hard." He glanced at her, so she continued. "It was hard not remembering. Then it was hard realizing no one reported me missing. And now, coming to grips with all that, I have to be suspicious of everyone I used to know because it appears someone wanted me dead."

He reached across and took her hand, lifting it to his lips, placing a sweet kiss on her fingers. "We'll get them, babe. I promise."

Her anger slid away, knowing how much he cared and was doing his best to protect her.

Jolted out of her thoughts, a wide door swung open to one of the baggage areas. The room was buzzing with activity as handlers made sure the luggage was heading in the right directions TSA and dogs were moving about.

Several people looked up as she walked into the room. Glancing around quickly, she breathed a sigh of relief as she recognized several faces. Two of the baggage handlers came jogging over.

"Miss Gracie! You back?"

Grinning, she was pulled into a hug. "Hey, Marcel. No, I'm just visiting."

"We heard you left for another job. Where'd you go?"

"Um," she stammered, "I was in an accident. That's why I was gone."

She watched in fascination as Marcel's face morphed from happy to angry. His eyes narrowed as they glanced over her head to someone behind her. "That asshole Preston told us you went somewhere else."

Licking her lips, she shrugged. "Well, I didn't. I just needed to heal."

"Goddamn, mother-fu—"

"Grace?"

She turned around, seeing Carter standing there with his dog. Squeezing Marcel's hand, she walked over to Carter.

"Hi," she said, plastering a smile on her face.

Blaise observed the exchanges carefully. Carter did not appear shocked…but maybe surprised she was here.

"Um, wow," Carter stammered. "It's…um…good to see you."

"It's nice to be back."

At her words, he said, "Back? You're coming back?"

"Well, not right now, but—"

"Grace. Bernie just told me you were here." Preston stepped through a side door and approached, his gaze jumping between her face and Blaise's.

"Preston," she said, cocking her head to the side, wondering how he would greet her.

Stepping forward, he nervously glanced to Blaise before looking back at her. "I heard you were in an accident. I'm sorry."

"Well, it was a bit of a shock to hear that you told others that I had taken a different job," she accused lightly, with a fake smile on her face.

Preston blushed as Carter's gaze bore holes into his. "Yes, well, it seemed best. You know, so that people wouldn't think you just walked out and quit."

"It worked out well for you two, didn't it?" Blaise interjected, his expression as hard as his tone.

Carter looked down at his feet, chewing on the inside of his mouth as Preston glared. Pretending to take a phone call, Preston walked away.

"I saw Jocelyn the other day," Grace said, curious as to what Carter's reaction would be after hearing about their awkward fling.

Grimacing, Carter's gaze shot back to her face. Shaking his head, he responded, "What a bitch. I thought she was a friend, but she's a piece of work."

Her eyebrows rose, confusion on her face as she

waited to see if more explanation was forthcoming.

"We got drunk one night and the next morning she was talking shit. I had applied for the job at the TSA in Charlestown airport. It's little, but it was a job. You had this job lined up and she was working for her dad in Albert County. But the greedy bitch took the Charlestown job too. Hell, it's not like she needs the money. Daddy keeps her in an apartment and a big ass car." His hands on his hips, he shook his head. "Damn sorry about your accident, Grace. I mean, it's no secret I wanted this job, but—"

A shout from across the large room was heard and, called back to work, Carter shot her a regretful look before walking away.

Back in Blaise's SUV, she turned to him and said, "Okay, you're the investigator. Tell me what you think."

He pursed his lips for a moment, gathering his thoughts. It was hard to know what to say—*Do I tell her all of my suspicions or allow her some peace. But, damnit, someone tried to kill her.* "I think that any of those three in there could have had something to do with you going up the mountain. Whether or not you saw something, heard something, decided to explore something on your own…I don't know. But there's got to be a link."

"If that's true, then that means one of them was involved in the drug trade," she thought out loud. She had not allowed herself to believe that a possibility, but she knew she needed to be open to any revelations. "Maybe I'll start remembering more about that night, now that almost everything else has come back."

STARING DOWN AT the new license in her hand, Grace slipped it into her new wallet. Smiling, she felt her independence growing every day as she gained pieces of her life back. Blaise had assisted in having her driver's license replaced, but today would be her first solo drive.

"Are you sure?" he asked, walking into the kitchen to say goodbye before leaving to meet at Jack's. He had taken her out for drives, to make sure she remembered how to drive as well as the laws, and she had passed with flying colors. *Somehow that seemed easier than having her drive by herself.*

"It's only a few miles," she pouted when she saw his expression. "I'll be fine and I promise to take care of your old truck."

"I don't give a fuck about that heap, but this'll be the first time you've driven by yourself since the accident."

Her face softened, looking up into his concerned one. Gifting him with a small smile, she nodded, "I'll be fine. I've got to start somewhere." Her fingers moved across his smooth cheek, once more astonished at the handsome man who had rescued her.

He pulled her in, wrapping his arms in an enveloping hug. Kissing the top of her head, he admitted," I just worry, babe."

"I know…that's why I love you."

As soon as the words left her mouth, she stopped breathing. *I didn't mean to say that…not now…not like this. Oh, God, he's going to think I'm some kind of clingy nutcase—*

"You love me?" he asked, pushing her body back slightly so he was able to peer into her face, his eyes searching hers.

"I…didn't mean…" Blushing, she felt her face grow hot, her body taut.

A slow grin curved the corners of his mouth until he was full-out smiling. Looking up at him, her heart pounding, she pulled in her lips. *Please, God…let the floor open up now.*

"I love you, too," he admitted, his smile now lighting his face.

"Wha…what?" she breathed.

"I knew it a while back, babe. I just couldn't rush you. Not when you had no idea who you were. I needed to give you time to discover you…before I could ask you to discover us."

"You love me too?" she whispered again, almost afraid the words were a dream.

He leaned down, his lips almost touching hers, his breath warm across her face. "Yeah, I do. Grace Marie Kennedy. I love you."

Throwing her arms around his neck while lifting to her toes, she captured his lips. Sealing, searing, white-hot kiss. Taking over, Blaise angled his head, dipping his tongue into her mouth, tasting cinnamon sugar. Grinning at Grace's love of Cinnamon Toast Crunch cereal for breakfast, he relished her flavor.

After a moment, he slowly pulled back, her arms unwilling to let him go. Gifting a little kiss on the corners of her mouth before leaning up again, "Oh, girl, I wanna take you upstairs, lay you down on the bed, and not come up for air until tomorrow."

"Can't we?" she murmured, her kiss-swollen lips still tingling.

Just then a horn sounded from outside. Sighing, they separated, gazes still holding fast. "Marc's here," he said. Adopting a stern expression, he ordered, "Now, be good and be safe today out on the road."

Smiling, she watched as he walked through the front door, down the steps and over to Marc's truck. Lost in thought, she was not sure which she liked more—the way his ass looked in his jeans as he walked away…or the way he swaggered confidently when he came home. Deciding both were equally delectable, she jumped when Marc honked again. Caught ogling, she blushed as she waved at the retreating vehicle.

Looking down at the dogs, she said, "Okay, guys, let's get everyone fed."

Hours later, sitting on a back deck chair with her feet up, Grace snoozed in the warm, early afternoon sun. Gypsy and Ransom lay at her feet also enjoying the warm day. She and Gypsy were heading out to the nursing home later, but for now, she allowed her mind to clear and the gentle breeze to carry her worries away.

Faces swam in front of her...Bernie, Preston, Carter, Jocelyn, Douglas, her parents, the K-9 training center, RIA, Blaise...

I'm going up...curvy roads...but beautiful vistas. Where are they going? The radio was playing. Dusk was falling. It was hard to see the driveways between the trees. Where did they go? Did I lose them?

Taillights ahead, barely glowing red, turning left between tall trees. Gypsy's eyes stared back at me through the rearview mirror. What am I doing, girl?

I turned. The night had settled. I circled my car around before parking near the dark house so I would be able to drive out easier. What is this place? The only vehicle in sight is a large, white SUV parked next to the house.

Gypsy is barking, clawing to get out. I open the door and she bounds out, running around the house. I can't see her. I shout a command and she reluctantly comes back to me, still agitated.

She never gets this way unless...there are drugs around. Why are they here? Who are they meeting?

A shout. A gunshot. Gypsy runs to me, standing in front protectively. Shit, shit, shit, I scream. Turning, I make it to my car. Another shot rings out. Oh, Jesus, help me.

I throw open my door, shouting for Gypsy to get in.

Gunning the engine, I race down the driveway, the darkness and curves keeping me out of sight of the shooter.

Racing, racing, racing…noooooo!

Jolting awake, Grace felt the pressure of weight on her chest. Pushing desperately to scramble from the chair, she tumbled to the ground, the weight now off but licking her face. *Gypsy.* Oh, thank God.

Continuing to lie on the deck, her dog anxiously nuzzling her, she sucked in air as her erratic breathing slowed.

I did go up on the mountain. Gypsy knew there were drugs. But why did I go there? What made me suspect something? Who was I following? Why can't I pull up a face…or even a body?

Finally, with no more answers coming, she gently pushed Gypsy and Ransom to the side. Standing, she debated on what to do. Glancing at her watch, she knew she had little time before meeting Bethany at the nursing home.

"Come on, Gypsy. Let's go make some people happy." Locking up, she opened the squeaky driver door, allowing the dog to jump in. "In the back," she ordered, smiling as Gypsy jumped over to the area just behind the bench seat.

CHAPTER 28

GYPSY MADE HER rounds to each of the rooms in the assisted living facility, obediently following Grace's instructions.

"Oh, there's my pretty girl," one woman cooed, patting the dog's head as Gypsy sat still by the wheel-chair.

"Mrs. McDougal, she really loves you," Grace said, smiling at the older woman.

"Oh, it must be because I had a lot of dogs myself over the years."

"That, or the fact that you're slipping her treats," Bethany laughed.

Mrs. McDougal grinned as she looked up. "Well, the fact that I know to have treats is because my dogs trained me well."

Moving down the hall, they rang the buzzer to enter the memory care facility. Glancing over at Bethany, Grace noticed her friend's eyes were not as bright as usual.

"Is everything okay with your Gram?"

Bethany did not answer for a moment, sucking in

her lips as she blinked back tears. Shaking her head, she replied, "No, not really. Honestly, if it wasn't for Gypsy's visits, I don't know that she would respond too much. She's gone downhill so quickly. It was just a year ago that she was living in the cabins. Granted," she admitted, "not doing so great there, but still, with some help, we were okay."

The two women stopped in the hallway, Gypsy sitting obediently at Grace's feet, and embraced.

"I'm glad Gypsy and I can help a little," Grace said.

"Oh, you do!" Bethany enthused. "When Gypsy comes, Gram seems to wake up and knows there is a dog there. She doesn't do that with people much anymore."

"Well, then come on, Gypsy. Let's go wake up Gram," Grace said, smiling at Bethany.

An hour later, leaving Gram's room, the two women hugged goodbye.

"I'm going to stay for a bit," Bethany said. "But, as always, thank you."

Stepping out of the building, Gypsy began prancing around, excited to be getting back into the truck. Grinning, Grace unlocked the door and opened it for the dog to jump in first. Reaching back into her purse, she searched for her sunglasses.

Gypsy barked just as a hard object poked Grace's back and a voice by her ear commanded, "Get in the truck and secure your dog, or else your dog dies. Right here. Right now."

Whirling around, she looked up in fright at the tall man standing behind her. Dark hair, slicked back. Reflector sunglasses hiding his eyes from her view. *Unknown…but familiar.* Dropping her gaze she saw the gun pointing at her, but as Gypsy barked again, she watched in horror as he pointed the gun at her dog.

Swallowing deeply, while barely breathing, she stammered, "Wh…who…"

"Shut up and do as I say."

Her mind rushing, she could not think of what to do, other than obey. "Quiet," she spoke, her eyes pleading Gypsy to obey. She did not disappoint. The large dog immediately stopped barking and sat down on the truck seat, staring at her mistress.

"Put her in the back," the man ordered, his gun never wavering from the dog, as he indicated the covered truck bed.

"I…can't. It's locked. I don…don't have the key." Working to calm her breathing, she held up the one truck key for him to see.

"Then tie her leash behind the seat and I'll keep my gun on her. One move…one mistake on your part and you'll watch your dog die."

With shaking hands, she ordered Gypsy to jump over the bench seat and secured her leash to the seat belt. "Stay," she said softly. Glancing up, she saw the man climb into the passenger seat and twist to the side facing her, keeping his weapon trained on Gypsy.

"Now drive."

MITCH SHOOK HIS head, frustration pouring off him as he said, "Finally got someone at DEA to tell me what they had on the Savine farm. Looks like they've made a connection with a branch of the Sinaloa cartel. What they're following is a trace from planes in Mexico flying into the United States…passing inspections…then flying to smaller airstrips where they unload the drugs. Smaller planes can then fly between the small, private, unregulated airstrips to distribute along the pipeline."

Rearing back, Blaise growled, "So what the fuck are they waiting on? They could go in anytime."

"They've been working on this for over a year and don't want to move too fast. Getting Savine will only shut down his little part. They are after the cartel."

"So we sit around with drug runners one county over and do nothing," Jude bit out, his frustration matching everyone else's.

"You got a name for me to check?" Luke said. "Give me something…anything that I can possibly link to the vehicle that ran Grace off the road."

"Ricardo Guzman has legally entered the country, under the guise of managing a trading company. He's a cousin in the Guzman family cartel and has been watched since arriving here. He has been known to fly in and out of Virginia and he has been seen at the Savine farm. So far, he's the highest one on the totem pole."

"What else does the DEA need on these guys to

step in?" Cam asked, back on the job for the first day since becoming a father. Fear pierced his heart at the idea of any of the cartel operating near where his wife and baby girl rested.

Luke, popping antacids into his mouth like candy, looked down as his computer indicated a message. Grinning, he knew who was there. Several months ago, a mystery tech genius contacted him, offering help with a case. He had not been able to ascertain their name, location, or how they knew what he was working on.

He wanted to meet one day, but his mystery helper always said it was too dangerous. Knowing how many persons worked freelance for the government...or criminals...he did not want to endanger them any more.

Looking at his messages, he read:

Check connection between Guzman, Martinez car rental.

"Bingo," Luke said under his breath, typing out a quick thank you.

No problem.

Deciding to approach something more personal, he typed: **How are you? Safe?**

For now.

You always help me. Seems like a one-sided friendship.

For a long minute, there was no response and Luke assumed his helper was unable...or choosing not...to respond. Finally, one more message came in.

When I need you, I'll let you know.

Anytime, anyplace Luke promised.

After another minute, one last message pinged.

Maybe soon.

Before he had time to process the ramifications of that message, Jack walked into the room. "What have you got?" Jack asked, looking over Luke's shoulder at what he was pulling up.

"Should be a hit between this Guzman and a car rental place nearby. Whatever it is, won't be immediately visible...let me do some digging."

"According to the DEA, Guzman doesn't drive a rental while here," Mitch said, interested in what Luke was finding.

"Maybe it's not for him," Bart speculated. "Maybe it's for someone else around here who does his bidding."

"Got it!" Luke declared, excitement pouring off him. "Guzman uses an alias but keeps a vehicle at Martinez Auto Rental. A white Range Rover. Fuji White Range Rover."

Within a few minutes, Luke's magic fingers tapped into the security video feed for the rental facility.

"Go back. Go back to the night Grace was hit,"

Blaise called out, filled with renewed vigor.

It took a while, but the Saints and Mitch looked on expectantly as the video feed ran across the screen.

"Holy fuck," Blaise shouted, shock running through his system. His sentiments were felt around the room. Grabbing his phone, his call went to Grace's voice mail. Glancing at the time, he looked up quickly. "Jack, call Bethany. Grace was with her this afternoon at the nursing home."

Jack immediately complied, nodding when he got hold of his wife. "Hey, babe. Is Grace still with you? No? When did she leave? Okay. No, no. I'll talk to you when you get here." Disconnecting, he pinned Blaise with his gaze. "Bethany is still with her grandmother, but Grace and Gypsy walked out about ten minutes ago."

"Then why won't she pick up?" he groused, trying her phone again.

"You said this was her first time driving since the accident," Patrick commented. "Maybe she's too nervous to talk and drive at the same time."

Nodding, Blaise agreed, "Yeah, you're probably right." Standing, he said, "Jack, I'm heading back home. I want to make sure she gets there all right."

"Good idea."

Mitch piped back up, saying, "I've just alerted the DEA of what Luke has found. I'm running a check on them as well. We need to coordinate tomorrow, to plan our move. I'll talk to my superiors right now."

Blaise turned around as Marc called out his name. "Let us hear that she got home," his friend said. Nodding, Blaise hustled up the stairs.

HEART HAMMERING INSIDE her chest, Grace tried to keep her eyes on the road, while simultaneously glancing into the rearview mirror at Gypsy in the back, and the man sitting beside her…still holding the gun.

The road curved upward and she quickly recognized the road she had been on the night of her accident.

"Wh…where are we going?"

After a long pause she thought he wasn't going to answer, when she finally heard him say, "You know where."

Shaking her head slightly, she said, "No, no I don't." Her fingers clutched the steering wheel, her knuckles turning white. She could feel his hard gaze burning into her, so she continued, "I don't remember anything. I had an accident…on this road…but I don't…"

"You don't remember anything about that night?"

Shaking her head again, she said, "I didn't know who I was. Amnesia from a concussion."

"Well, I'll be damned." Silent for a moment, he added, "If this had been done correctly, you wouldn't have even been involved."

She opened her mouth to question him further

when he barked, "Turn left here."

As she turned onto the gravel drive flanked by thick foliage and trees, she slowed the truck as a memory assaulted her.

I've seen this man before. He was at the airport. He's the one I followed here that night—

"Park here," he ordered, startling her out of her thoughts. Glancing to the side, she noticed his eyes were on the small house. Another man walked out— tall, dark, light blue polo shirt and dark slacks. And his expression…murderous.

"What are you doing, you moron? Why did you bring her here?"

"We need to get rid of her…her and the dog," the man next to her quickly explained as he got out of the truck, still pointing the gun at her.

"You could have done that anywhere," came the sharp retort.

As the two men argued, Grace grew lightheaded, her vision blurring. For once she tried to keep the memory from coming, but to no avail.

I saw him…at the airport…with…with…

Planes were landing and taking off. The main airport was over to the right, with the smaller private planes disembarking at hangars to the left.

Douglas Wilkins stepped around a large, white SUV, walking with a man. Tall, dark haired, and distinguished. I lifted my hand to wave but did not want to interrupt. Their heads were bent closely together, deep in conversation. They began walking toward a long, sleek car…black with dark, tinted windows.

Gypsy and I walked toward Douglas, passing by the white SUV, when Gypsy began to pace excitedly. Instinctively, my eyes moved to her, letting her have more of a lead. Rushing around the car, nose working, she made her way toward the back and began digging at the vehicle. Scratching and whimpering, I stared…knowing what was there. All the training…I knew. Drugs. Why had Douglas gotten out of a vehicle with drugs?

Before I had a chance to ponder what to do, I observed Douglas turning to walk back to the SUV. Silently commanding Gypsy to follow, we backed away, moving out of sight behind other cars in the parking lot.

As the SUV pulled out of the parking lot, I ordered Gypsy back into my car and followed.

CHAPTER 29

"**G**RACE?" BLAISE CALLED out, jogging into his house. He had noticed the truck was not parked in front of the garage, but hoped against hope she was home. Racing through the room and out toward the kennels calling her name, his stomach sank with the realization she was not there.

Pulling out his phone, he tried once more, but just like the past hour it rang and rang before going to voice mail.

Dialing Jack, his strident voice croaked, "She's not here. She's not picking up. Get Luke on it. I'm coming back."

On the other end, Jack immediately barked orders to Luke and the others still there. "Get Mitch back on," he added to Monty.

By the time Blaise pulled up to the front of Jack's place, Marc was there, ready to brief him.

"Luke's got her. She's up on the mountain…the Savine place. Mitch already has DEA and his FBI team alerted and on their way. Come on, you're with me."

The rest of the Saints were coming around in their

vehicles, with Luke, Jude, and Jack in their specially equipped van.

Throwing himself up into Marc's SUV, the caravan roared down the drive.

GRACE'S MIND STRUGGLED with the memory of her former trainer in a vehicle with drugs. The memory of her first trip up the mountain replayed, this time with more clarity.

As I followed discreetly, I continued to mull over the possibilities. Who better to disguise someone coming into the country with drugs than someone trained...and one with a dog that's been trained not to react? Oh, Jesus, Mr. Wilkins, what have you gotten yourself into?

The road climbed higher and higher, the twists and turns unfamiliar. Dusk was falling but I did not turn on my headlights, wanting to stay unnoticed. Thank goodness my car is black and their SUV is white. Hopefully, I'll stay hidden, and their bright colored vehicle is easier to follow!

I noted when the vehicle slowed, turning to the left between trees. I braked, crawling up to the now visible gravel drive between two trees...almost hidden. What do I do? Looking at Gypsy sitting on the back seat, eyes bright, eagerly awaiting whatever my command would be.

Sitting in my car, I debated what to do, when a sheriff's car drove by. Rolling my window down, I waved him over. Glancing back, I said, "Gypsy, we're in luck!"

"You having car trouble, miss?" the young, female

deputy asked.

Whipping my head around at the familiar voice, I cry out, "Jocelyn! Oh, thank God!"

Jocelyn, eyes wide, stared at me, shock on her face. "Grace? What are you doing up here?"

"I needed to pick up something from the Charlestown TSA office since I live near there and," I climbed out of the car, "you won't believe what I saw!" Looking toward her official car, I saw K-9 on the side and saw a large dog inside. "Oh, thank God, you've got Torch."

"Grace, slow down, you're not making any sense." Jocelyn put her hands on my arms, giving me a little shake. "Come on, let's head toward town and you can tell me what is going on."

"No, no, we can't leave. We need to call for back-up...or the DEA...or...or..."

"What are you talking about?"

"I followed a white SUV from the Charlestown airport to here. I know there are drugs in it because Gypsy detected them! And the vehicle belonged to Douglas Wilkins! He was talking to a man before he got into the SUV and he turned in here." I knew I sounded fantastical but was grateful it was Jocelyn and not some strange deputy, thinking I had too much to drink!

She turned toward the lane, biting her lip, before saying, "Let's check it out. I'll go in and you follow me. They won't do anything when they see a police car. I'll call for backup on the way."

"Are you sure?" Her plan sounded off...but she's the deputy. Watching as Jocelyn climbed into her vehicle, I

followed down the dark, wooded lane until we came to a clearing circling a small house.

Adrenaline coursing through my veins, I hoped the back-up she called for was soon to arrive. As she alighted from her car, Jocelyn grabbed Torch's leash, calling for me to do the same with Gypsy.

Blindly following her instructions, I opened the door, allowing Gypsy to hop down next to me, her tail wagging as she pranced around eager to work. Looking up, I noticed the house was dark, but lights shown from a structure further down the lane. Continuing to follow Jocelyn, we walked down the path, coming to a lighted barn, the white SUV parked outside.

"Jocelyn," I whispered, grabbing her arm. "What are you doing? Don't we need the backup?"

Her gaze cut over to me, barely discernable in the darkness, as she said, "Just follow my lead. I've got this."

The wide door to the barn opened, exposing a small airplane inside. Two men were loading packages into the seat, while a third man—the tall, distinguished man I had seen at the Charlestown airport—stood, appearing to monitor the activities. And next to him...Douglas Wilkins!

Gypsy began whimpering again, straining at the leash to get to the plane. Drugs!

The four men's faces turned in unison toward us. One of the men by the plane angrily shouted, "What the fuck are you doing? Why did you bring her here?"

"I didn't bring her, you idiot! I found her at the end of the lane! She followed Douglas here from the airport!"

Jocelyn? No! How could you be part of this? Now that the light from the barn illuminated the area, I looked at the hard face of my former friend and her dog...that's not Torch. Of course! She needs a look-alike that's not trained for drug detection.

Her vision clearing, Grace came out of her memory, glancing around at her surroundings, seeing the two men still talking angrily. Hearing a familiar voice, she turned her head toward the sound. *Holy shit. Jocelyn!* The similarities between what had occurred the night of her accident and her current situation slammed into her.

"What's going on? Joe, why did you bring her here?" Jocelyn asked.

Joe Savine. I didn't recognize him earlier, but that was who Blaise had me try to identify. Oh, why won't my memory work when I need it to! Steeling her spine, she refused to let them see her quivering.

"How deep into this are you, Jocelyn?" Grace bit out, her voice hard with anger.

The other woman quickly turned toward Grace, her expression unsure. "Grace, I...you wouldn't understand. I needed to do this...I had to."

"Had to? Had to what? Protect drug runners? Get them through customs? Help smuggle?" Grace shot a disgusted look at the men, still standing by the plane. "Seems like we've met before, and I just now remember everything. You tried to kill me."

Joe Savine grinned but his face held no mirth—

only danger. "It wasn't me who ran you off the road," he said, his eyes cutting over to Jocelyn.

"Shut up!" Jocelyn screamed, causing Gypsy to shift protectively.

"You?" Grace asked, still incredulous over her former friend's involvement. "That was you chasing me?"

"I had to, don't you see? I had to get rid of you once you discovered what was happening."

"Yeah, but you bungled it," Joe accused. "You even climbed down the ravine to grab her purse and supposedly checked to see that they were dead."

"There was so much blood," Jocelyn cried. "I thought she had to be dead!"

The tall, distinguished man, silently watching the proceedings, finally spoke as he made his way to the plane. "You two can bicker all you want, but I'm keeping my schedule." Stopping, he nodded his head toward Grace and said, "This time, make it permanent memory loss...and clean up your mess. Or the next accident will be you!"

~

RENDEZVOUSING AT BOB Davison's farm, the old man met the Saints as they pulled up to his barn. Hustling out, he made his way directly to Marc and said, "You take what you need, son." Turning, Bob placed his hand on Blaise's shoulder. "I lost my love to cancer about five years ago. I'll do whatever you need to help you hang on to yours."

Stepping back, Bob's gaze danced around as the men immediately went to work. DEA and FBI vehicles arrived, with Mitch stepping out of one. Hustling over to Jack's group, he said, "I've got point on this, but DEA is here for support. What have we got?"

A woman, wearing a dark jacket with DEA emblazoned on the back, hurried over. "Carin Torgensen," she introduced. "We've got confirmation Ricardo Guzman came into the country and our informant had him heading to the Savine farm. We're assuming he's going to try to load up the drugs he brought in and take them out in a much smaller plane."

Luke called from inside the heavily equipped van. "Her tracer has her at the Savine farm. I'm pulling up visuals and they're close to real time. DEA sent a drone over once they discovered their satellites were being interrupted. Foliage is heavy but there's a clearing where the house is located. I have a lock on Blaise's truck and a deputy car, number on top is twelve, K-9."

Before he could finish, two Albert county sheriff cars sped up Bob's lane, dust flying as they came to a halt. Antonio Montez bolted out of one of the cars, his face dark with anger. "What the hell is going on? This is my county. Why wasn't I notified?"

Mitch stepped up to him, saying, "Sir, you'll have to stand down. We have evidence indicating that your daughter, Jocelyn Montez, is colluding with drug runners from Mexico through the Charlestown airport and Joe Savine's airstrip."

The Sheriff, visibly paling, stepped backward in shock. Shaking his head, he repeated, "No, no. Not her. No."

Another agent moved the Sheriff to the side, as Mitch turned back to Blaise. "DEA is monitoring them from the air, but we don't want to go in until we know what's happening with Grace."

"We got this," Blaise answered, pulling on the Kevlar with the rest of the Saints. Looking over at Marc, he said, "You going in?"

Nodding, Marc said, "I'll coordinate with DEA, but I'm going to head on up…with Bob's assistance."

The older man stepped forward, saying, "You got it, son."

The rest of the Saints armed themselves and, leaving Marc and Luke, they climbed into three of their SUVS and left Bob's farm. Within a few minutes, they arrived at the turnoff for the Savine farm. Parking along the road, they alighted and, with night vision goggles, they jogged down the lane and into the woods nearby.

Blaise cleared his mind, readying himself for the mission. He stumbled once, cursing inwardly. *Who am I kidding? This isn't a mission. This is Grace. This is all about Grace.* Steadying his resolve, he continued forward. Hearing shots fired in the distance, his heart stumbled as his steps had earlier.

~

GRACE, HORRIFIED AT the revelations, watched as the

tall man climbed into the plane. Nudged by Gypsy's head, she tightened her grip on the dog's leash. She understood Gypsy's desire to get to the plane, knowing drugs were onboard. *Think. Slow down and think.* As the two remaining men glared at Jocelyn, the one with the gun now with his arm pointing downward, she knew it was her chance. Shooting a fleeting glance toward the dark woods just to the right of the barn, where the illumination no longer penetrated, she knew what she had to do.

"Follow," she commanded softly, and whirled around, running into the darkness, momentarily out of sight of the group inside.

Avoiding the underbrush, she ran just inside the woods lining the path. A gunshot ricocheted close by and she instinctively ducked. "Go, go," she encouraged the large dog running beside her, each trying to protect the other. More gunshots fired her way as yelling from behind met her ears, but she refused to stop.

Blindly running she made it to the clearing, the still unlit house to the left. Sprinting to her truck, she yelled for Gypsy to jump in as her hand landed on the handle. The ping of gunshot hitting the vehicle next to her hand caused her to jump back, stumbling to the ground as Gypsy planted herself in front of her. The following gunshot met its target and Grace watched in horror as her beloved dog fell to the ground at her feet, blood coating her fur.

CHAPTER 30

JOCELYN WALKED OVER to where Grace scrambled over Gypsy, trying to stop the flow of blood.

"No, no, no, baby," Grace cried, tears streaming down her face.

"You shouldn't have followed me," Jocelyn accused, her expression tangled in fear and regret. "None of this would have happened," she said, her hand shaking as it held the gun.

Ignoring the ramblings of the woman over her, Grace jerked her t-shirt over her head and placed it on the wound, applying pressure.

"Stop," Jocelyn said. "She's gonna die, and fuck it all, Grace, so are you. I've got no fucking choice."

"Why? Why?" Grace screamed, her chancing a glance up at the woman she no longer knew.

Before Jocelyn had an opportunity to speak, more crashing through the woods was heard as Joe came into view, barely visible in the dark as he ran around the house toward them. Suddenly the woods came alive as shadows appeared, moving, circling around the group.

The sound of a small engine plane was heard in the

distance, coming closer. Unable to discern why the pilot would be returning, Grace shook herself, only caring about the animal dying in her arms. Laying her head down on the ground next to Gypsy, she stared into the amber eyes that peered back at her. Trusting. Loving.

The shadows formed into men, dark clothing and blackened faces obscuring their identities and striking fear into Joe and Jocelyn. Their weapons trained on the pair, Mitch called out, "FBI. Drop your weapons."

Joe immediately complied, but Jocelyn stood still, staring dumbly at the large assembly. Unaware of what was behind her, Jocelyn's body slammed to the ground as she was hit in the back.

"You fucking bitch!" Grace screeched, standing with a large, heavy stick in her hand. Bringing it down again on the woman's prone body, she hit her over and over, continuing to roar. "You tried to kill me and my dog! You left us for dead! You fucking bitch!"

Blaise rushed around the vehicle, jerking off his goggles, seeing Grace out of control with Gypsy at her feet. His heart in his throat, he grabbed Grace from behind, pinning her arms to her sides as he repeated, "Babe, It's me. I've got you. I've got you." It took several repetitions for the words to sink in, stilling her struggling body. "Let it go, babe. We've got Jocelyn. Let it go."

Dropping the stick, she cried, "Blaise! She killed Gypsy." As her body gave out, shaking with grief, he was the only thing holding her up.

He did not want to let her go but knew she would want him to see to the dog. Signaling to Chad, he shifted her body to his friend's arms, saying, "Get her a goddamn shirt to put on."

Cam already had a blanket out for Grace and he wrapped it around her as Chad continued to hold her close. Jude quickly shucked his Kevlar and pulled his black t-shirt over his head, walking to Chad.

"Come on, Grace. Let's get you dressed," he said softly, sliding the material over the distraught woman's head and weaving her arms through the holes.

"Patrick!" Blaise shouted. "Get the first aid field equipment and I need light!"

Patrick ran to the Saints' SUV that Monty had driven up. Rushing back, he leaned over Blaise's shoulder, adjusting the lights over the man desperately working on the dog. Gypsy whimpered, shocking everyone.

Jolted by the sound, Grace began fighting Chad's arms. "Let me go!" she cried, her tear-stained face turned toward the light now illuminating the man she loved as he worked to save the dog that had protected her and held her heart.

Chad set her feet gently on the ground but kept his hands on her shoulders as she scrambled over to Blaise. Leaning down, he cautioned, "Let him work, Grace. Give Blaise room to work."

Blaise looked up at Grace, his expression unreadable to all but her. She saw the warmth in his eyes. "Grace, she's alive, but barely. I've got to get her to a hospital."

"Where can we go?" she asked, emotion choking her voice.

From around the corner of the house, Marc came running. "Got here as soon as I could," he panted, looking down at the scene in front of him. Glancing over at Jack, he said, "Flew Bob's old plane right in, stopping Ricardo on the runway. Mitch and the DEA's got him now."

"Can you get me out of here?" Blaise asked, his hand covered in blood as he knelt by Gypsy.

"Yeah, no problem. There's a farm next to my property, about two miles from you. I can land us there and get you to your place."

Quickly unpacking a gurney from their emergency supplies, Jude and Patrick bent to assist placing Gypsy onto the carrier. Both men stood, easily jogging down the path, carrying the injured dog toward the plane.

Blaise turned to Grace, stepping back as her body slammed into his. He desperately wanted to wrap his arms around her, hold her while reminding himself that he did not have to perform emergency surgery on her. She encircled his waist with her arms, holding her cheek against his pounding heartbeat.

"I want to go too," she pleaded.

"Baby, you can't. There's not enough room on the plane." He looked down at her anguished face as she stared in horror up at him.

"Blaise, I have to—"

"Grace, listen to me, sweetheart. I've got to go. I've got to get her to my clinic. I've got another vet who'll come help and bring blood. I promise you, I'll do everything in my power to save her but I can only do that if you let me go." He felt her nod as her arms loosened from around him.

She stepped back, tears flowing freely. "I know. Go. Please go."

With a quick kiss, that he wanted to be so much more than a hurried goodbye, he ran after the others heading to the plane.

With her arms wrapped around her waist as she stood in Jude's huge t-shirt hanging over her blood-stained jeans, she was instantly surrounded by the remaining Saints.

Stepping up, Jack bent to capture her attention. "Let's go, honey. We'll get you down the mountain and to Blaise's place before you know it."

The group hustled over to the SUVs and Chad assisted Grace into the back seat. Bart climbed in on the other side, with Cam riding shotgun as Chad pulled out.

Bart, glancing to the side at Grace, noticed her hands in her lap, twisting together nervously. "Blaise'll do everything he can," he assured. Catching her thankful smile, he added, "Gotta tell you, girl, seeing you beatin' the shit outta Jocelyn while half-dressed and screamin…'bout the craziest thing I've ever seen."

Blushing, Grace grinned. "I'm glad you enjoyed the show." She saw a smile pass between Chad and Cam in the front seat, and she added, "Don't know that Blaise was so thrilled."

"Grace, when he gets over being scared as fuck about that gun going off on you, he'll think it was sexy as hell!"

A giggle escaped, in spite of her anxiety, and she looked out the window smiling as the SUV expertly hurtled down the mountain road. Her memories back, she now knew what had happened that night. As she stared out of the window into the deep ravine on the side, she could not hold back the flood of memories. This time, not of what had occurred that night, but what had happened since. With Blaise at her side…she was whole.

~

BLAISE SAT IN the back of the tiny plane, Gypsy squeezed onto a blanket at his feet. Marc flew expertly, occasionally glancing back as he got updates from Blaise as to Gypsy's condition. Blaise spoke softly to the large dog, glad that she was stable for the moment. He had given her pain medication and inserted an IV before they took to the air. Closing his eyes for a moment, he felt his breath choke in his throat as he allowed his thoughts to stray back to when he and the Saints entered the woods.

With their night vision goggles, they quickly traversed through the dark woods, seeing a house in the background and several vehicles parked in front. Suddenly, the sound of a shot resounded, breaking the silence of the night. Fear gripped his heart as he stumbled. Recognizing his truck, he saw a figure running from the woods, a dog by her side. Grace! Thank God!

Attempting to keep his mind on the mission, he noticed the other Saints circling around. Just then another shot rang out, and this time, he saw Grace drop to the ground. His heart stopped as he rushed forward, forsaking all caution to reach her side.

Before he could reach her, she began screaming about Gypsy. Unsure if she was hurt or her dog had been shot, he continued to race through the woods. Running around a tangle of trees he came into the clearing from behind his truck. As he bolted around, he was shocked to see Grace, in her jeans and bra, pummeling Jocelyn with a large stick, screaming at her.

A quick glance to the ground indicated it was Gypsy that had been injured. Grabbing Grace from behind, he warred between wanting to clutch her to his body, feeling with every inch of his being the sensation of having her alive and well in his arms, and the desire to shake her for putting herself in danger by attacking someone holding a gun.

But as she broke down in his embrace, her grief overwhelming her, he knew he would have done the same.

"Almost there," Marc said. "Jack called the neighbors and they've put out lights on the field.

Blaise knew Marc had flown in combat and for the CIA for years. He had no doubt his friend would be able to land anywhere and, within a few minutes, Marc proved just that. The landing was bumpy, but they soon came to a stop and taxied over to a waiting SUV. Within fifteen minutes they were at his house, Marc jumping out of the vehicle to assist. Another car was already in the driveway and the occupant was standing in Blaise's doorway.

"Good to see you, Annie. Thank God you got here."

The pretty red-haired veterinarian smiled, saying, "Glad to see you again too." Her eyes dropped to the bundle in his arms, as she followed him into his back room. Once inside, she quickly moved around to begin assisting, hooking up the anesthetic machine to the IV line Blaise had already inserted.

She glanced up at Marc and smiled. "Hey, I'm Annie Douglass. You must be one of the Saints."

Cocking his head to the side, Marc nodded curiously. Blaise, focused solely on Gypsy, made no introduction, so Annie continued. "My husband is Shane Douglass, with the Richland Police Department. And we're good friends with the Alvarez Security men…they used to serve with Jack."

Nodding, Marc greeted, "Nice to meet you. Glad you could help us out."

"I've got a clinic not too far from here and Shane's

home with the kids." Looking over at Blaise, she said, "But he said you owe him a beer for getting me out this time of night."

Finally looking up, Blaise smiled. "Done." Pulling the surgery table over to him, he said, "Now let's get this bullet out of my woman's dog."

BY THE TIME Grace ran through the front door, Bethany was waiting for her in Blaise's living room.

"It's okay, they're working on her," Bethany hurried to explain, wanting to reassure her friend as quickly as possible, noting her long black t-shirt that was obviously one of the Saints, as well as her blood-covered jeans and arms.

"I've got to get to her," Grace said, trying to push past her. The other Saints crowded the room as well.

"Let's get you cleaned up first," Bethany suggested, but Grace refused.

"Don't you see?" Grace pleaded, her eyes filling with tears as she looked at the full room. "For weeks, Gypsy was my only friend. The only connection to who I used to be. She stayed with me. Protected me. Never left my side...not once." Her face crumpled as she whispered, "So I can't leave her side now."

Nodding Bethany hugged Grace quickly, tears in her own eyes, and then let her pass down the hall toward the clinic room. Stopping at the closed door, Grace hesitated, placing her forehead and hand on it.

Silent prayers filled her as she thought about the weeks that Gypsy was there for her. *Please God...if You care about animals and I believe you do...please take care of her.*

Sucking in a shaky breath, Grace opened the door and walked in. Blaise was stitching Gypsy as a beautiful woman in a lab coat monitored one of the machines connected to the dog.

"You must be Grace," the woman smiled, looking up. "I'm Dr. Douglass. Annie."

Rushing forward, she looked down at Gypsy peacefully sleeping. "How is she?"

Blaise smiled at her, though the lines on his face indicated his fatigue. "I can't fucking believe it, but I think she's going to be fine. The bullet missed all her organs and mostly went through the muscle. She lost a lot of blood, but Annie brought some from her clinic."

"Oh, thank you," Grace effused, her eyes not leaving his until he dropped his gaze reluctantly back to Gypsy. Grace stepped over to the woman, wanting to touch Gypsy, but uncertain what was allowed.

Annie's smile warmed Grace's heart as she nodded, "You can touch her. It's okay. She's sedated and, I promise, she's not in pain."

Bending down, Grace laid her hand gently on Gypsy's shoulder before continuing the rest of the way down. Placing her head right next to the still dog, she breathed in her scent, nuzzling her fur. Silent tears began to fall, dropping onto Gypsy's coat.

Annie blinked back tears of her own as she watched the agony play out in front of her. Glancing over at Blaise, she saw tears sliding down his face as he completed the stitching. Reaching over, she touched his shoulder, whispering, "I've got this. Go to her."

Nodding his thanks, Blaise looked up as he placed the suturing materials back on the tray and pulled off his bloodied gloves. Standing behind Grace, crowding into the small space, stood the rest of the Saints. Every one of them. And, more than a few, quickly blinking while swallowing hard.

Walking around, his work on Gypsy now done, he focused on the woman holding his heart. He bent his body over hers, plastering her back to his front, laying his head next to hers. Whispering into her ear, he murmured comfort as his huge arms encircled her. After a moment, he raised up, lifting her upper body as he moved.

She turned, her cheek pressed against his chest, her arms holding tightly around his waist. The couple stood, silent…no words could possibly convey their emotions.

Annie quietly turned off the anesthesia machine and removed the endotracheal tube. Giving silent instructions to the men in the room, Chad and Jude walked over and assisted her in lifting Gypsy down to a soft pad on the floor. Bethany stepped forward and whispered to Annie, "I'll help clean up in here. Just show me what to do."

Marc came up to the couple in the middle of the room and said softly, "Blaise, you need to take care of Grace now. You've done all you can for Gypsy. Go get Grace, and you, cleaned up. We're here for now. Come back down when you're ready."

Blaise felt, rather than heard, his friend's concern, but knew he needed to see to Grace. "Babe, come with me and, I promise, we'll be right back to be at her side."

With that, he bent to scoop her up in his arms, carrying her out of the room and up the stairs. Kissing the top of her head as he walked into the bathroom, he glanced at their reflection in the mirror. Exhausted, bloody, complete total messes. And yet, seeing them together, he knew he was looking at the most beautiful sight in the world.

CHAPTER 31

STEPPING INTO THE warm shower after stripping both of them, Blaise maneuvered Grace where the water would hit her back. Taking the shower gel, he lathered his hands and then smoothed them over her body.

She leaned her head back allowing the water to cascade from her hair to her toes. Her gaze pinned his with unspoken words of love. A tremulous smile curved her lips as she took a shuddering breath. Letting it out slowly, she finally said, "Thank you."

He moved closer, his hands now washing her hair, fingers massaging her scalp, keeping his gaze on her. "Babe, thank *you.*"

Her brow crinkled in question as she asked, "For what?"

Bending down, he whispered, "For staying alive." His voice shook and he captured her lips before she could see the tears forming in his eyes once more.

For several long minutes, they stood, bodies pressed together, arms holding fast, as their lips met. Taking away fear. Soothing grief. Passion mixed with love.

Finally, pulling back, he said, "I want to take you to bed. I want to hold you in my arms all night long and never sleep for fear of losing one minute of my life not seeing you."

Her easy smile pierced his heart, and he reluctantly added, "But we have a houseful of people downstairs who want to check on us. But when they leave…"

"Then I guess we'd better get down there," she agreed, still grinning. "The sooner they can check on us, the sooner we can get on with our lives."

BY THE TIME Grace and Blaise made it downstairs, Angel, Sabrina, Dani, and Evie had arrived and Mitch was just walking into the house. The group had moved into the living room where drinks and snacks the women had brought were being enjoyed.

Annie stepped over to the couple and hugged Grace. "We weren't properly introduced earlier. I'm Annie Douglass, a friend of Blaise's. He's helped me out when I had rescue animals that needed to be boarded so I was glad to have a chance to pay him back."

"Please sit down and have some refreshments," Grace offered, waving her hand toward the breakfast bar loaded with goodies.

"Thanks, but I need to get home. My husband, Shane, is sitting up waiting for me while keeping an eye on our kids." She hugged Blaise before saying her goodbyes to the rest of the group.

Mitch walked over next, saying, "Grace, we'll have to have an official statement from you, but I'd love to go over more of what you know combined with what we know, if that's all right."

Blaise started to protest, but Grace placed her hand over his chest and said, "Honey, I really want to do this. I know we're all exhausted, but I'm ready."

Kissing the top of her head, he moved into the living room, settling down in one of the comfortable chairs with her in his lap, unwilling to be apart from her.

Once everyone had sat down, covering all of the furniture and most of the floor space, Mitch rubbed his hand over his tired face and smiled at Grace. "Why don't you tell us what you remember now? We'll start with that."

Sucking in a deep breath, she nodded, looking at the expectant faces of the crowd. The crowd of friends...ones who cared...ones who charged out into the night to save her. An emotion jolted right to her very marrow...*I'm not alone anymore.* Armed with that knowledge, she plunged ahead.

"I now remember what happened that night, although I don't understand why or who all was involved." Casting her mind back, she could now see the events taking place. "One of the TSA secretaries asked if I would deliver a package to the TSA at the Charlestown Airport since I lived nearby. It was not a problem and, in fact, I thought I might see Jocelyn. I arrived there and was walking towards what I thought was the terminal when I saw Douglas Wilkins. Before I could greet him, I could see he was deep in conversation with a tall, well-dressed man and I didn't want to interrupt. They walked to another vehicle and as Gypsy and I neared the white SUV, Gypsy indicated there were drugs there. Not sure what to do, we moved out of sight and then watched as Douglas got into his vehicle and drove away. So I followed him."

Blaise grunted underneath her, drawing her attention to his glare. "Babe, you never fuckin' go after someone on your own. You always have someone take your back."

"I know that now, but—"

"No buts about it," he continued. "That was reckless."

Glaring back, she retorted, "Do you want to hear my story or not?"

The others cried, "Yes," in unison, causing her to smirk in triumph at Blaise. He shot her a warning glance, which only made her smile wider.

"I followed him and waited on the road after he turned down a lane. A deputy car came by and asked if I needed help. It turned out to be Jocelyn. I guess I now understand why she was in the area, but at the time, I simply thought it was a stroke of luck. I told her what I'd seen and she told me to follow her and she was calling for backup. Obviously, she didn't and I was following her blindly, assuming she would never lead me into danger."

She quieted, her mind now remembering the event clearly. A gentle squeeze from Blaise brought her back to reality. Blushing, she said, "Sorry. It's so weird to actually remember everything now."

"You take your time," Bethany said. "Don't let these men bully you into talking more than you want."

Laughing at the incredulous expression Jack had on his face as he stared at his wife, Grace said, "No, it's fine." Allowing the moment of mirth to ease her thoughts, she continued. "Once we got there, we went to the barn and there were several men loading packages from the white SUV into the plane."

"That would have been Joe Savine," Mitch supplied. "He legally owns the property but has ties to the cartel. Also, Ricardo Guzman, the highest member of the cartel we've been able to capture was the tall, distinguished man you saw with Douglas."

Digesting this information, the group turned back to Grace, eager to hear the rest of her story.

"It only took a moment for me to realize Jocelyn was part of the group and that she had not called for backup. While they argued, I took off running with Gypsy at my side." Shaking her head, she said, "This'll sound weird since I haven't been able to remember anything for so long, but tonight was like déjà vu." She saw the understanding expressions on all the Saints and their women, as they stayed riveted to her.

"I managed to get to my car, with Gypsy jumping into the back seat as trained, and I sped off. I thought I was okay, at least, to get to a town. Then, well, you know the next part. What I didn't find out until tonight was that it was Jocelyn who was in the white SUV chasing me down the mountain. She's the one who bumped me off the road. And she climbed down the ravine to see if I was dead. Assuming we were, she took my purse and phone." Heaving a deep sigh, she added, "And left me for dead. I suppose it was her luck that, when I woke up, I had no memory."

Blaise drew her attention as he said, "I wonder if that's why you were so afraid of going to the police. Subconsciously you associated fear with the uniform."

Her gaze held his warmly as she saw the agonizing concern etched into his face. Reaching up, she cupped his jaw, her thumb smoothing the creases. Turning back to Mitch, she admitted, "So that's all I know. All I remember. But now can you fill in some of the *hows and whys* for me?"

Mitch leaned forward in his chair, resting his forearms on his knees, piercing her with his gaze. "Absolutely, but first, I've got to say that you have been amazing throughout all of this. From the moment you climbed out of that ravine, before any of us knew you, to right now...you took care of yourself perfectly. You...and Gypsy."

Smiling widely, she nodded her thanks. "I don't think I could have done it without her. Not to begin with. And then without you," she added turning back to Blaise.

A slight squeeze acknowledged his feelings as his heart overflowed once more.

"So what I can add at this time for all of you, but especially for Grace," Mitch began, "is that DEA had the Savine farm on their radar for about six months but didn't want to get just him. They wanted the man higher up on the totem pole and that was Ricardo Guzman, a cousin to the Guzmans of the Sinaloa Cartel that Cam and Miriam were escaping last fall. They were hard to catch because the Cartel can afford to pay, and pay well, to keep their business secret."

Leaning back, he continued, "They finally got a break when an informant told them that Ricardo was coming into the country to oversee a shipment himself. What they now know is that Jocelyn was the person who would take her pretend drug dog to the Charlestown airport when called and would pass the shipments coming in from the private planes. We don't know why yet, but the money the cartels flash around is addictive. She would sign off on their paperwork and that was the extent of what she had been involved in…until you made an appearance. Frightened of both being discovered and facing the ire of the cartel, she had to eliminate you."

Shuddering, Grace leaned back against Blaise's firm chest as his arms enveloped her.

"You okay, babe?" he whispered.

She nodded rather than answered, and he shot Mitch a look. Catching the need to hurry it along, Mitch said, "Douglas was on their payroll as well. He would recruit willing dog handlers who could be trusted by the cartel. He was also in on the deliveries and made trips to the Savine farm."

The group released a collective sigh as the investigation came to a close...at least for the Saints. Mitch stood, saying, "Well, I'm heading out now. Grace, we'll get the official statement from you tomorrow. For now, I've got serious as shit report writing to finish."

Jack stood and walked Mitch out of the house and down to his vehicle. Looking at their FBI contact, who had become a good friend, Jack said, "You ready to quit? Ready to try something new?"

Chuckling, Mitch said, "Yeah...more than you know. Got some things going on...some family issues. I've got some decisions to make, but I'll fill you in on them at a later time."

"You know you've got a place here with us," Jack said. "I'd be proud to call you a Saint."

Grinning, Mitch acknowledged, "I'd be proud to work with you, Jack. Hell, with all of you. But not sure life's gonna take me in that direction."

Nodding, Jack met his friend's gaze and smiled. "Understood. You do what you've got to do, but always remember...no matter where you go, you've got Saints at your back."

THE CROWD HAVING left, lingering only long enough for handshakes and hugs, Blaise alarmed the house with Ransom at his heels. Looking down, he said, "Come on boy, let's go find Grace and Gypsy."

Walking into the clinic room, his eyes immediately landed on Grace as she sat cross-legged on the floor next to Gypsy, who was comfortably resting. Struck with the comparison to the first time Grace had been in his clinic room with Gypsy, he could not believe all of the changes that had occurred since then. Talon was curled up in Grace's lap sleeping. Grace lifted her gaze to Blaise as he walked in and sat across from her.

"Do you really think she's doing okay?" Grace asked, her face a mixture of concern and trust.

Complete and total trust in him. He felt the punch to his gut at her expression. "I think she's going to be fine. She'll sleep well tonight." Looking down at his watch, "What little of the night there is left."

She tried to stifle a yawn but was unable to hide her exhaustion. Standing, he took her hand in his and pulled her gently up after scooping Talon from her lap and sitting the sleepy kitten on the blanket next to Gypsy. "Let's go to bed. She'll rest for several more hours and then I'll get up and check on her."

Sleep did not come easily to either of them. After watching her toss and turn, Blaise finally rolled his large body over hers, pinning her to the bed, holding his weight up on his forearms. Brushing the hair back from her face, he peered down at her, memorizing her face, relishing the feel of her body underneath his.

Lifting her arms to his shoulders, she dug her fingernails in slightly, the feel of his heavy body on hers comforting.

"We're not sleeping, babe," Blaise stated the obvious.

Grinning, she responded, "You got something to take our minds off everything that happened?"

Pressing his erection against her hips, he nodded. "Yeah, I can think of one or two things that might just make us forget."

She giggled, squeezing his shoulders. "Blaise, I've been trying to remember for a very long time and now you want me to forget?" she teased.

Leaning closer, until his lips were a breath away from hers, he said, "You deserve nothing but good memories, sweetheart. So yeah, I want to take away all your bad ones."

His lips touched hers, soft and gentle to begin with, before taking them possessively, erasing her cares and worries. And then, with his body rocking hers into the wee hours of the morning, he gave her nothing but perfect, new memories and a promise of forever.

CHAPTER 32
A YEAR LATER

"PERFECT," GRACE SAID to the trainee. "Keep your animal calm and quiet as they approach the person in the wheelchair." Nodding encouragingly to the young woman, Grace scanned the others in the circle. After she completed the training for companion dogs for the elderly, she became a certified trainer herself.

"I heard you used to be trained for security with a drug-sniffing dog," one of the trainees said, clearly impressed and eagerly waiting for her explanation into the career shift.

Smiling, she nodded. "I was. It's a noble profession, but," giving a little shrug, she continued, "sometimes life takes us in different directions than we originally thought."

"I'd think that going from that action packed world to this would be kind of a downer," he continued.

"Not at all," she replied. "Now that I truly understand myself, I like the direction my life has taken."

Just then, Gypsy trotted over, nuzzling her mistress' hand as the class ended.

Squatting, she threw her arms around her dog's neck, burying her face in Gypsy's thick fur. "We know, don't we girl. We know who we are...who we love...and who loves us."

Just then a car honked and Gypsy barked. Standing, Grace smiled as the tall, handsome man came stalking straight toward her. Her dog went bounding toward him, receiving the first attention as Grace's heart sung. *Yeah I know who I am, who I love, and who loves me. No more mystery.* Running, she jumped into Blaise's arms, safe in his embrace.

SEVERAL YEARS LATER

THE TREES IN the park were in full green regalia as the summer sun beamed warmly on the families enjoying the weekend. A large pond, surrounded on three sides by thick trees, sported picnic tables and benches along the perimeter.

Two small children were running around the grass, laughing and playing with a large German Shepherd cavorting with them. A woman sat on a blanket in the shade, keeping an eye on the activities.

A man saw them from the distance and began to approach. The children were too entertained to notice him. The dog, growing slightly deaf, did not hear him approach either. His eyes dropped to the woman on the blanket. Long, dark hair blowing behind her in the breeze. A pink top with white shorts showed off her beautiful body…one he knew intimately. He halted as the scene in front of him stole his breath for a moment. Everything he wanted…needed…was right in front of him.

The woman called out, "Ben! Beth! Careful…not too rough. Gypsy's getting a little old to play so hard."

As the children fell to the grass, still rolling with the dog, she smiled as she saw the man approach, his hands full. He was huge…tall and broad. With his square jaw and blond hair, he could have stepped from the pages of one of her historical romance novels. Pushing her sunglass back on her head, she watched his natural swagger. Closer and closer he came until he was directly in front of her, looking down.

"Could you use some food, Miss?" he asked, his eyes twinkling.

"What did you bring?" she asked.

"You said to surprise you, so I brought…" he knelt down, placing the containers on the blanket, "hot dogs!" Leaning over to place a soft, meaningful kiss on her lips, he added, "I seem to remember you were partial to hot dogs from the food trucks."

A smile greeted his words, but before she could respond, the children saw their dad and ran over, arms waving as they tackled him. Gypsy ambled over and lay down on the blanket with Grace, placing her head on her mistress' lap.

As the family ate the simple meal, Grace caught Blaise's gaze and smiled. He had done what he promised...erased her bad memories, only leaving her with the ones that mattered. Good friends...family...and love.

THE END

BONUS SCENE
MITCH

THE SAINTS FINISHED their meeting, but before they dispersed, Jack said, "Got Mitch coming by. He said he wanted to talk to us and wanted to do it in person. I told him to come on over."

Bart grinned, saying, " 'Bout time he left the Bureau and came with us."

Monty was quiet, unsure of what his friend's plans were, but had to admit to himself that he was curious.

"We can head on up. It'll be informal," Jack said, standing.

Several minutes later, the Saints were sitting in Jack and Bethany's living room, the oversized, comfortable furniture perfect for their sizes. Bethany had snacks on the counter and the men had helped themselves.

Opening the door, she greeted Mitch with a hug, inviting him in and then motioning toward the living room. "They're all waiting. Well, eating and waiting," she laughed, handing him a plate.

Making his way in, Mitch greeted the others. They ate, the companionable conversation surrounding them for several minutes. Finally, Mitch pushed his plate back and said, "I know Jack told you all that I wanted to let you know what was going on with me and, well, I consider you all friends...so I wanted to do it this way."

Gaining the undivided attention of the other men in the room, he said, "The only one of you who know this is Monty, but I guess you could say that law enforcement's been in my blood. My grandfather was the Police Chief of a town on the Eastern Shore of Virginia and when he grew too old to handle the job, my dad, who'd been an officer, became the Chief. That's where I was born and raised. Both of those men were at my graduation from the FBI academy and I swear, they nearly popped their buttons with pride...more so than at my college graduation."

Chuckling at the memory, he grew quiet, a pensive expression on his face. "I loved being an FBI agent. I'd like to think I was a good one—"

At that, he was interrupted by the immediate affirmations from all around.

"But, just as each of you, I found the agency to be ponderous at times. Slow to change. Slow to react. So, I confess, I've become a bit disenchanted. I've considered resigning and joining you, but," he quickly held up his hand before the celebration could begin, "that's not in the cards."

The Saints looked at him, disappointment mixed with curiosity on their faces.

"My dad's had a couple of heart episodes in the past

six months and has decided that he needs to step down from being the Police Chief. And…" he drawled out, "the town council has asked me to come back home and take over."

"Wow," Bart said, shaking his head. "I'm sorry about your father, but that's a big change."

"More than you know," Mitch admitted. "The Eastern Shore is one of the poorest counties in Virginia. So, I'd be going from an agency with almost everything I need at my disposal, to a town that will be able to pay salaries and run the sheriff's department, but will have nothing left over for frills."

Whistling, Cam asked, "Can you just take a leave of absence from the Bureau for family emergency?"

Nodding, Mitch answered, "You know, I actually thought about that. But what kind of Chief would I be…what kind of man would I be…if I took the job with one foot already out the door?"

Leaning back, he continued, "It'd mean leaving a large, major area in Virginia with a university and two hospitals, and moving to a small town with a clinic and thirty miles to the closest hospital. Leaving the salary I'm getting now and going back to a bare-bones department with a bare-bones salary."

A small grin curved the corners of his mouth as he added, "But it also means I can help the town that helped shape me into the man I am. I'll be back around family and it gives me a chance to assist my parents as they deal with my dad's convalescence. It also gives me a chance to connect with a group of guys I graduated from high school with and we all joined the military, scattering with various deployments. Most did a tour or two overseas and moved back home."

Looking out of Jack's huge floor to ceiling windows with the Blue Ridge Mountains in the vista, he said, "You know, Jack, the first time I saw your place, I thought this view was one of the best in the world. But, I gotta tell you, the sunsets over the Chesapeake Bay from Baytown will steal your breath away." Moving his gaze around the room, "It's time for me to go home…really home."

"When do you leave?" Bethany asked, her face kind with understanding. Having given up her marketing career in Richland to help run the cabin rental property with her grandmother, she completely understood the challenge, and reward, Mitch was facing.

Smiling, he said, "I've turned in my notice and will leave in two weeks. I've already started packing up my apartment and will have movers come to move everything. My grandfather had a small house just outside of town, just fifty yards from the beach. It's where I stay when I go there to visit."

He stood up, hands on his lean hips, and said, "Hate like hell to get all sentimental on you, but I gotta say it." Pinning them with his gaze again, he said, "I have never, and I mean never, worked with a better group of people than you all in this room. Each and every one of you have made a difference in not only my job, but the lives of so many. Keep doing what you're doing…and know that whenever you need a vacation, you just have to come out to the Eastern Shore. Not much there but I'll show you a good place to relax."

With that, he moved to the door, followed by the others. Saying goodbye, he hugged all ten men and then Bethany, and jogged down the front steps to his jeep.

Pulling out of Jack's long scenic drive, he flipped open his sunglasses and slid them onto his face. Smiling, he turned on the radio, blasted a country song and headed off for his next adventure.

Please follow Mitch as his story begins the amazing new series, Baytown Boys.

Luke's story in the Saints Protection & Investigations will soon follow.

Discover Annie and Shane's story in Love's Taming.

If you enjoyed Remember Love, please leave a review!

Keep up with the latest news and never miss another release by Maryann Jordan.
Sign up for her newsletter here!
goo.gl/forms/ydMTe0iz8L

Other books by Maryann Jordan

(all standalone books)

All of my books are stand-alone, each with their own
HEA!! You can read them in any order!

Saints Protection & Investigation

*(an elite group, assigned to the cases no one else wants...
or can solve)*

Serial Love

Healing Love

Revealing Love

Seeing Love

Honor Love

Sacrifice Love

Protecting Love

Alvarez Security Series

*(a group of former Special Forces brothers-in-arms now
working to provide security in the southern city
of Richland)*

Gabe

Tony

Vinny

Jobe

Love's Series

(detectives solving crimes while protecting the women they love)

Love's Taming

Love's Tempting

Love's Trusting

The Fairfield Series

(small town detectives and the women they love)

Carol's Image

Laurie's Time

Emma's Home

Fireworks Over Fairfield

I love to hear from readers, so please email me!

Email

authormaryannjordan@gmail.com

Website

www.maryannjordanauthor.com

Facebook

facebook.com/authormaryannjordan

Twitter

@authorMAJordan

MORE ABOUT MARYANN JORDAN

As an Amazon Best Selling Author, I have always been an avid reader. I joke that I "cut my romance teeth" on the historical romance books from the 1970's. In 2013 I started a blog to showcase wonderful writers. In 2014, I finally gave in to the characters in my head pleading for their story to be told. Thus, Emma's Home was created.

My first novel, Emma's Home became an Amazon Best Seller in 3 categories within the first month of publishing. Its success was followed by the rest of the Fairfield Series and then led into the Love's Series. From there I have continued with the romantic suspense Alvarez Security Series and now the Saints Protection & Investigation Series, all bestsellers.

My books are filled with sweet romance and hot sex; mystery, suspense, real life characters and situations. My heroes are alphas, take charge men who love the strong, independent women they fall in love with.

I worked as a counselor in a high school and have been involved in education for the past 30 years. I recently retired and now can spend more time devoted to my writing.

I have been married to a wonderfully patient man for 34 years and have 2 adult very supportive daughters and 1 grandson.

When writing, my dog or one of my cats will usually be found in my lap!

ACKNOWLEDGEMENTS

In writing Remember Love, I researched the use of dogs for search and rescues, drug and explosives detection, and police work. I tried to be as accurate as possible with my descriptions and use of characters, but readers, please realize that some creative license was used to make the story flow.